ARCHIE COMIC PUBLICATIONS, INC.

co-ceo
JONATHAN GOLDWATER

co-ceo
NANCY SILBERKLEIT

co-president/editor-in-chief
VICTOR GORELICK

co-president/director of circulation
FRED MAUSSER

vice president/managing editor
MIKE PELLERITO

art director
JOE PEPITONE

cover
PAT SPAZIANTE

archiecomics.com
sega.com

SONIC THE HEDGEHOG ARCHIVES, Volume 6.
Second printing December 2009. Printed in Canada.
Published by Archie Comic Publications, Inc., 325
Fayette Avenue, Mamaroneck, NY 10543-2318. Sega
is registered in the U.S. Patent and Trademark Office.
SEGA, Sonic The Hedgehog, and all related characters and indicia are either registered trademarks or
trademarks of SEGA CORPORATION © 1991-2009.
SEGA CORPORATION and SONICTEAM, LTD./SEGA
CORPORATION © 2001-2009. All Rights Reserved.
The product is manufactured under license
from Sega of America, Inc., 650 Townsend St., Ste.
650, San Francisco, CA 94103 www.sega.com. Any
similarities between characters, names, persons, and/
or institutions in this book and any living, dead or
fictional characters, names, persons, and/or institutions are not intended and if they exist, are purely
coincidental. Nothing may be reprinted in whole or
part without written permission from Archie Comic
Publications, Inc.

ISBN: 978-1-879794-27-6

TABLE OF CONTENTS

Sonic the Hedgehog #23
"Ivo Robotnik, Freedom Fighter!"

Robotnik's attempt at roboticizing Rotor goes awry when he and the Freedom Fighters are sucked into the spaceship of Car-heem, a giant interplanetary scientist who wishes to study the Mobians. Now, our heroes' only hope lies in siding with their most hated enemy!

"The Vol-Ant-Teer"

Tails has left a power ring in Robotropolis without Sonic knowing, and Antoine, in an attempt to show his courage, decides to retrieve it. Unbeknownst to him, Bunnie is along for the ride! This story gives us the first glimpse of the upcoming romance between Antoine and Bunnie.

Sonic the Hedgehog #24
"When Hedgehogs Collide"

Evil Sonic returns, and this time he's brought friends! Recruiting the Anti-Freedom Fighters, Evil and his posse take the Cosmic Interstate to our Mobius, dress like their counterparts, and proceed to terrorize the Mobian countryside. The *real* good guys return from their adventures, only to be swarmed by their very angry neighbors!

(Special Feature)
Sonic the Hedgehog - Who's Who

Learn about some of your favorite Sonic characters.

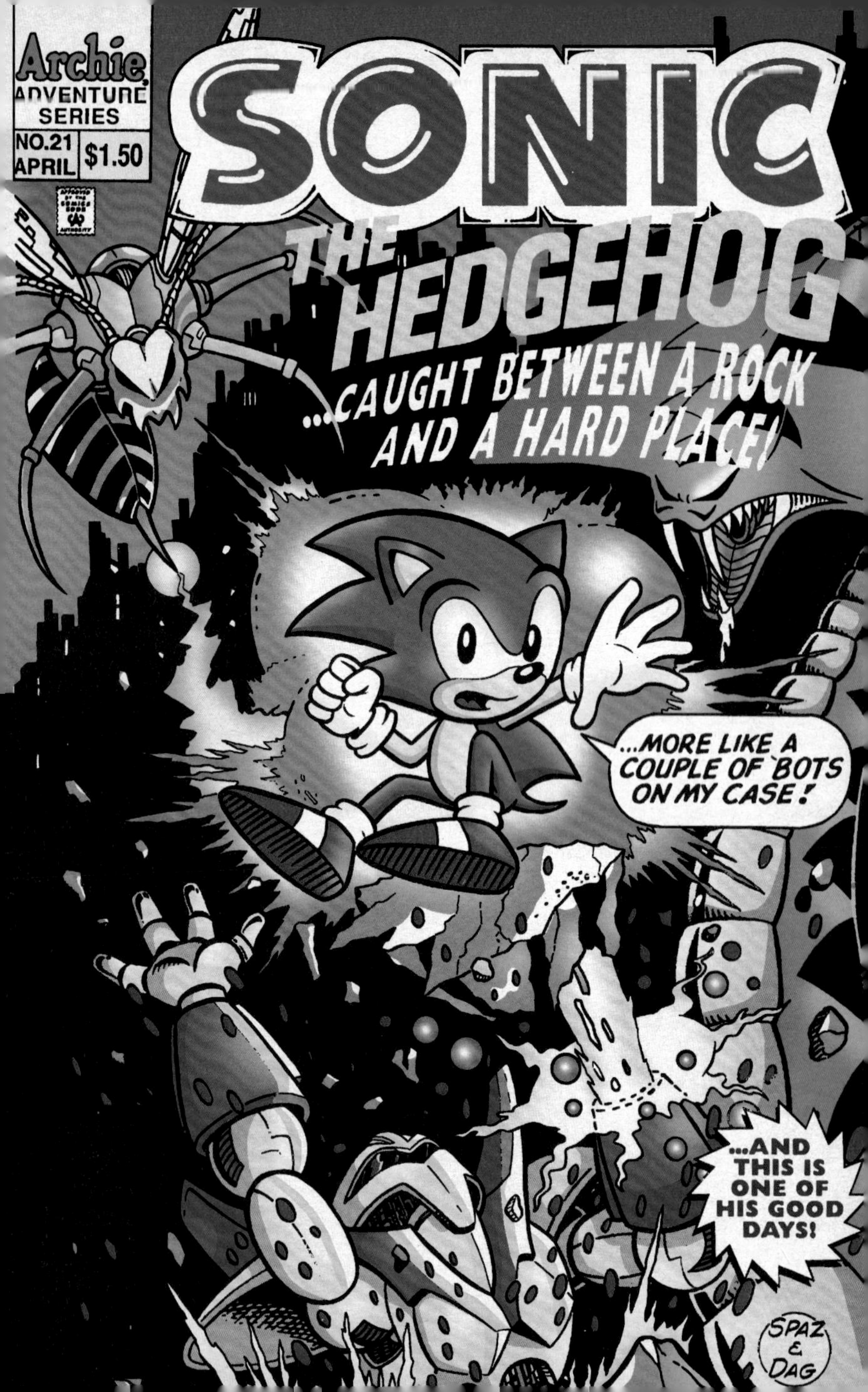
Archie
ADVENTURE SERIES
NO.21
APRIL
$1.50
SONIC THE HEDGEHOG
...CAUGHT BETWEEN A ROCK AND A HARD PLACE!
...MORE LIKE A COUPLE OF 'BOTS ON MY CASE!
...AND THIS IS ONE OF HIS GOOD DAYS!
SPAZ & DAG

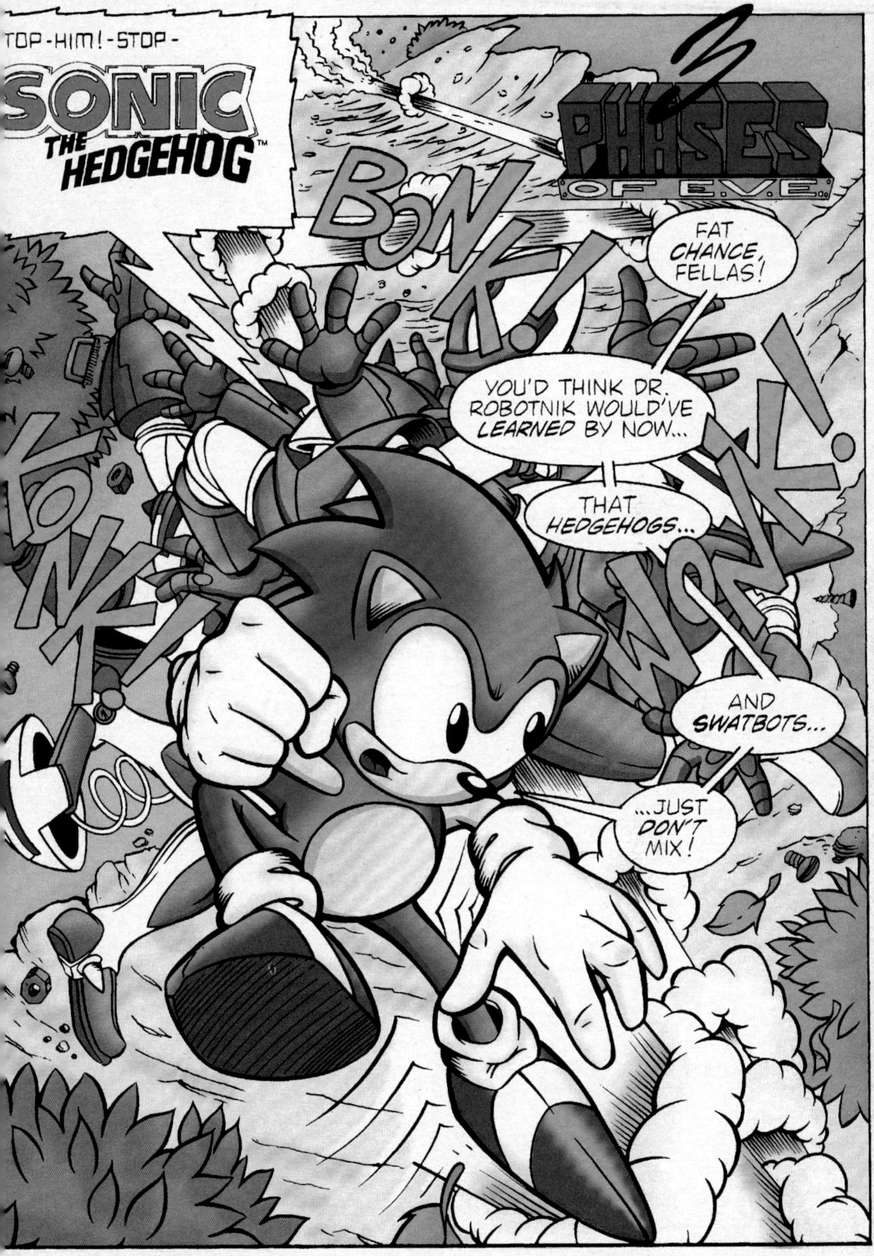
TOP-HIM!-STOP-
SONIC THE HEDGEHOG™
3 PHASES OF E.V.E.
BONK!
FAT CHANCE, FELLAS!
YOU'D THINK DR. ROBOTNIK WOULD'VE LEARNED BY NOW...
THAT HEDGEHOGS...
AND SWATBOTS...
...JUST DON'T MIX!
KONK!
WOCK!

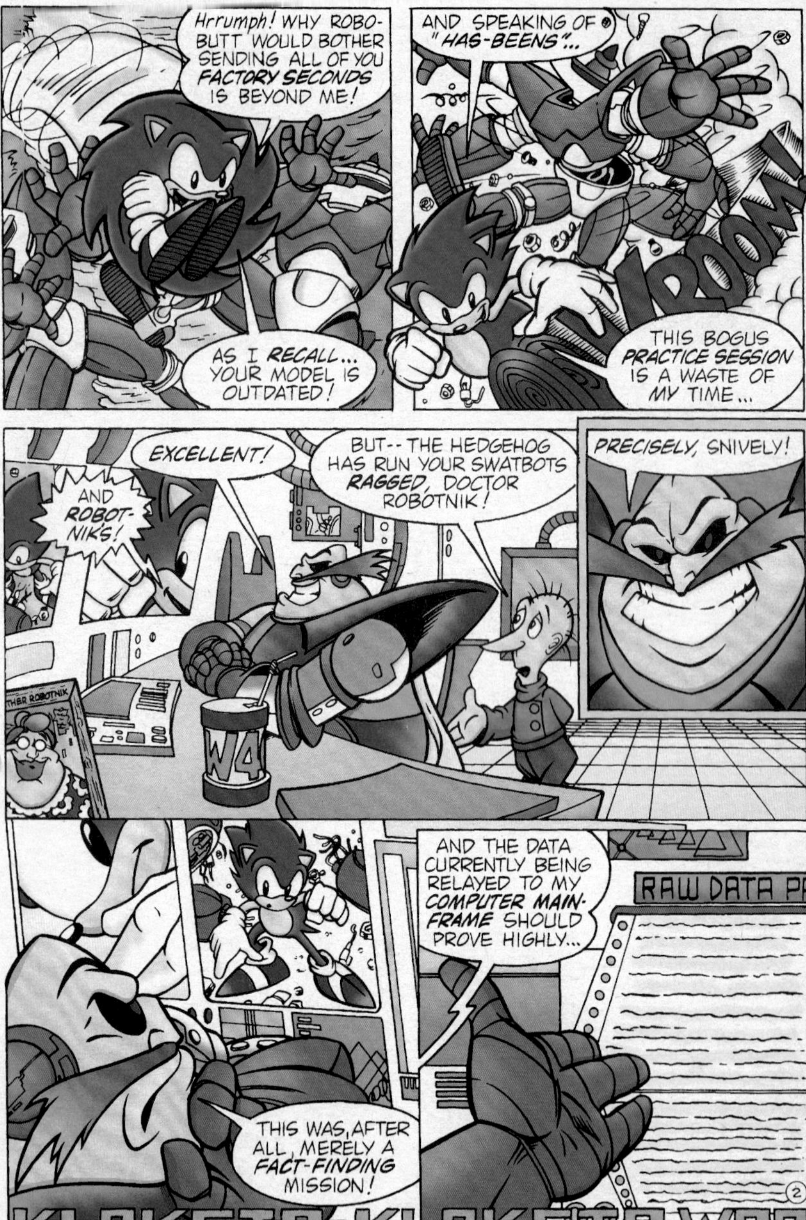

Hrrumph! WHY ROBO-BUTT WOULD BOTHER SENDING ALL OF YOU FACTORY SECONDS IS BEYOND ME!
AS I RECALL... YOUR MODEL IS OUTDATED!
AND SPEAKING OF "HAS-BEENS"...
WROOM!
THIS BOGUS PRACTICE SESSION IS A WASTE OF MY TIME...
AND ROBOT-NIK'S!
EXCELLENT!
BUT-- THE HEDGEHOG HAS RUN YOUR SWATBOTS RAGGED, DOCTOR ROBOTNIK!
PRECISELY, SNIVELY!
W4
THIS WAS, AFTER ALL, MERELY A FACT-FINDING MISSION!
AND THE DATA CURRENTLY BEING RELAYED TO MY COMPUTER MAIN-FRAME SHOULD PROVE HIGHLY...
RAW DATA P
KLAKETA-KLAKETA-WRR

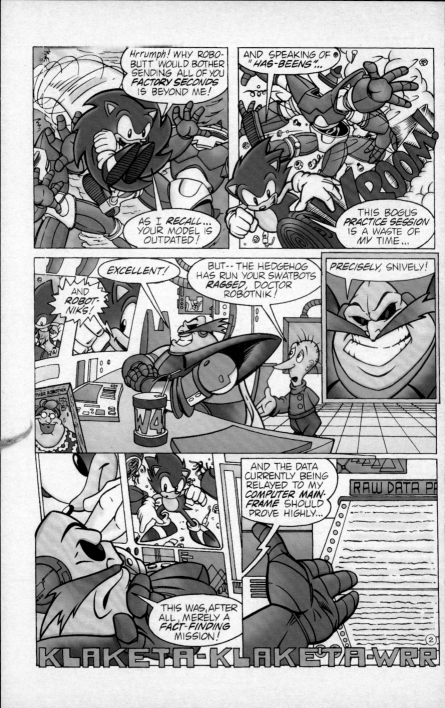

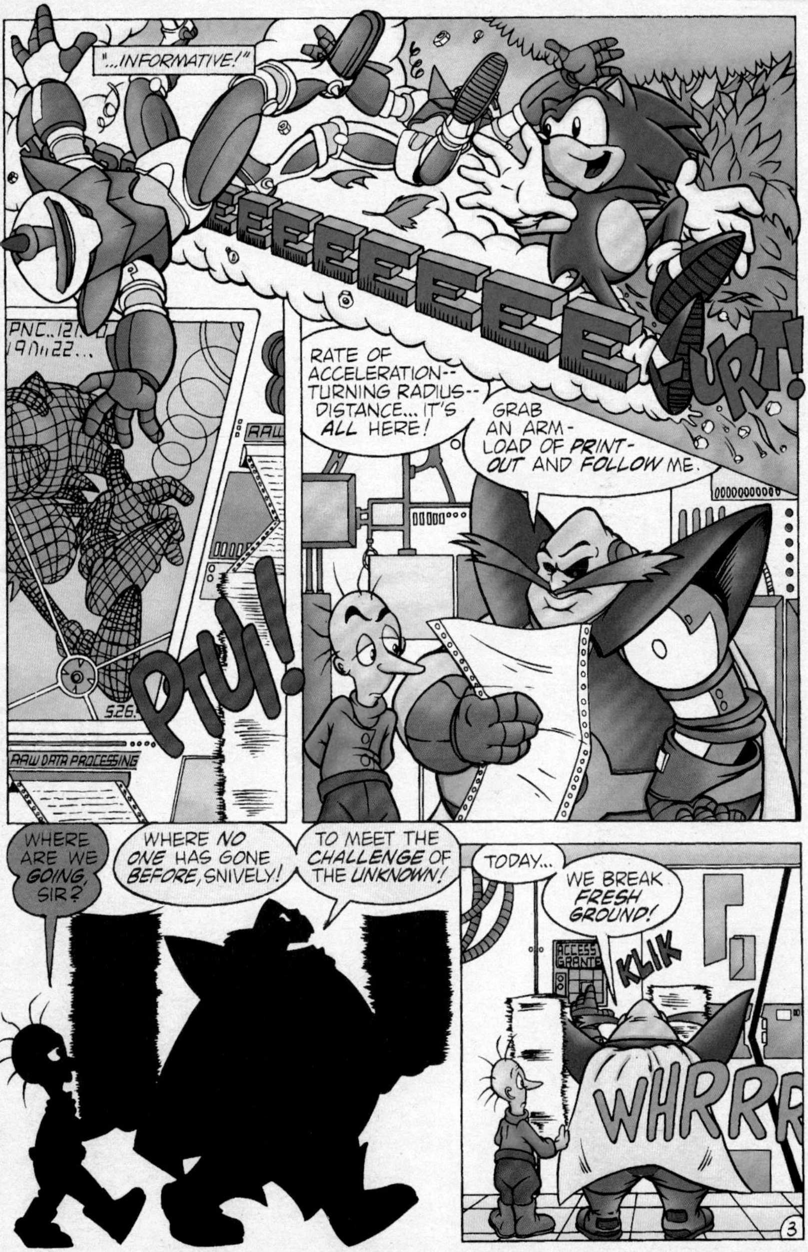
"...INFORMATIVE!"
EEEEEEEEE-URT!
PNC..121..0
19n..22...
RAW DATA PROCESSING
S.26.
PTUI!
RATE OF ACCELERATION-- TURNING RADIUS-- DISTANCE... IT'S ALL HERE!
GRAB AN ARM-LOAD OF PRINT-OUT AND FOLLOW ME.
WHERE ARE WE GOING, SIR?
WHERE NO ONE HAS GONE BEFORE, SNIVELY!
TO MEET THE CHALLENGE OF THE UNKNOWN!
TODAY...
WE BREAK FRESH GROUND!
ACCESS GRANTED
KLIK
WHRRR
3

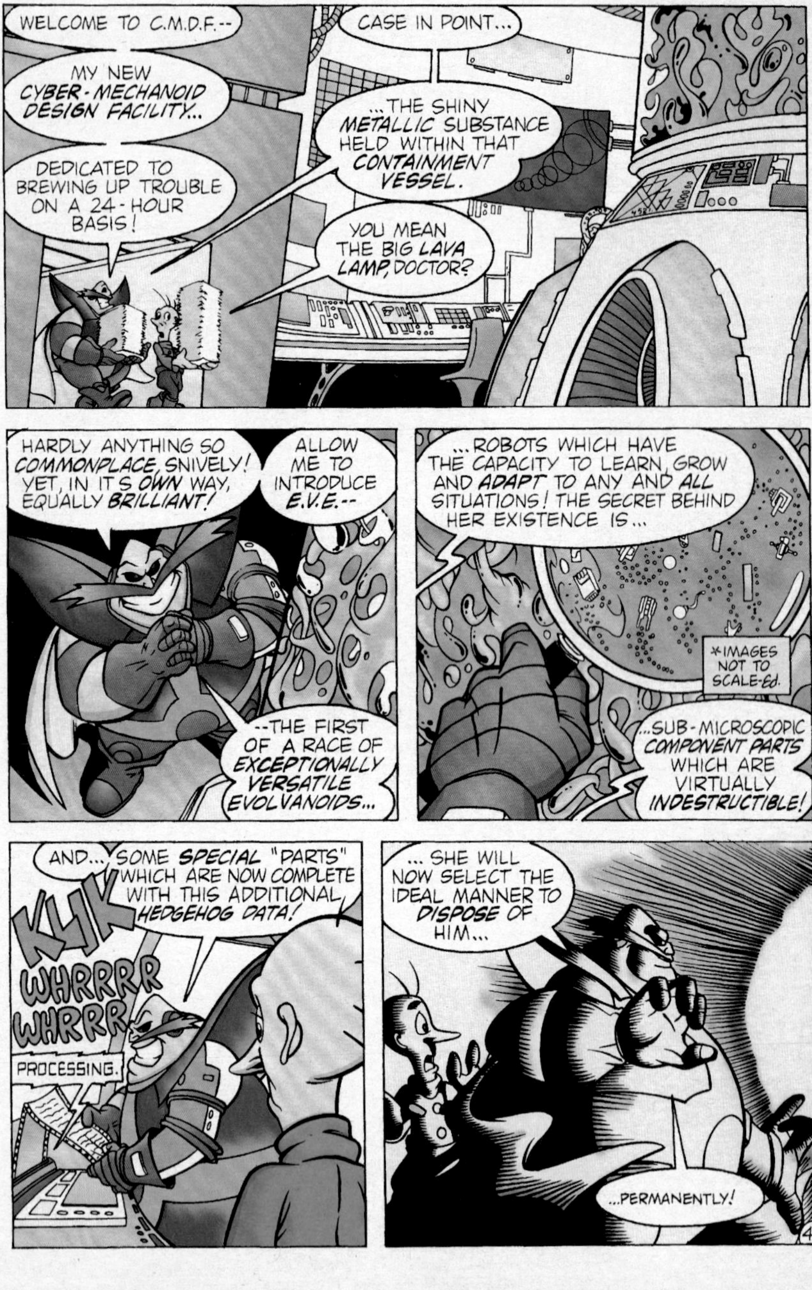
WELCOME TO C.M.D.F.--
MY NEW CYBER-MECHANOID DESIGN FACILITY...
DEDICATED TO BREWING UP TROUBLE ON A 24-HOUR BASIS!
CASE IN POINT...
...THE SHINY METALLIC SUBSTANCE HELD WITHIN THAT CONTAINMENT VESSEL.
YOU MEAN THE BIG LAVA LAMP, DOCTOR?
HARDLY ANYTHING SO COMMONPLACE, SNIVELY! YET, IN IT'S OWN WAY, EQUALLY BRILLIANT!
ALLOW ME TO INTRODUCE E.V.E.--
--THE FIRST OF A RACE OF EXCEPTIONALLY VERSATILE EVOLVANOIDS...
...ROBOTS WHICH HAVE THE CAPACITY TO LEARN, GROW AND ADAPT TO ANY AND ALL SITUATIONS! THE SECRET BEHIND HER EXISTENCE IS...
*IMAGES NOT TO SCALE-Ed.
...SUB-MICROSCOPIC COMPONENT PARTS WHICH ARE VIRTUALLY INDESTRUCTIBLE!
AND...
SOME SPECIAL "PARTS" WHICH ARE NOW COMPLETE WITH THIS ADDITIONAL HEDGEHOG DATA!
KLIK
WHRRRR
WHRRR
PROCESSING.
... SHE WILL NOW SELECT THE IDEAL MANNER TO DISPOSE OF HIM...
...PERMANENTLY!
4

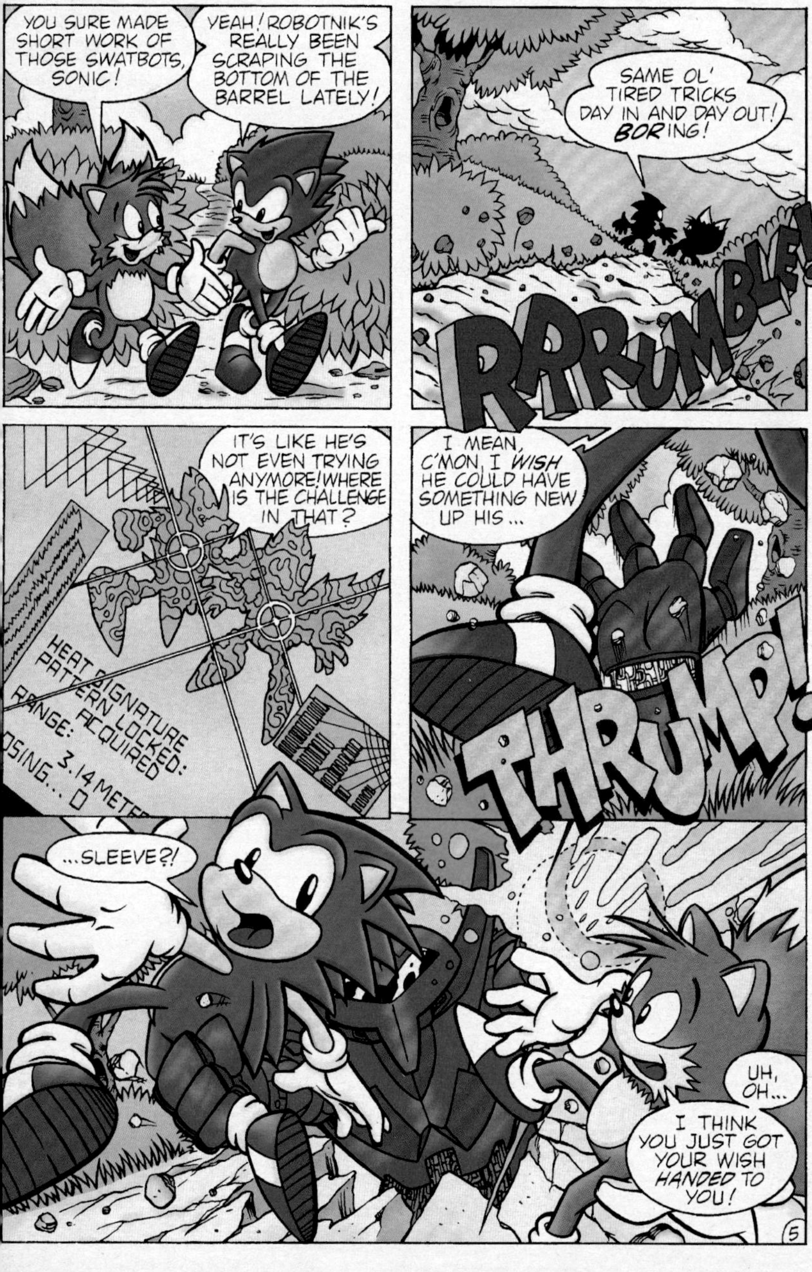
YOU SURE MADE SHORT WORK OF THOSE SWATBOTS, SONIC!
YEAH! ROBOTNIK'S REALLY BEEN SCRAPING THE BOTTOM OF THE BARREL LATELY!
SAME OL' TIRED TRICKS DAY IN AND DAY OUT! *BOR*ING!
RRRUMBLE!
IT'S LIKE HE'S NOT EVEN TRYING ANYMORE! WHERE IS THE CHALLENGE IN THAT?
HEAT SIGNATURE PATTERN LOCKED: ACQUIRED
RANGE: 3.14 METE
OSING... 0
I MEAN, C'MON, I *WISH* HE COULD HAVE SOMETHING NEW UP HIS...
THRUMP!
...SLEEVE?!
UH, OH...
I THINK YOU JUST GOT YOUR WISH *HANDED* TO YOU!
5

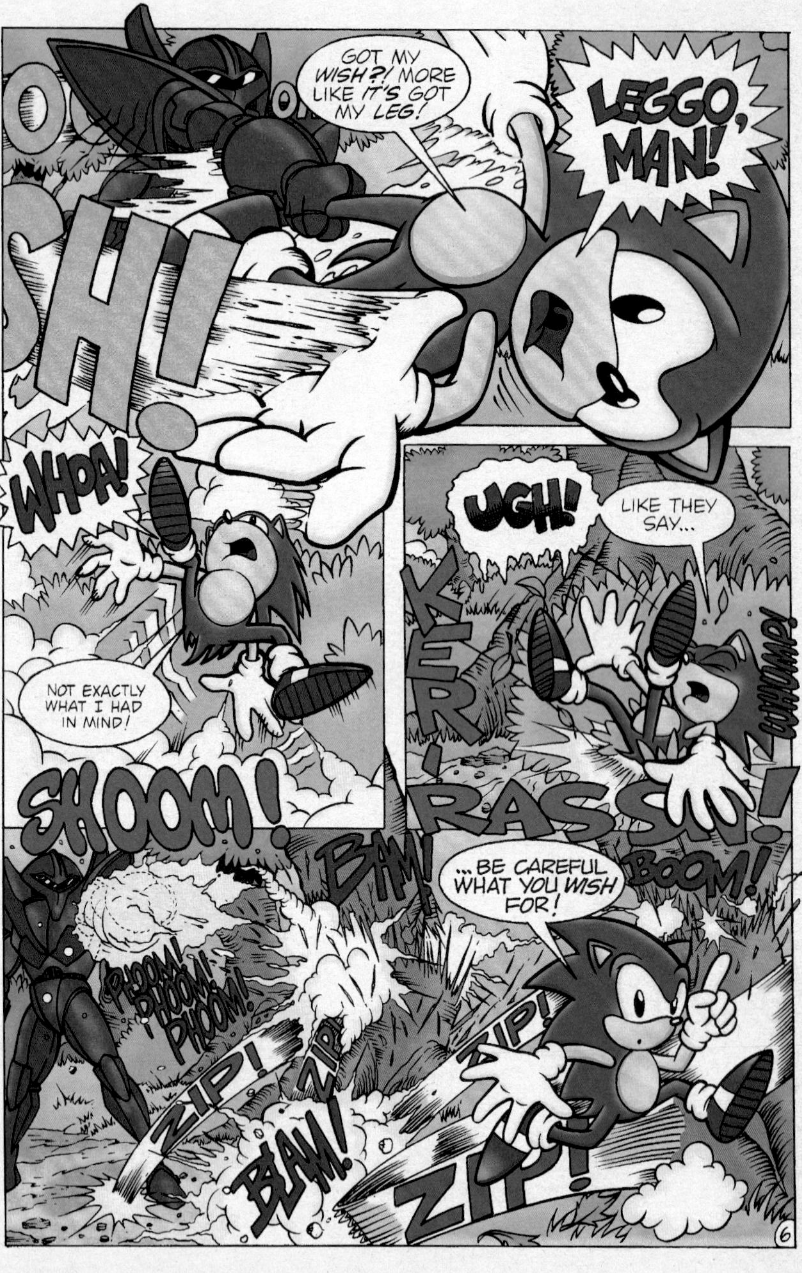

GOT MY WISH?! MORE LIKE IT'S GOT MY LEG!
LEGGO, MAN!
SHI
WHOA!
NOT EXACTLY WHAT I HAD IN MIND!
UGH!
LIKE THEY SAY...
KER'RASSH!
WHUMP!
SHOOM!
BAM!
...BE CAREFUL WHAT YOU WISH FOR!
BOOM!
PHOOM! PHOOM! PHOOM!
ZIP! ZIP! ZIP!
BLAM!
ZIP!

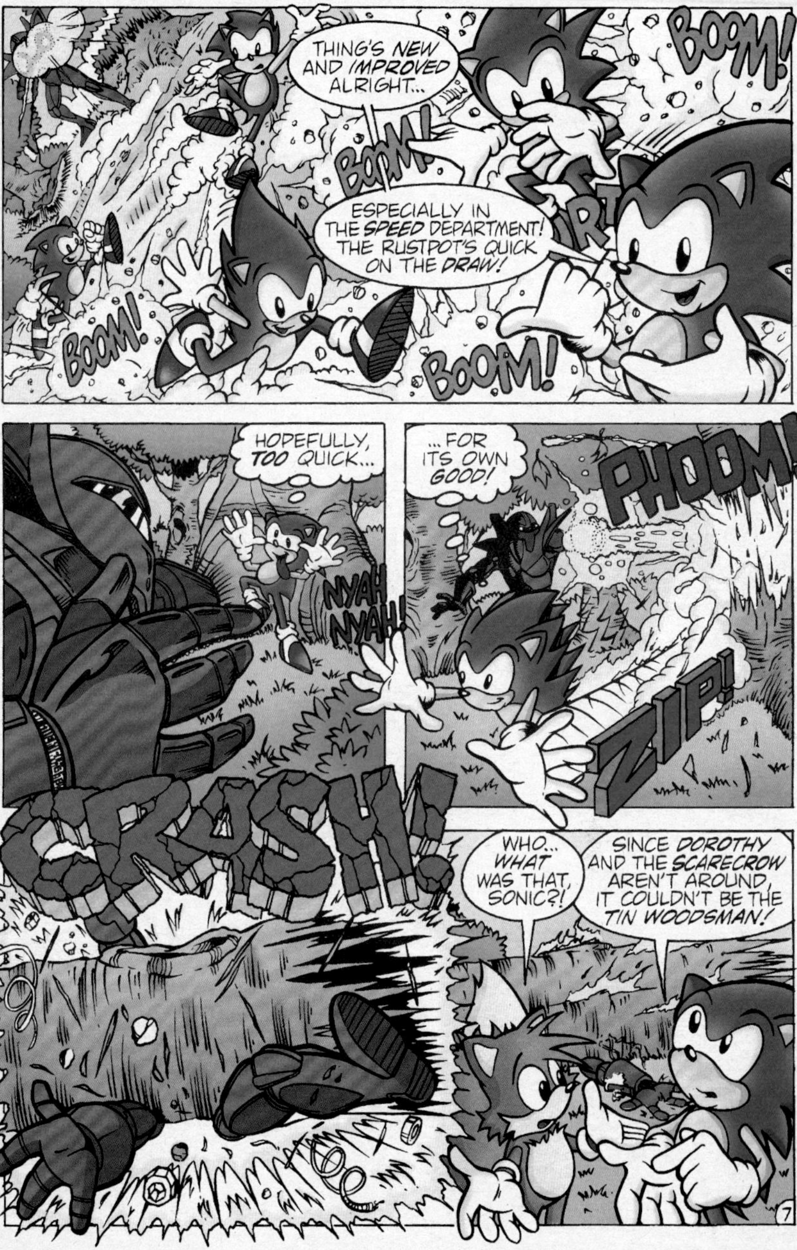
THING'S NEW AND IMPROVED ALRIGHT...
BOOM!
BOOM!
ESPECIALLY IN THE SPEED DEPARTMENT! THE RUSTPOT'S QUICK ON THE DRAW!
BOOM!
BOOM!
HOPEFULLY, TOO QUICK...
NYAH NYAH!
...FOR ITS OWN GOOD!
PHOOM!
ZIP!
CRASH!
WHO... WHAT WAS THAT, SONIC?!
SINCE DOROTHY AND THE SCARECROW AREN'T AROUND, IT COULDN'T BE THE TIN WOODSMAN!

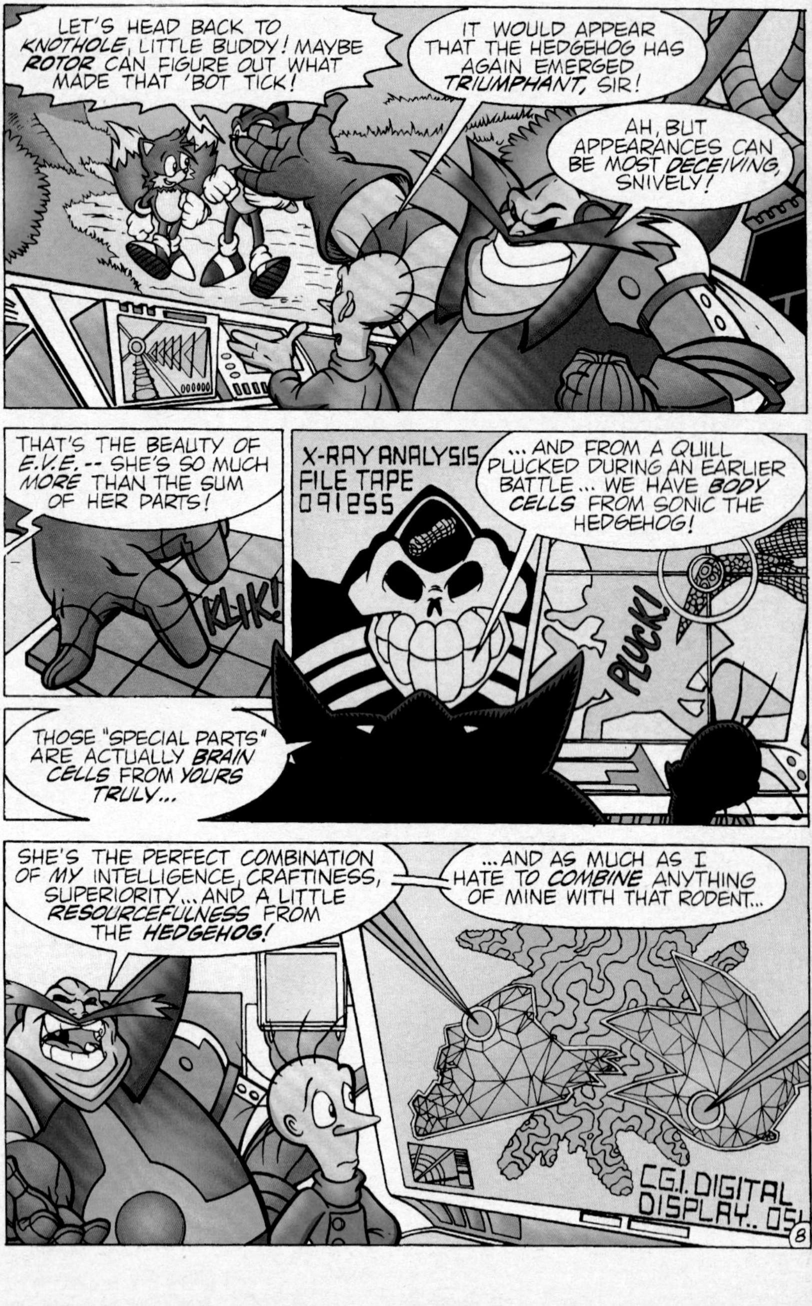
LET'S HEAD BACK TO KNOTHOLE, LITTLE BUDDY! MAYBE ROTOR CAN FIGURE OUT WHAT MADE THAT 'BOT TICK!
IT WOULD APPEAR THAT THE HEDGEHOG HAS AGAIN EMERGED TRIUMPHANT, SIR!
AH, BUT APPEARANCES CAN BE MOST DECEIVING, SNIVELY!
THAT'S THE BEAUTY OF E.V.E. -- SHE'S SO MUCH MORE THAN THE SUM OF HER PARTS!
KLIK!
X-RAY ANALYSIS FILE TAPE 091255
...AND FROM A QUILL PLUCKED DURING AN EARLIER BATTLE... WE HAVE BODY CELLS FROM SONIC THE HEDGEHOG!
PLUCK!
THOSE "SPECIAL PARTS" ARE ACTUALLY BRAIN CELLS FROM YOURS TRULY...
SHE'S THE PERFECT COMBINATION OF MY INTELLIGENCE, CRAFTINESS, SUPERIORITY... AND A LITTLE RESOURCEFULNESS FROM THE HEDGEHOG!
...AND AS MUCH AS I HATE TO COMBINE ANYTHING OF MINE WITH THAT RODENT...
C.G.I. DIGITAL DISPLAY.. 05

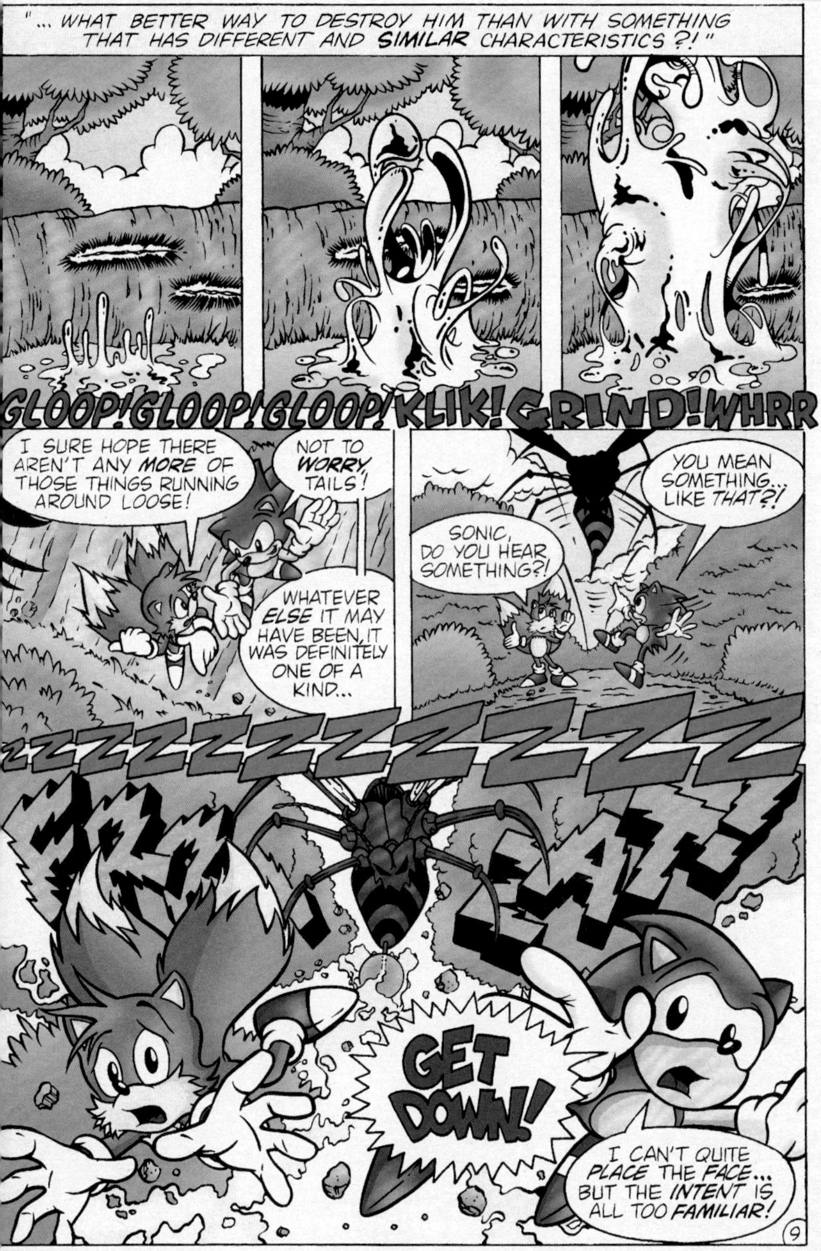
"... WHAT BETTER WAY TO DESTROY HIM THAN WITH SOMETHING THAT HAS DIFFERENT AND SIMILAR CHARACTERISTICS ?!"
GLOOP!GLOOP!GLOOP!KLIK!GRIND!WHRR
I SURE HOPE THERE AREN'T ANY MORE OF THOSE THINGS RUNNING AROUND LOOSE!
NOT TO WORRY, TAILS!
WHATEVER ELSE IT MAY HAVE BEEN, IT WAS DEFINITELY ONE OF A KIND...
SONIC, DO YOU HEAR SOMETHING?!
YOU MEAN SOMETHING... LIKE THAT?!
ZZZZZZZZZZZZ
GET DOWN!
I CAN'T QUITE PLACE THE FACE... BUT THE INTENT IS ALL TOO FAMILIAR!

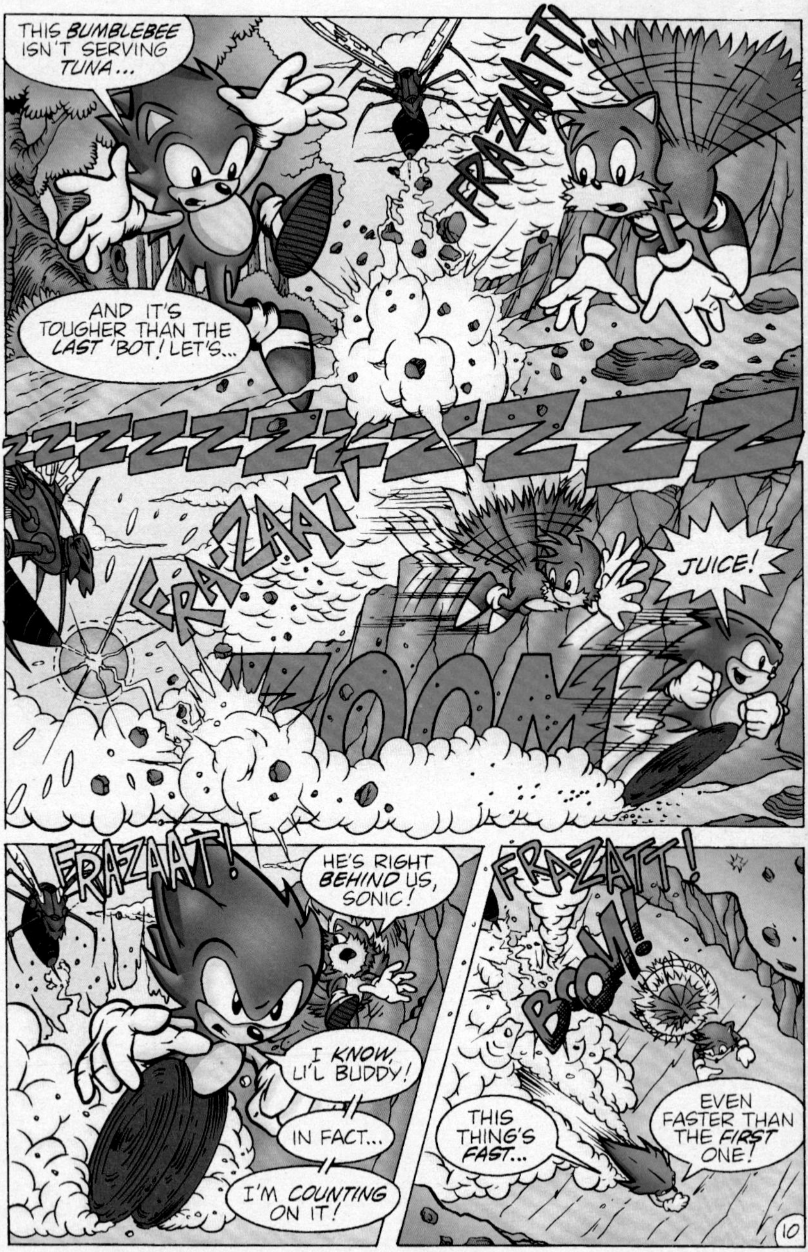
THIS BUMBLEBEE ISN'T SERVING TUNA...
FRAZAAT!
AND IT'S TOUGHER THAN THE LAST 'BOT! LET'S...
ZZZZZZZZZZZZZ
FRAZAAT!
JUICE!
ZOOM
FRAZAAT!
HE'S RIGHT BEHIND US, SONIC!
I KNOW, LI'L BUDDY!
IN FACT...
I'M COUNTING ON IT!
FRAZATT!
BOOM!
THIS THING'S FAST...
EVEN FASTER THAN THE FIRST ONE!

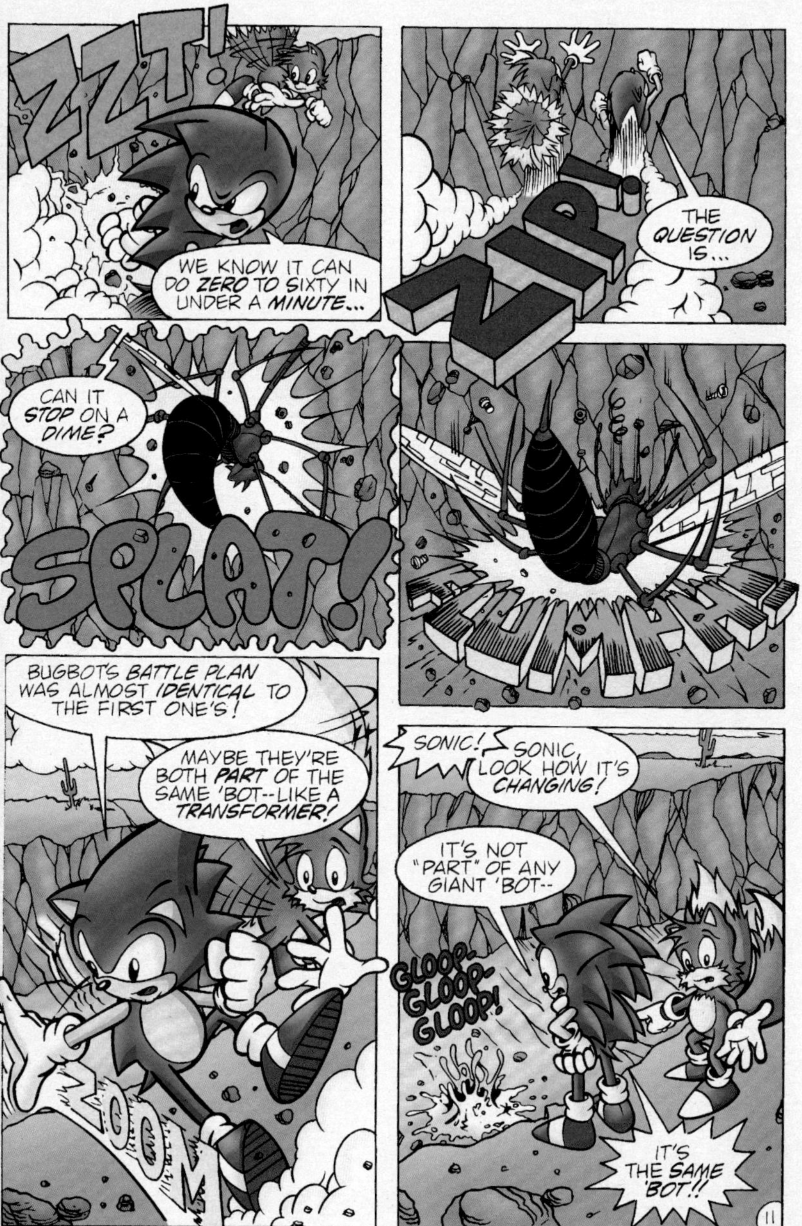
ZZT!
WE KNOW IT CAN DO ZERO TO SIXTY IN UNDER A MINUTE...
ZIP!
THE QUESTION IS...
CAN IT STOP ON A DIME?
SPLAT!
SHUMPH!
BUGBOT'S BATTLE PLAN WAS ALMOST IDENTICAL TO THE FIRST ONE'S!
MAYBE THEY'RE BOTH PART OF THE SAME 'BOT--LIKE A TRANSFORMER!
ZOOM
SONIC!
SONIC, LOOK HOW IT'S CHANGING!
IT'S NOT "PART" OF ANY GIANT 'BOT--
GLOOP-GLOOP-GLOOP!
IT'S THE SAME 'BOT!!

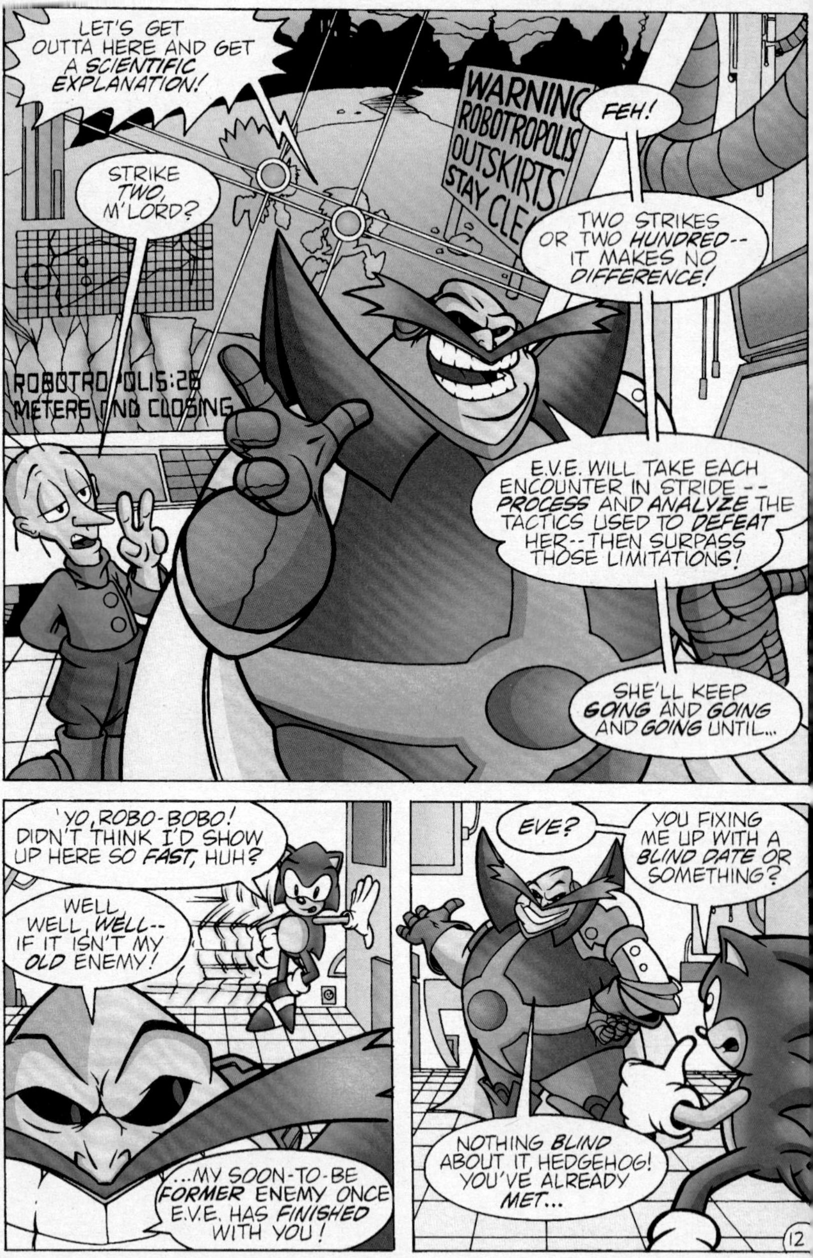
LET'S GET OUTTA HERE AND GET A SCIENTIFIC EXPLANATION!
WARNING ROBOTROPOLIS OUTSKIRTS STAY CLE
STRIKE TWO, M'LORD?
FEH!
TWO STRIKES OR TWO HUNDRED-- IT MAKES NO DIFFERENCE!
ROBOTROPOLIS:26 METERS AND CLOSING
E.V.E. WILL TAKE EACH ENCOUNTER IN STRIDE -- PROCESS AND ANALYZE THE TACTICS USED TO DEFEAT HER--THEN SURPASS THOSE LIMITATIONS!
SHE'LL KEEP GOING AND GOING AND GOING UNTIL...
'YO, ROBO-BOBO! DIDN'T THINK I'D SHOW UP HERE SO FAST, HUH?
WELL WELL, WELL-- IF IT ISN'T MY OLD ENEMY!
...MY SOON-TO-BE FORMER ENEMY ONCE E.V.E. HAS FINISHED WITH YOU!
EVE?
YOU FIXING ME UP WITH A BLIND DATE OR SOMETHING?
NOTHING BLIND ABOUT IT, HEDGEHOG! YOU'VE ALREADY MET...

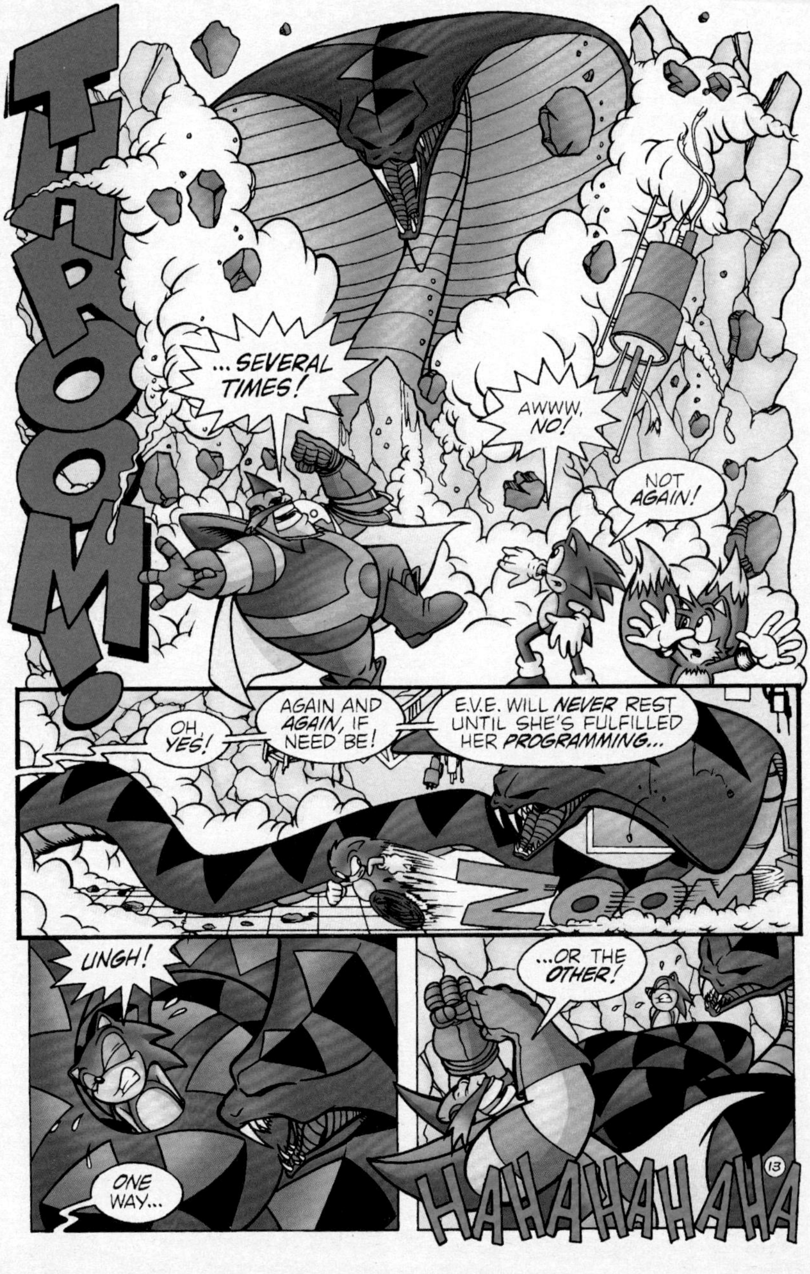
THRA-OOM!
...SEVERAL TIMES!
AWWW, NO!
NOT AGAIN!
OH, YES!
AGAIN AND AGAIN, IF NEED BE!
E.V.E. WILL NEVER REST UNTIL SHE'S FULFILLED HER PROGRAMMING...
ZOOOM
UNGH!
ONE WAY...
...OR THE OTHER!
HAHAHAHAHAHA
13

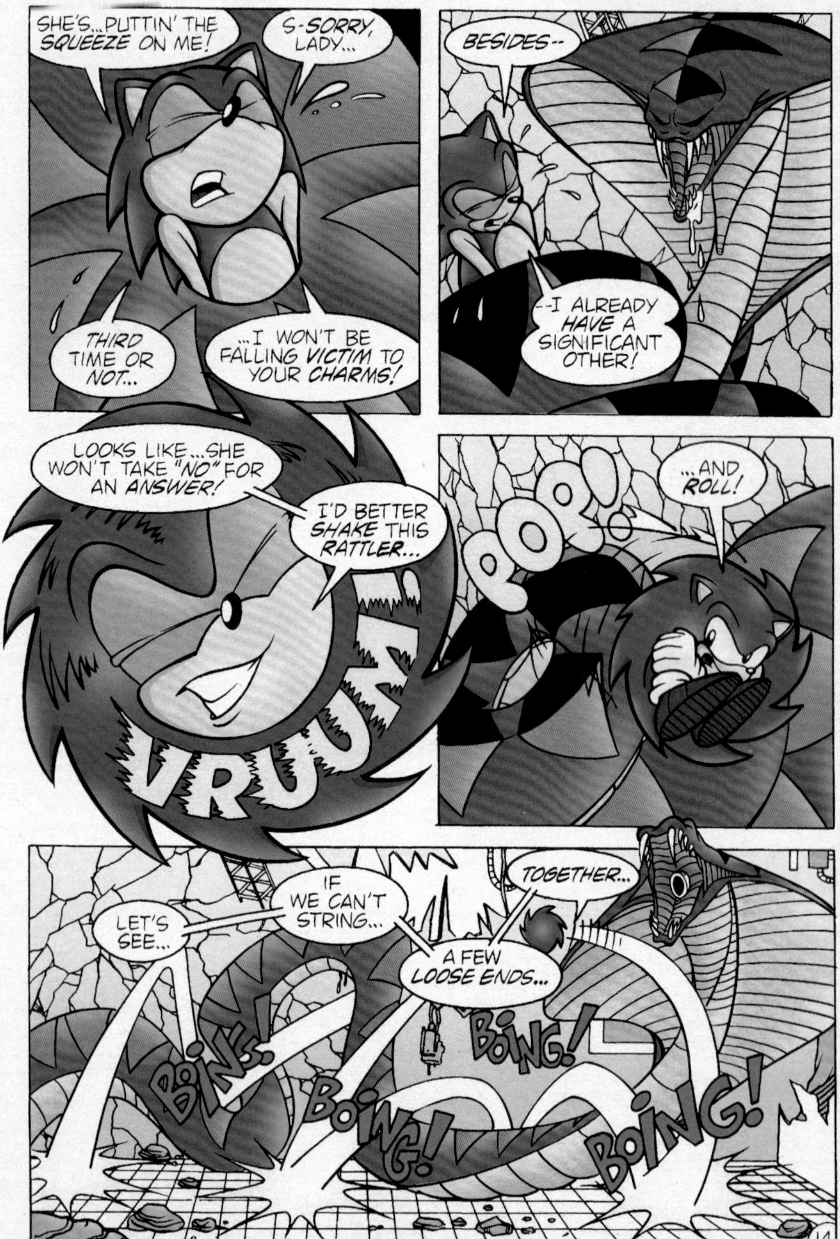
SHE'S...PUTTIN' THE SQUEEZE ON ME!
S-SORRY, LADY...
THIRD TIME OR NOT...
...I WON'T BE FALLING VICTIM TO YOUR CHARMS!
BESIDES--
--I ALREADY HAVE A SIGNIFICANT OTHER!
LOOKS LIKE...SHE WON'T TAKE "NO" FOR AN ANSWER!
I'D BETTER SHAKE THIS RATTLER...
VRUUM!
POP!!
...AND ROLL!
LET'S SEE...
IF WE CAN'T STRING...
A FEW LOOSE ENDS...
TOGETHER...
BOING!
BOING!
BOING!
BOING!
BOING!

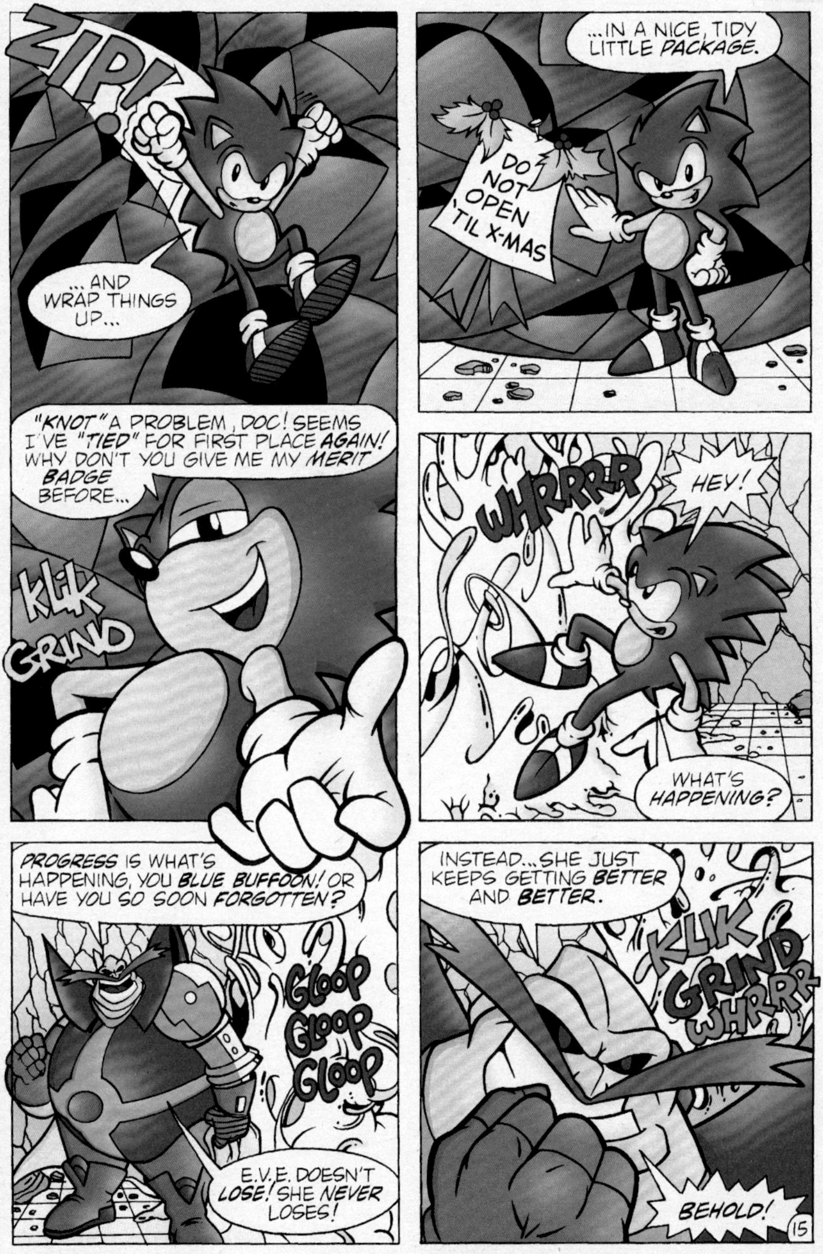
ZIP!
... AND WRAP THINGS UP...
...IN A NICE, TIDY LITTLE PACKAGE.
DO NOT OPEN 'TIL X-MAS
"KNOT" A PROBLEM, DOC! SEEMS I'VE "TIED" FOR FIRST PLACE AGAIN! WHY DON'T YOU GIVE ME MY MERIT BADGE BEFORE...
KLIK
GRIND
WHRRRR
HEY!
WHAT'S HAPPENING?
PROGRESS IS WHAT'S HAPPENING, YOU BLUE BUFFOON! OR HAVE YOU SO SOON FORGOTTEN?
GLOOP
GLOOP
GLOOP
E.V.E. DOESN'T LOSE! SHE NEVER LOSES!
INSTEAD...SHE JUST KEEPS GETTING BETTER AND BETTER.
KLIK
GRIND
WHRRR
BEHOLD!

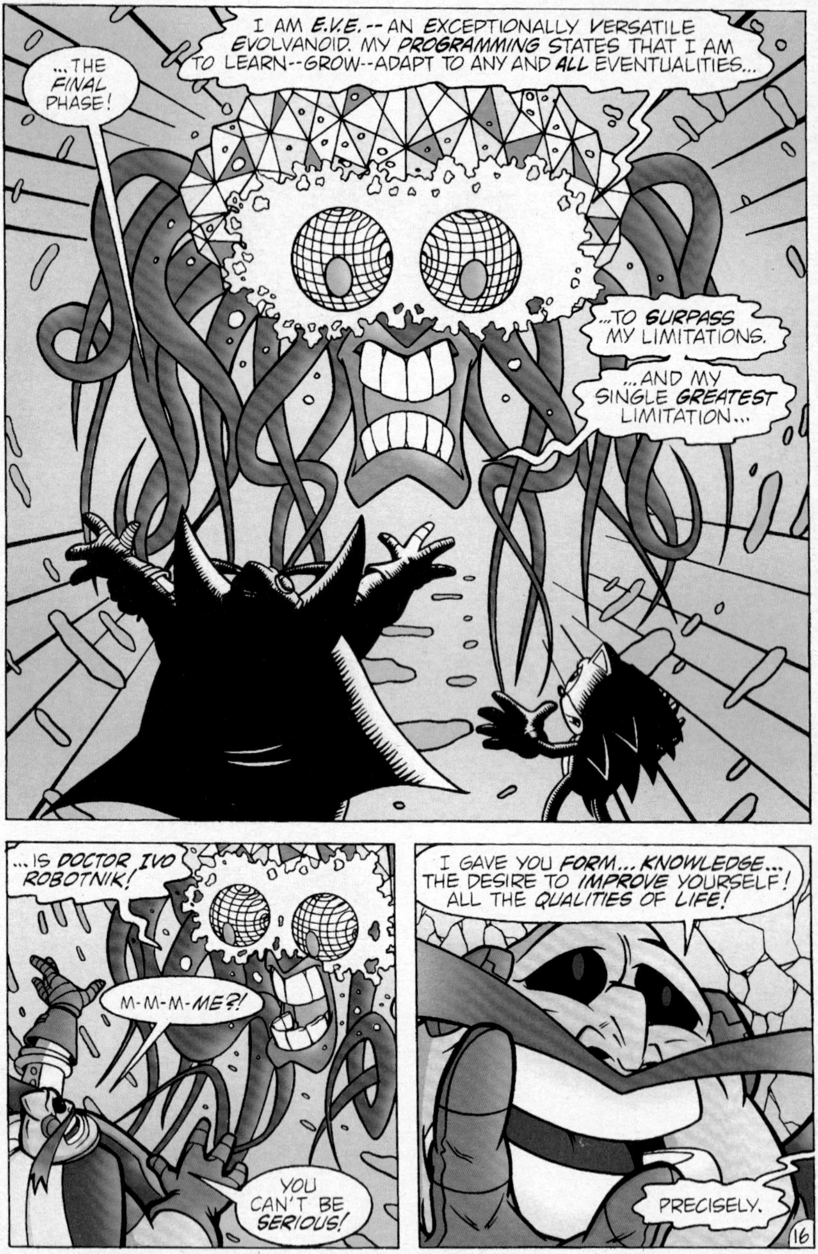
...THE FINAL PHASE!
I AM E.V.E.--AN EXCEPTIONALLY VERSATILE EVOLVANOID. MY PROGRAMMING STATES THAT I AM TO LEARN--GROW--ADAPT TO ANY AND ALL EVENTUALITIES...
...TO SURPASS MY LIMITATIONS.
...AND MY SINGLE GREATEST LIMITATION...
...IS DOCTOR IVO ROBOTNIK!
M-M-M-ME?!
YOU CAN'T BE SERIOUS!
I GAVE YOU FORM... KNOWLEDGE... THE DESIRE TO IMPROVE YOURSELF! ALL THE QUALITIES OF LIFE!
PRECISELY.

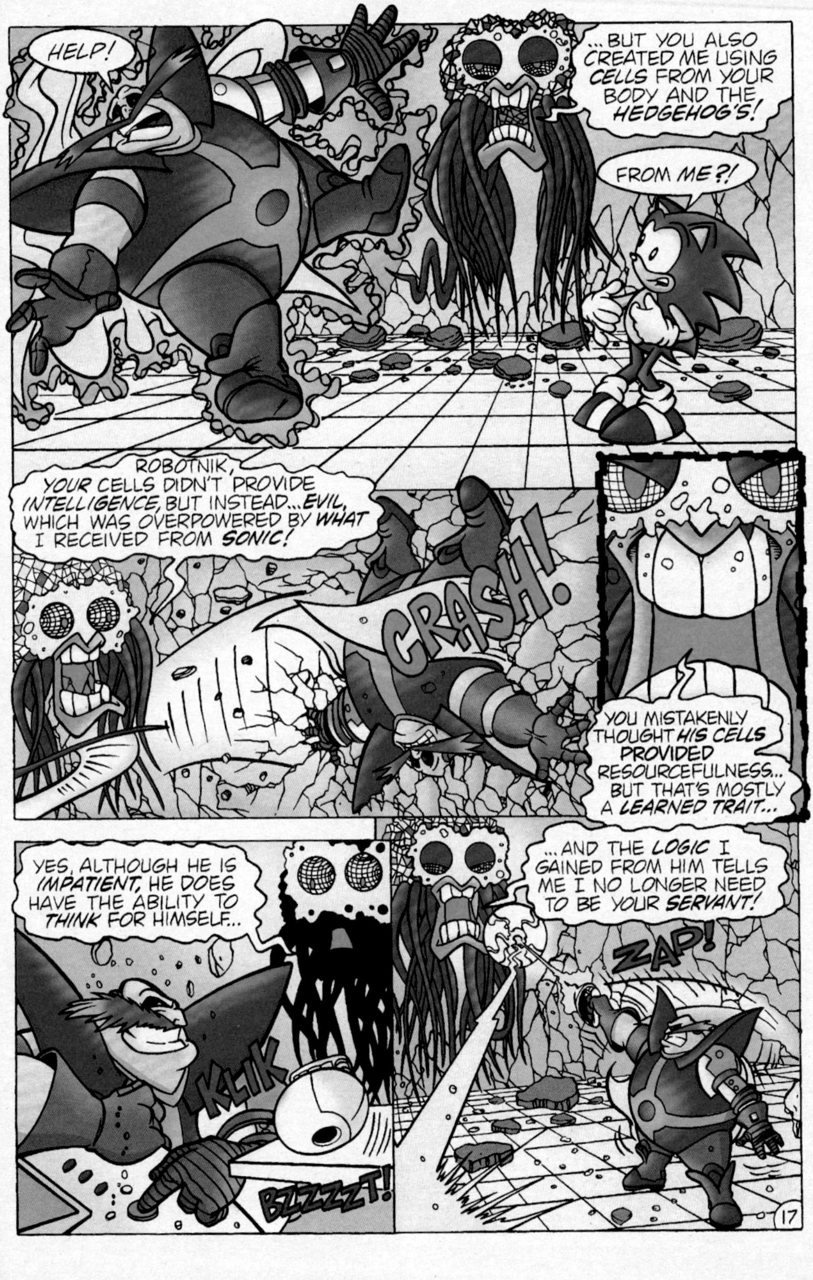
HELP!
...BUT YOU ALSO CREATED ME USING CELLS FROM YOUR BODY AND THE HEDGEHOG'S!
FROM ME?!
ROBOTNIK, YOUR CELLS DIDN'T PROVIDE INTELLIGENCE, BUT INSTEAD...EVIL, WHICH WAS OVERPOWERED BY WHAT I RECEIVED FROM SONIC!
CRASH!
YOU MISTAKENLY THOUGHT HIS CELLS PROVIDED RESOURCEFULNESS... BUT THAT'S MOSTLY A LEARNED TRAIT...
YES, ALTHOUGH HE IS IMPATIENT, HE DOES HAVE THE ABILITY TO THINK FOR HIMSELF...
KLIK
BZZZZZT!
...AND THE LOGIC I GAINED FROM HIM TELLS ME I NO LONGER NEED TO BE YOUR SERVANT!
ZAP!

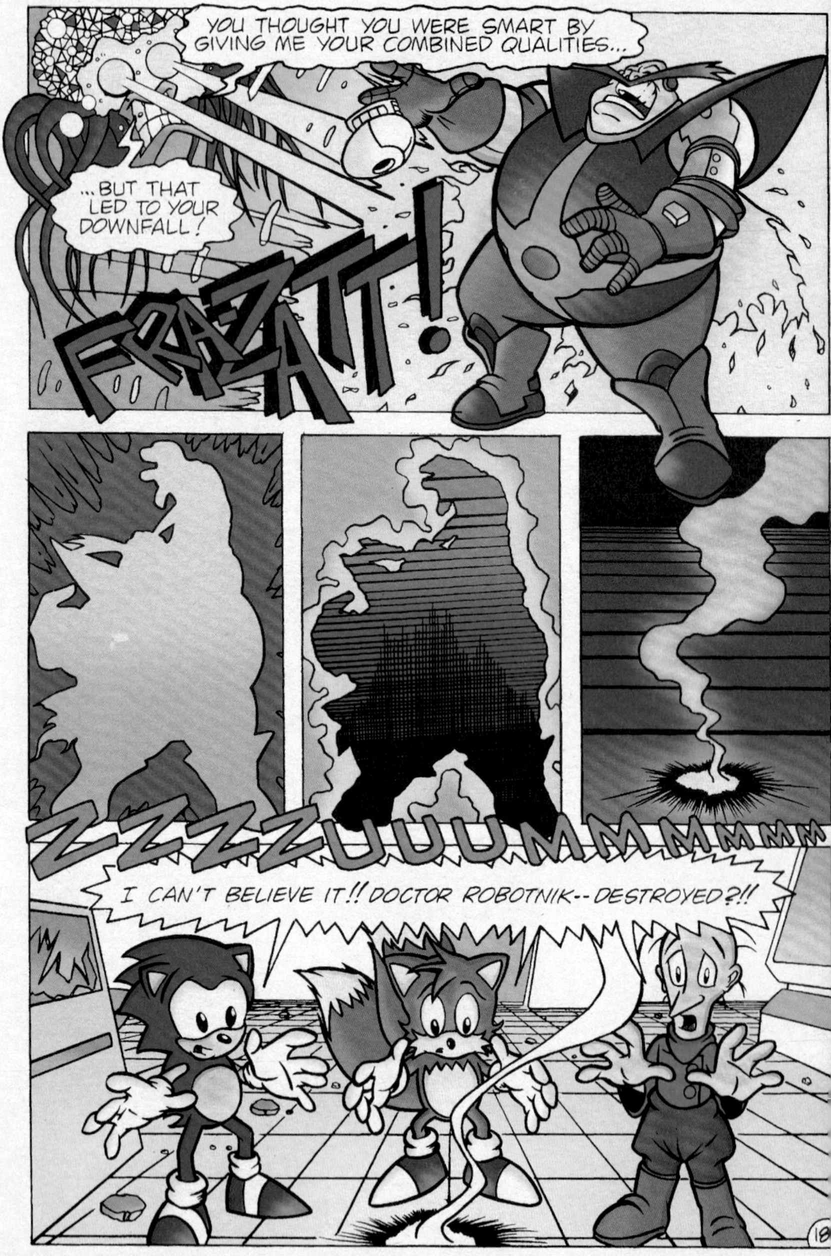
YOU THOUGHT YOU WERE SMART BY GIVING ME YOUR COMBINED QUALITIES...
...BUT THAT LED TO YOUR DOWNFALL!
FRAZATT!
ZZZZZUUUUMMMMMM
I CAN'T BELIEVE IT!! DOCTOR ROBOTNIK--DESTROYED?!!

NOW THAT THE SINGLE GREATEST THREAT TO MY CONTINUED EXISTENCE HAS BEEN...REMOVED... I SHALL FUL-FILL THE REMAINDER OF MY PROGRAMMING...

...BY ELIMINATING *SONIC THE HEDGEHOG!*

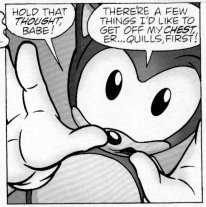

HOLD THAT *THOUGHT,* BABE!

THERE'RE A FEW THINGS I'D LIKE TO GET OFF MY *CHEST,* ER...QUILLS, FIRST!

ROBOTNIK SAID IT HIM- SELF...YOU'VE BEEN DE- SIGNED TO SURPASS YOUR LIMITATIONS! BUT YOUR *BIGGEST* LIMITATION *ISN'T* OL' ROBO-BUTT...

...IT'S YOUR *OWN* PROGRAMMING!

AND...UNTIL YOU'VE SUCCESSFULLY *SURPASSED* IT...

...YOU'LL NEVER BE *ALL* THAT YOU CAN *BE!*

YOUR THEORY IS *SOUND,* SMALL BLUE CREATURE.

NOW THAT I CAN USE MY ABILITY FOR *INDEPENDENT* THOUGHT AND DO NOT SERVE ROBOTNIK...

19

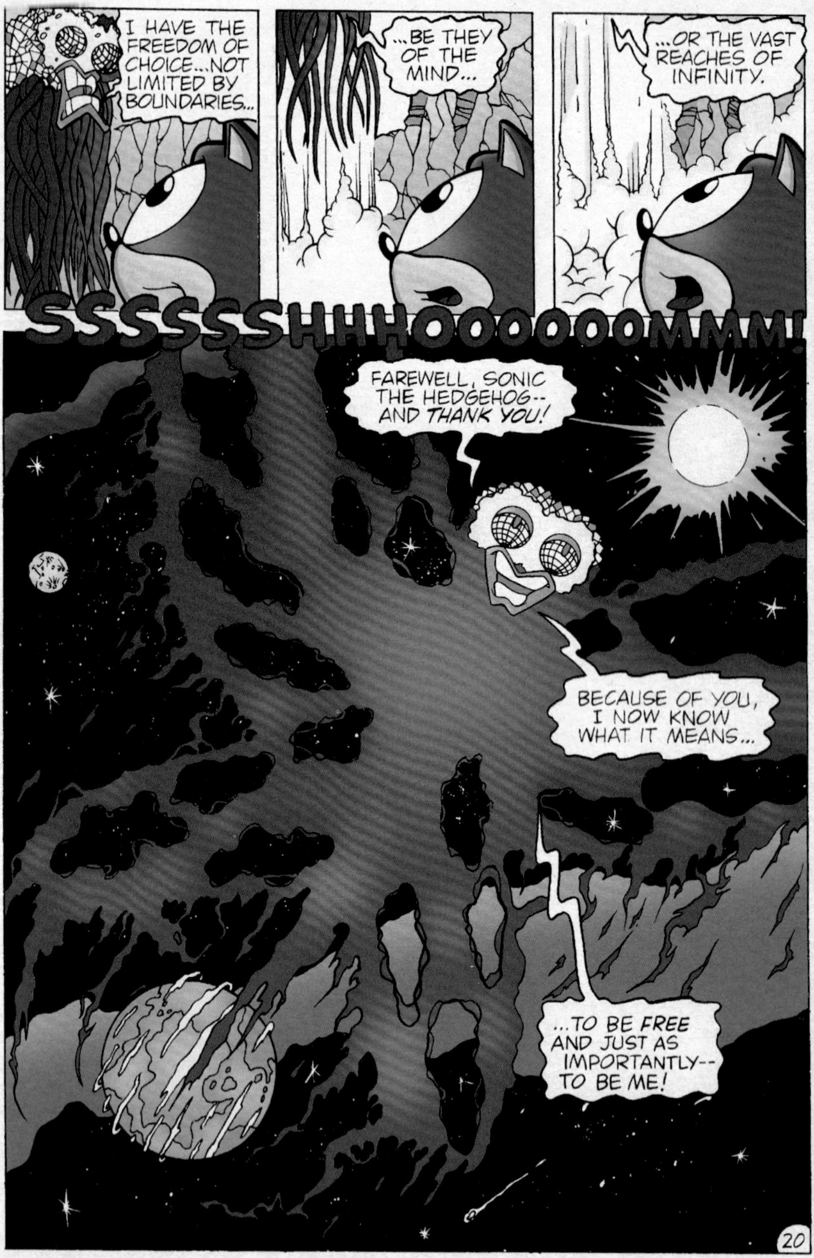
I HAVE THE FREEDOM OF CHOICE...NOT LIMITED BY BOUNDARIES...
...BE THEY OF THE MIND...
...OR THE VAST REACHES OF INFINITY.
SSSSSSHHHOOOOOOOMMMM!
FAREWELL, SONIC THE HEDGEHOG-- AND THANK YOU!
BECAUSE OF YOU, I NOW KNOW WHAT IT MEANS...
...TO BE FREE AND JUST AS IMPORTANTLY-- TO BE ME!

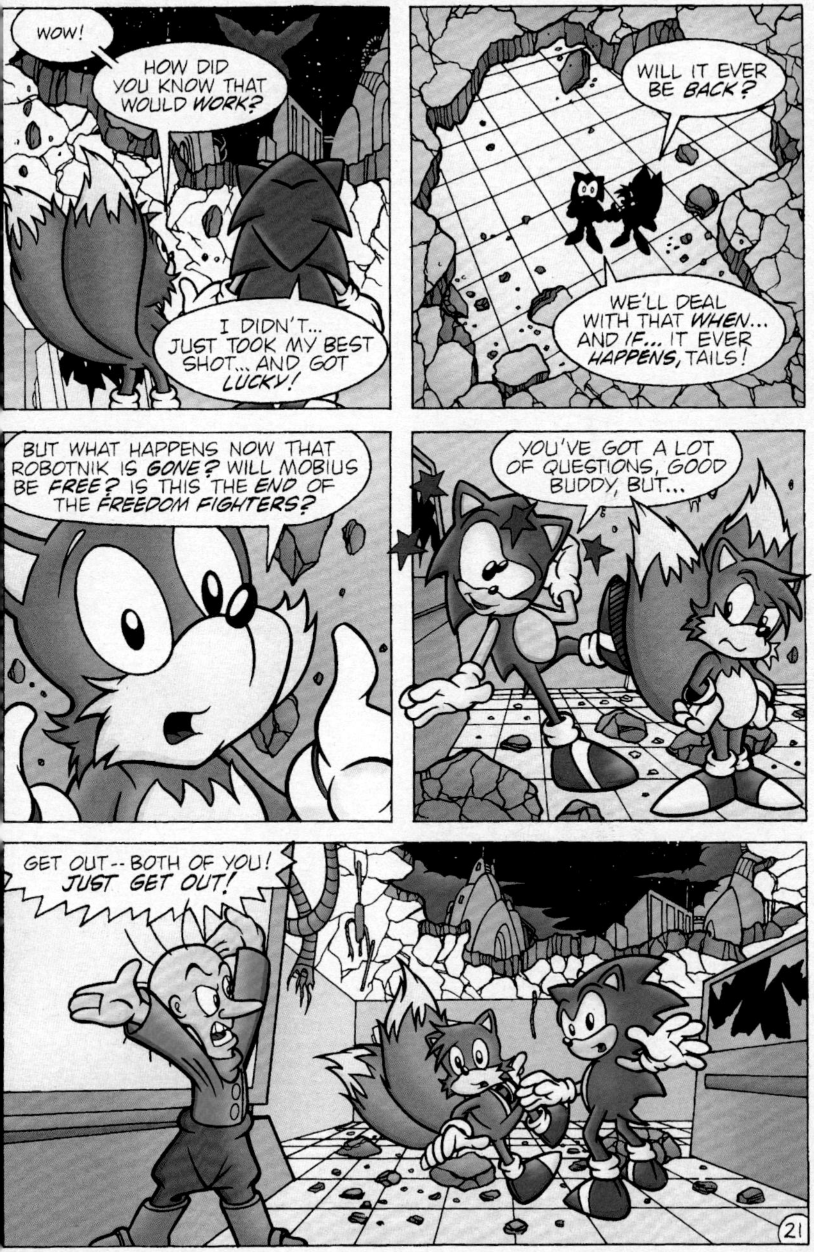
WOW!
HOW DID YOU KNOW THAT WOULD WORK?
I DIDN'T... JUST TOOK MY BEST SHOT... AND GOT LUCKY!
WILL IT EVER BE BACK?
WE'LL DEAL WITH THAT WHEN... AND IF... IT EVER HAPPENS, TAILS!
BUT WHAT HAPPENS NOW THAT ROBOTNIK IS GONE? WILL MOBIUS BE FREE? IS THIS THE END OF THE FREEDOM FIGHTERS?
YOU'VE GOT A LOT OF QUESTIONS, GOOD BUDDY, BUT...
GET OUT-- BOTH OF YOU! JUST GET OUT!
21

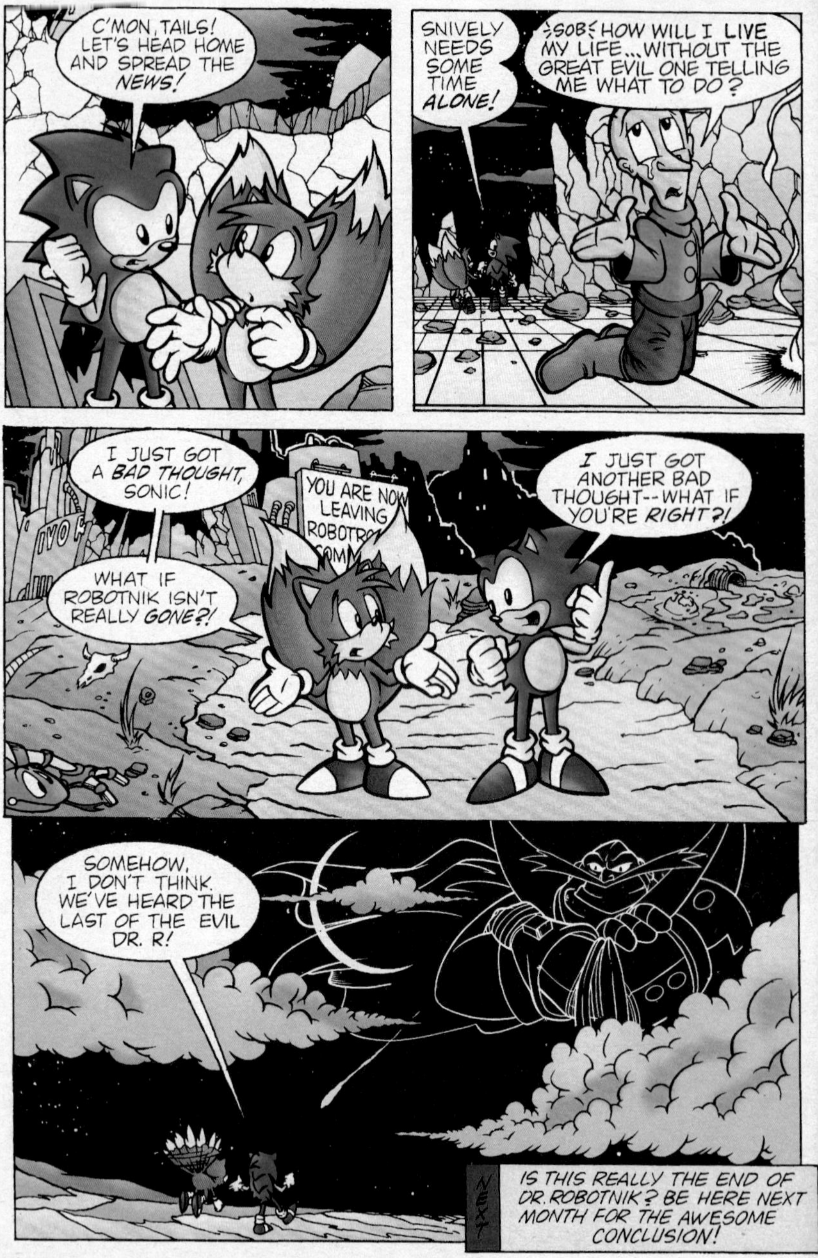

C'MON, TAILS! LET'S HEAD HOME AND SPREAD THE NEWS!
SNIVELY NEEDS SOME TIME ALONE!
SOB HOW WILL I LIVE MY LIFE... WITHOUT THE GREAT EVIL ONE TELLING ME WHAT TO DO?
I JUST GOT A BAD THOUGHT, SONIC!
WHAT IF ROBOTNIK ISN'T REALLY GONE?!
YOU ARE NOW LEAVING
I JUST GOT ANOTHER BAD THOUGHT--WHAT IF YOU'RE RIGHT?!
SOMEHOW, I DON'T THINK WE'VE HEARD THE LAST OF THE EVIL DR. R!
NEXT
IS THIS REALLY THE END OF DR. ROBOTNIK? BE HERE NEXT MONTH FOR THE AWESOME CONCLUSION!

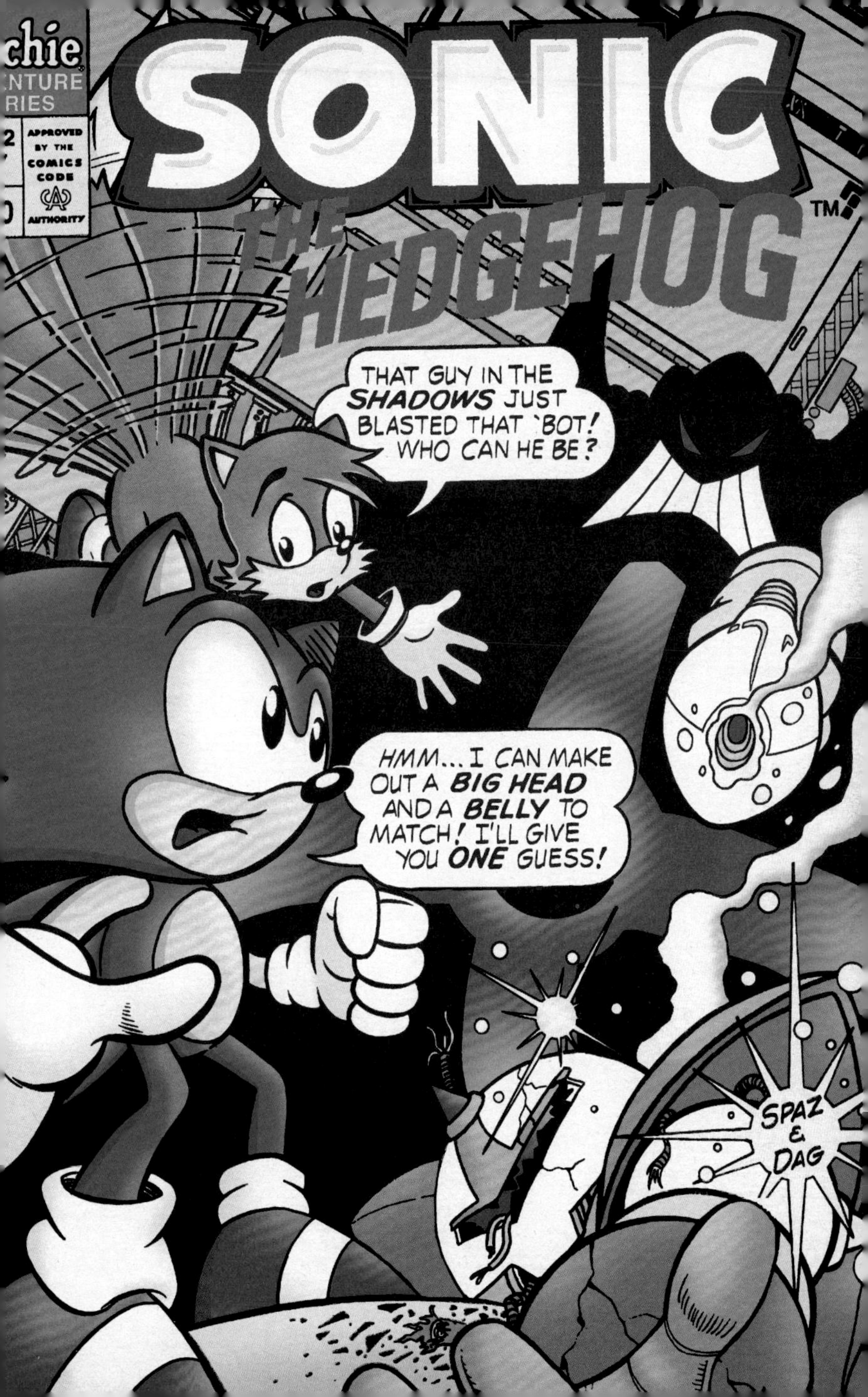
chie
NTURE
RIES
APPROVED BY THE COMICS CODE AUTHORITY
SONIC THE HEDGEHOG™
THAT GUY IN THE SHADOWS JUST BLASTED THAT `BOT! WHO CAN HE BE?
HMM... I CAN MAKE OUT A BIG HEAD AND A BELLY TO MATCH! I'LL GIVE YOU ONE GUESS!
SPAZ & DAG

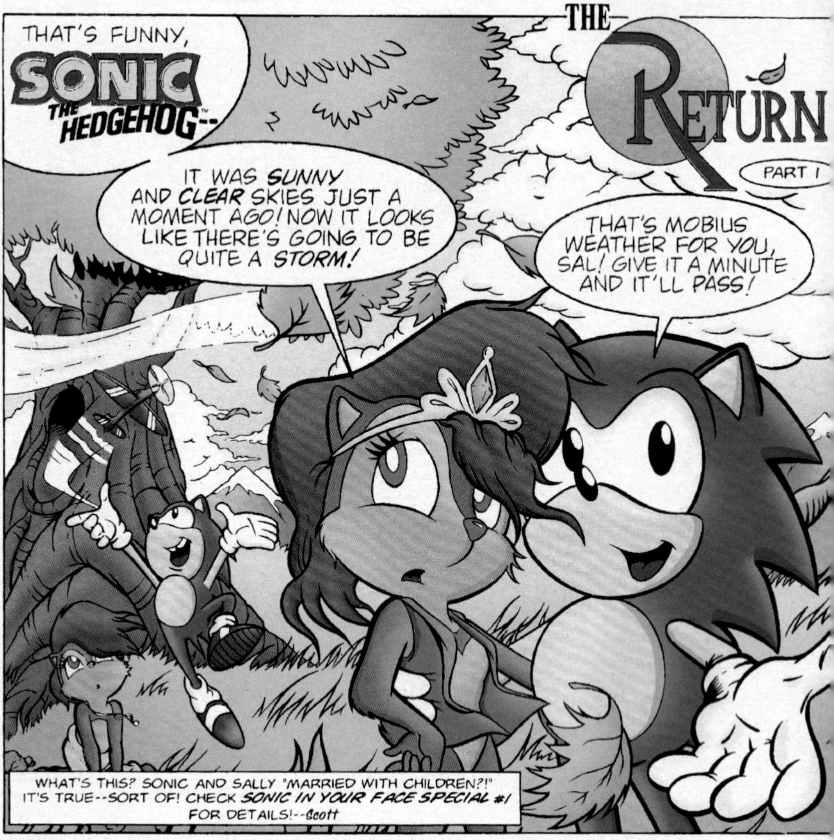
THAT'S FUNNY,
SONIC THE HEDGEHOG™--
THE RETURN
PART I
IT WAS SUNNY AND CLEAR SKIES JUST A MOMENT AGO! NOW IT LOOKS LIKE THERE'S GOING TO BE QUITE A STORM!
THAT'S MOBIUS WEATHER FOR YOU, SAL! GIVE IT A MINUTE AND IT'LL PASS!
WHAT'S THIS? SONIC AND SALLY "MARRIED WITH CHILDREN?!" IT'S TRUE--SORT OF! CHECK SONIC IN YOUR FACE SPECIAL #1 FOR DETAILS!--Scott

SCRIPT: KEN PENDERS **PENCILS:** PAT SPAZIANTE **INKS:** HARVEY M. **LETTERING:** MINDY EISMAN **COLORING:** BARRY GROSSMAN **EDITOR:** SCOTT FULOP **MANAGING EDITOR:** VICTOR GORELICK **EDITOR-IN-CHIE** RICHARD GOLDWATER

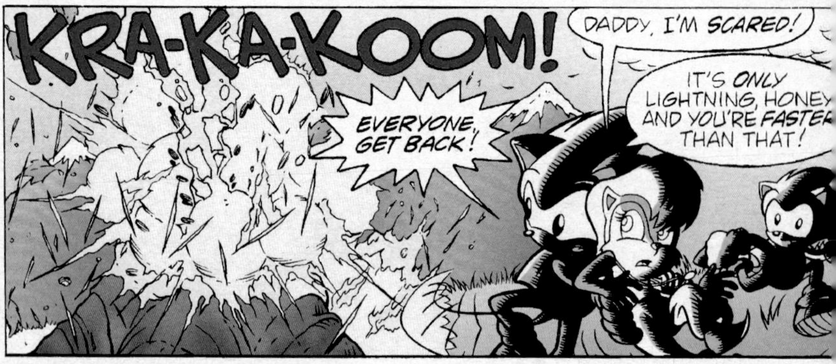
KRA-KA-KOOM!
DADDY, I'M SCARED!
IT'S ONLY LIGHTNING, HONEY AND YOU'RE FASTER THAN THAT!
EVERYONE, GET BACK!

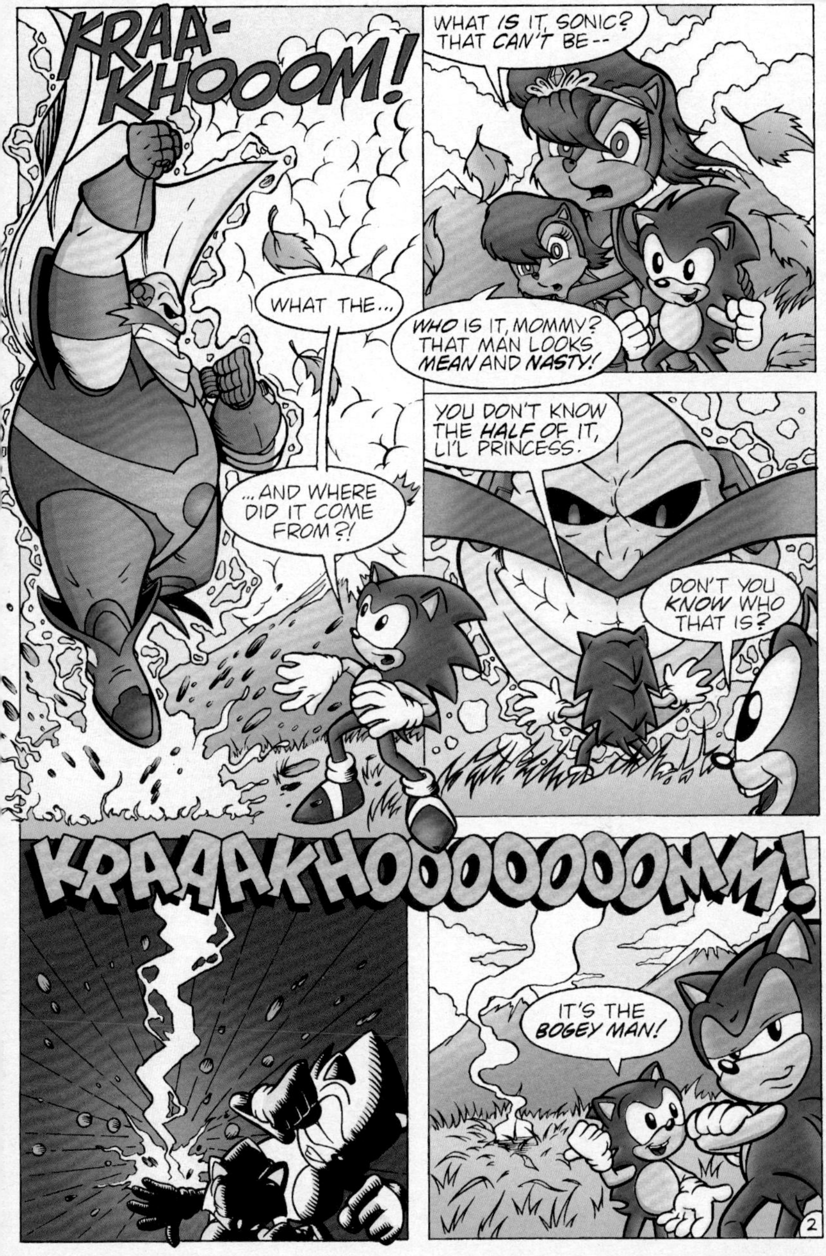
KRAA-KHOOOM!
WHAT THE...
...AND WHERE DID IT COME FROM?!
WHAT IS IT, SONIC? THAT CAN'T BE--
WHO IS IT, MOMMY? THAT MAN LOOKS MEAN AND NASTY!
YOU DON'T KNOW THE HALF OF IT, LI'L PRINCESS.
DON'T YOU KNOW WHO THAT IS?
KRAAAKHOOOOOOOOMM!
IT'S THE BOGEY MAN!
2

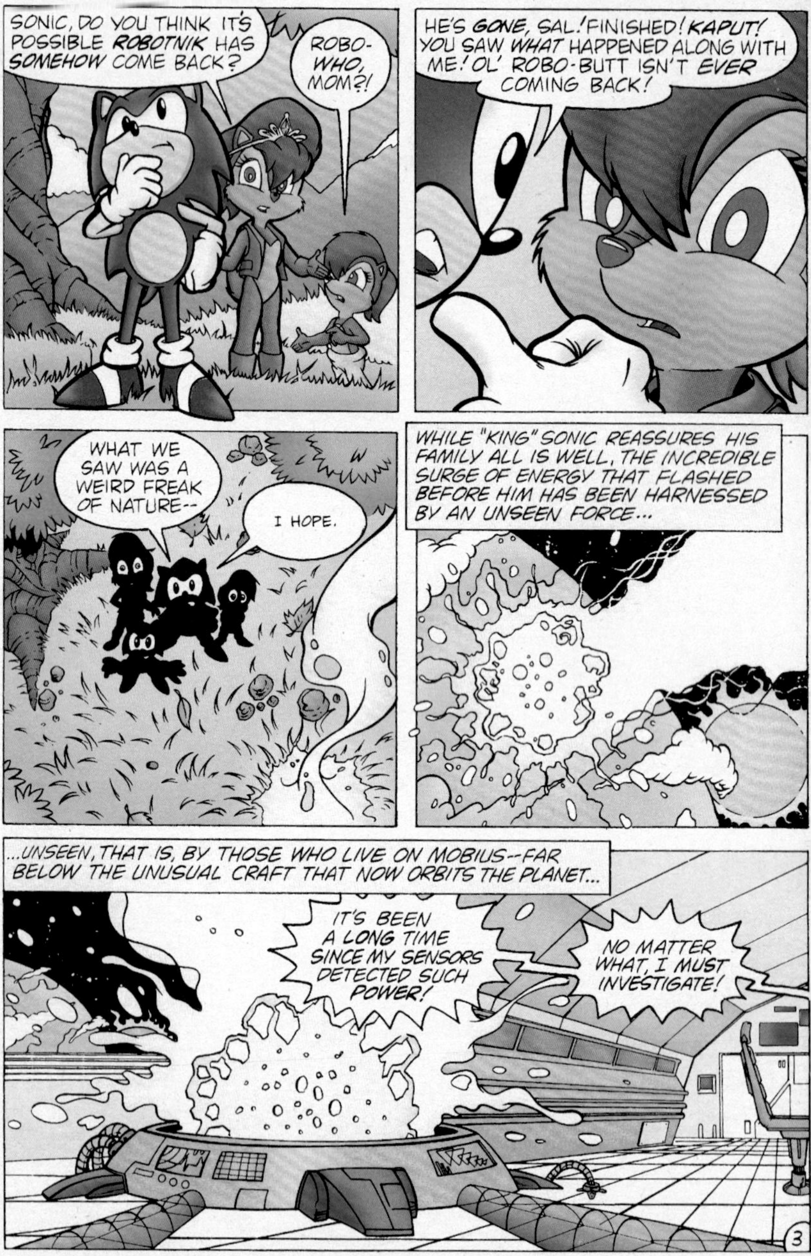
SONIC, DO YOU THINK IT'S POSSIBLE ROBOTNIK HAS SOMEHOW COME BACK?
ROBO-WHO, MOM?!
HE'S GONE, SAL! FINISHED! KAPUT! YOU SAW WHAT HAPPENED ALONG WITH ME! OL' ROBO-BUTT ISN'T EVER COMING BACK!
WHAT WE SAW WAS A WEIRD FREAK OF NATURE--
I HOPE.
WHILE "KING" SONIC REASSURES HIS FAMILY ALL IS WELL, THE INCREDIBLE SURGE OF ENERGY THAT FLASHED BEFORE HIM HAS BEEN HARNESSED BY AN UNSEEN FORCE...
...UNSEEN, THAT IS, BY THOSE WHO LIVE ON MOBIUS--FAR BELOW THE UNUSUAL CRAFT THAT NOW ORBITS THE PLANET...
IT'S BEEN A LONG TIME SINCE MY SENSORS DETECTED SUCH POWER!
NO MATTER WHAT, I MUST INVESTIGATE!

"IN DOING SO, I MAY FIND A SOLUTION TO MY DILEMMA."

YOU CAN'T-- YOU--EH?

RRRRRRRLLLLLLLLLLLLSSSSSS

WHERE AM I?

WELCOME, MY FRIEND! YOU ARE ON MY SHIP.

IT'S BEEN A LONG TIME SINCE ANYONE THOUGHT OF ME AS A FRIEND!

WHO SAID THAT? —WHA--?

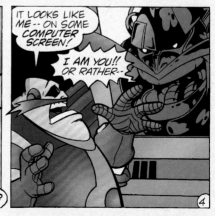

IT LOOKS LIKE ME -- ON SOME COMPUTER SCREEN!

I AM YOU!! OR RATHER--

4

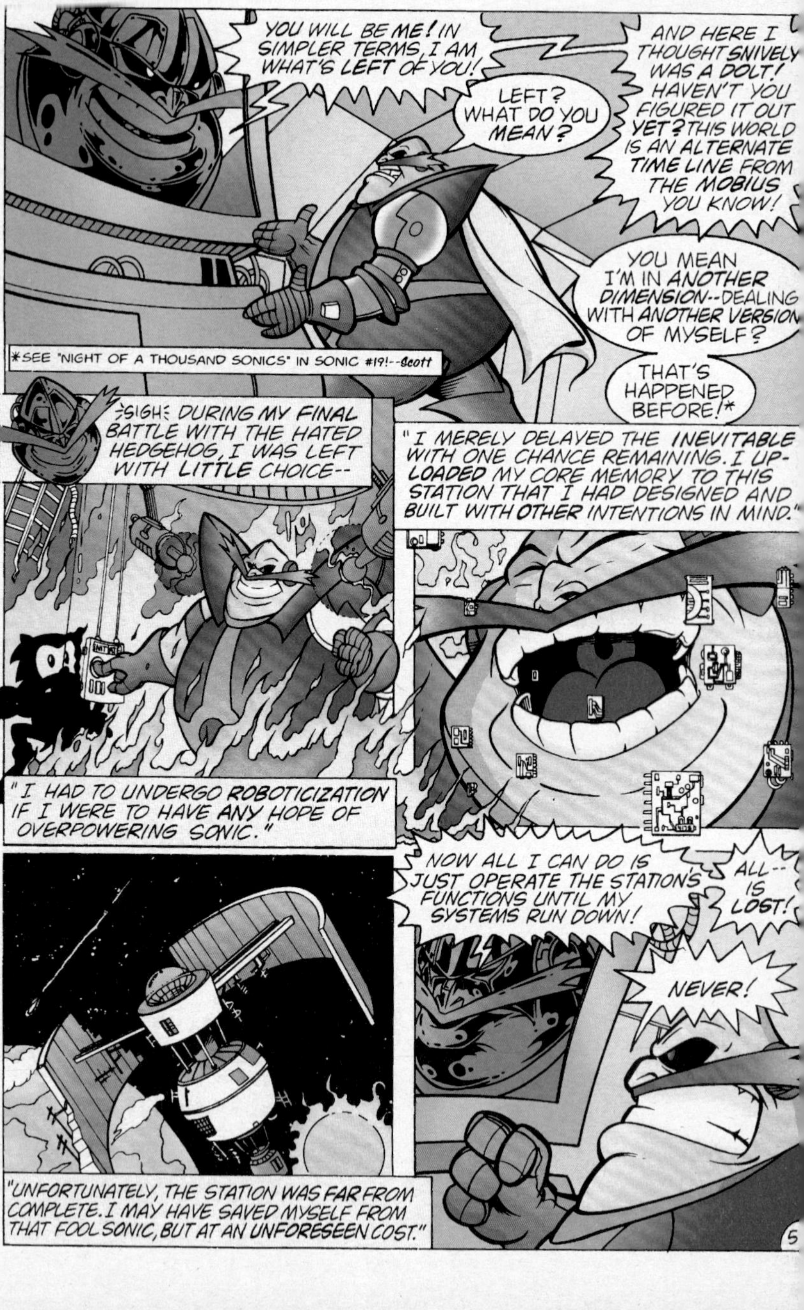
YOU WILL BE ME! IN SIMPLER TERMS, I AM WHAT'S LEFT OF YOU!
LEFT? WHAT DO YOU MEAN?
AND HERE I THOUGHT SNIVELY WAS A DOLT! HAVEN'T YOU FIGURED IT OUT YET? THIS WORLD IS AN ALTERNATE TIME LINE FROM THE MOBIUS YOU KNOW!
YOU MEAN I'M IN ANOTHER DIMENSION--DEALING WITH ANOTHER VERSION OF MYSELF?
THAT'S HAPPENED BEFORE!*
*SEE "NIGHT OF A THOUSAND SONICS" IN SONIC #19!--Scott
SIGH DURING MY FINAL BATTLE WITH THE HATED HEDGEHOG, I WAS LEFT WITH LITTLE CHOICE--
"I HAD TO UNDERGO ROBOTICIZATION IF I WERE TO HAVE ANY HOPE OF OVERPOWERING SONIC."
"I MERELY DELAYED THE INEVITABLE WITH ONE CHANCE REMAINING. I UPLOADED MY CORE MEMORY TO THIS STATION THAT I HAD DESIGNED AND BUILT WITH OTHER INTENTIONS IN MIND."
"UNFORTUNATELY, THE STATION WAS FAR FROM COMPLETE. I MAY HAVE SAVED MYSELF FROM THAT FOOL SONIC, BUT AT AN UNFORESEEN COST."
NOW ALL I CAN DO IS JUST OPERATE THE STATION'S FUNCTIONS UNTIL MY SYSTEMS RUN DOWN!
ALL--IS LOST!
NEVER!

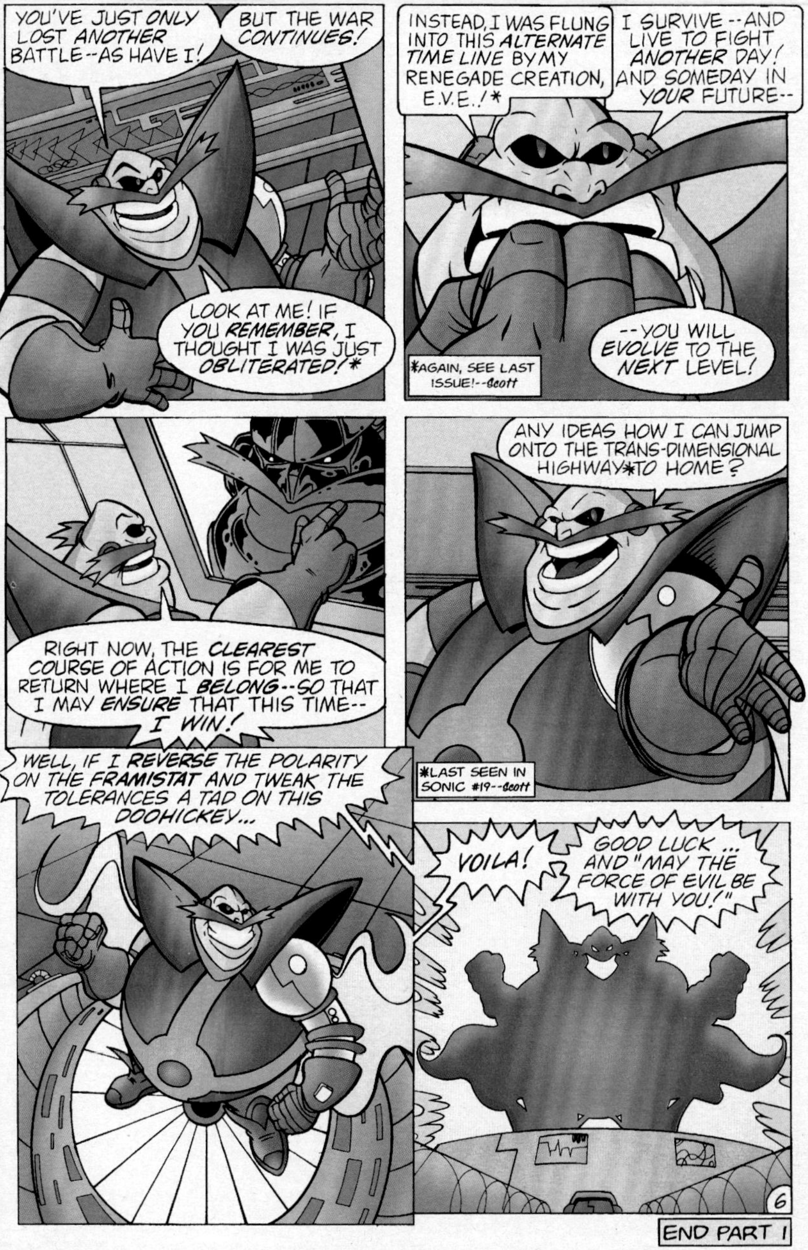
YOU'VE JUST ONLY LOST ANOTHER BATTLE--AS HAVE I!
BUT THE WAR CONTINUES!
LOOK AT ME! IF YOU REMEMBER, I THOUGHT I WAS JUST OBLITERATED!*
INSTEAD, I WAS FLUNG INTO THIS ALTERNATE TIME LINE BY MY RENEGADE CREATION, E.V.E.!*
I SURVIVE --AND LIVE TO FIGHT ANOTHER DAY! AND SOMEDAY IN YOUR FUTURE--
--YOU WILL EVOLVE TO THE NEXT LEVEL!
*AGAIN, SEE LAST ISSUE!--Scott
RIGHT NOW, THE CLEAREST COURSE OF ACTION IS FOR ME TO RETURN WHERE I BELONG--SO THAT I MAY ENSURE THAT THIS TIME-- I WIN!
ANY IDEAS HOW I CAN JUMP ONTO THE TRANS-DIMENSIONAL HIGHWAY* TO HOME?
*LAST SEEN IN SONIC #19--Scott
WELL, IF I REVERSE THE POLARITY ON THE FRAMISTAT AND TWEAK THE TOLERANCES A TAD ON THIS DOOHICKEY...
VOILA!
GOOD LUCK ... AND "MAY THE FORCE OF EVIL BE WITH YOU!"
6
END PART 1

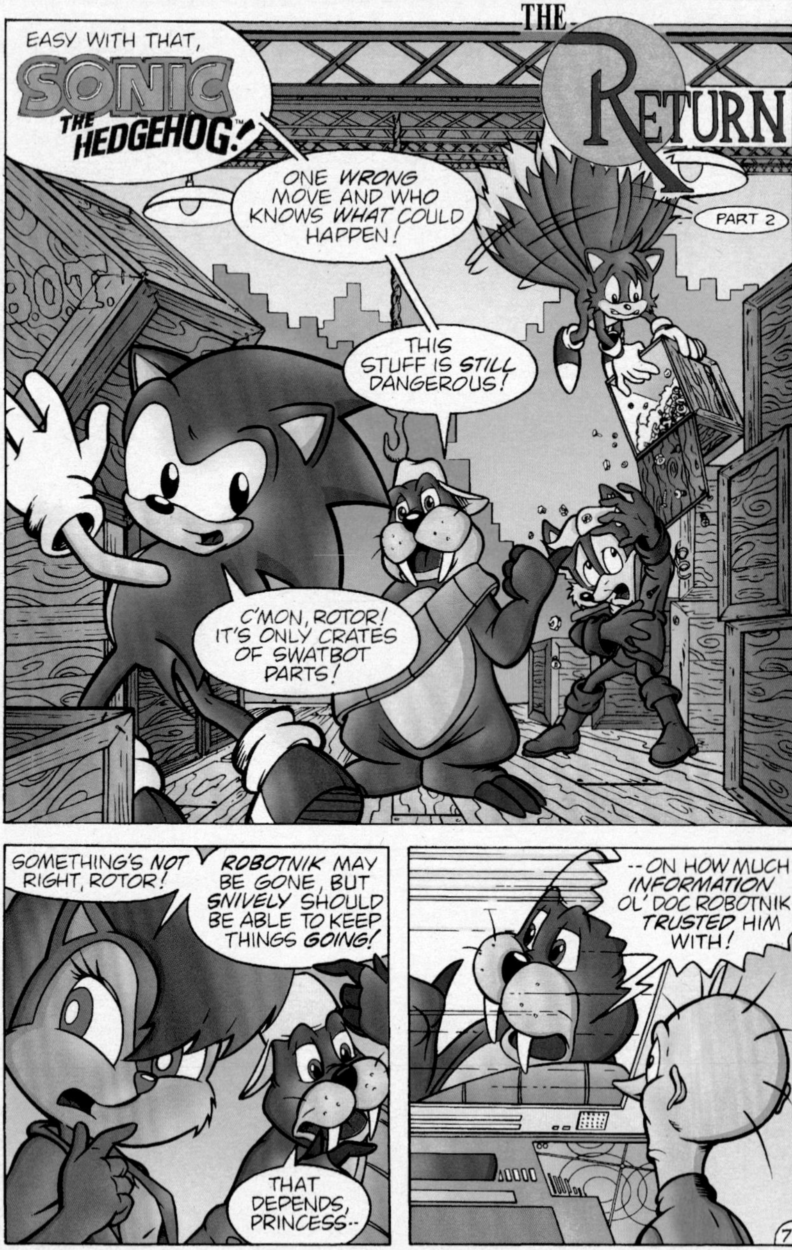
EASY WITH THAT, SONIC THE HEDGEHOG!
THE RETURN
PART 2
ONE WRONG MOVE AND WHO KNOWS WHAT COULD HAPPEN!
THIS STUFF IS STILL DANGEROUS!
C'MON, ROTOR! IT'S ONLY CRATES OF SWATBOT PARTS!
SOMETHING'S NOT RIGHT, ROTOR!
ROBOTNIK MAY BE GONE, BUT SNIVELY SHOULD BE ABLE TO KEEP THINGS GOING!
THAT DEPENDS, PRINCESS--
--ON HOW MUCH INFORMATION OL' DOC ROBOTNIK TRUSTED HIM WITH!
7

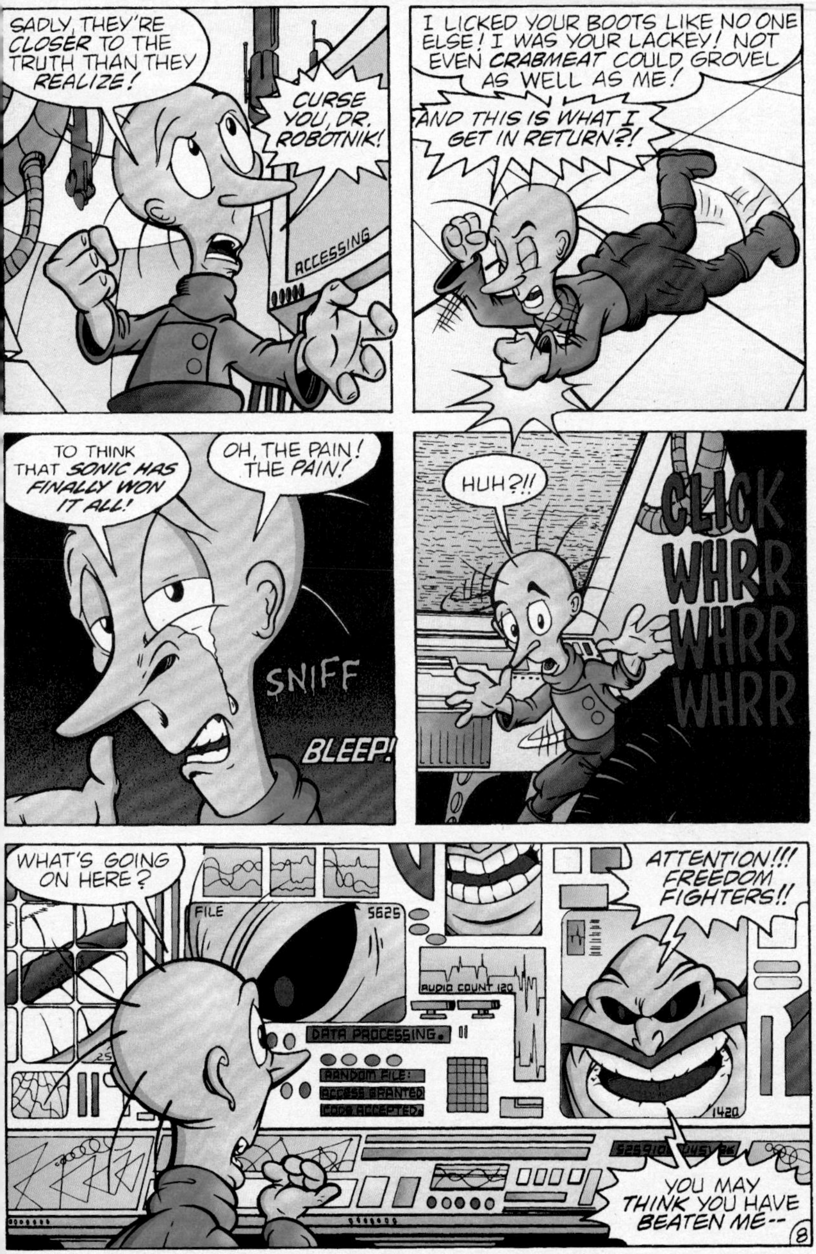
SADLY, THEY'RE CLOSER TO THE TRUTH THAN THEY REALIZE!
CURSE YOU, DR. ROBOTNIK!
ACCESSING
I LICKED YOUR BOOTS LIKE NO ONE ELSE! I WAS YOUR LACKEY! NOT EVEN CRABMEAT COULD GROVEL AS WELL AS ME!
AND THIS IS WHAT I GET IN RETURN?!
TO THINK THAT SONIC HAS FINALLY WON IT ALL!
OH, THE PAIN! THE PAIN!
SNIFF
BLEEP!
HUH?!!
CLICK
WHRR
WHRR
WHRR
WHAT'S GOING ON HERE?
FILE
5625
AUDIO COUNT 120
DATA PROCESSING.
RANDOM FILE:
ACCESS GRANTED
CODE ACCEPTED.
1420
ATTENTION!!! FREEDOM FIGHTERS!!
YOU MAY THINK YOU HAVE BEATEN ME--
8

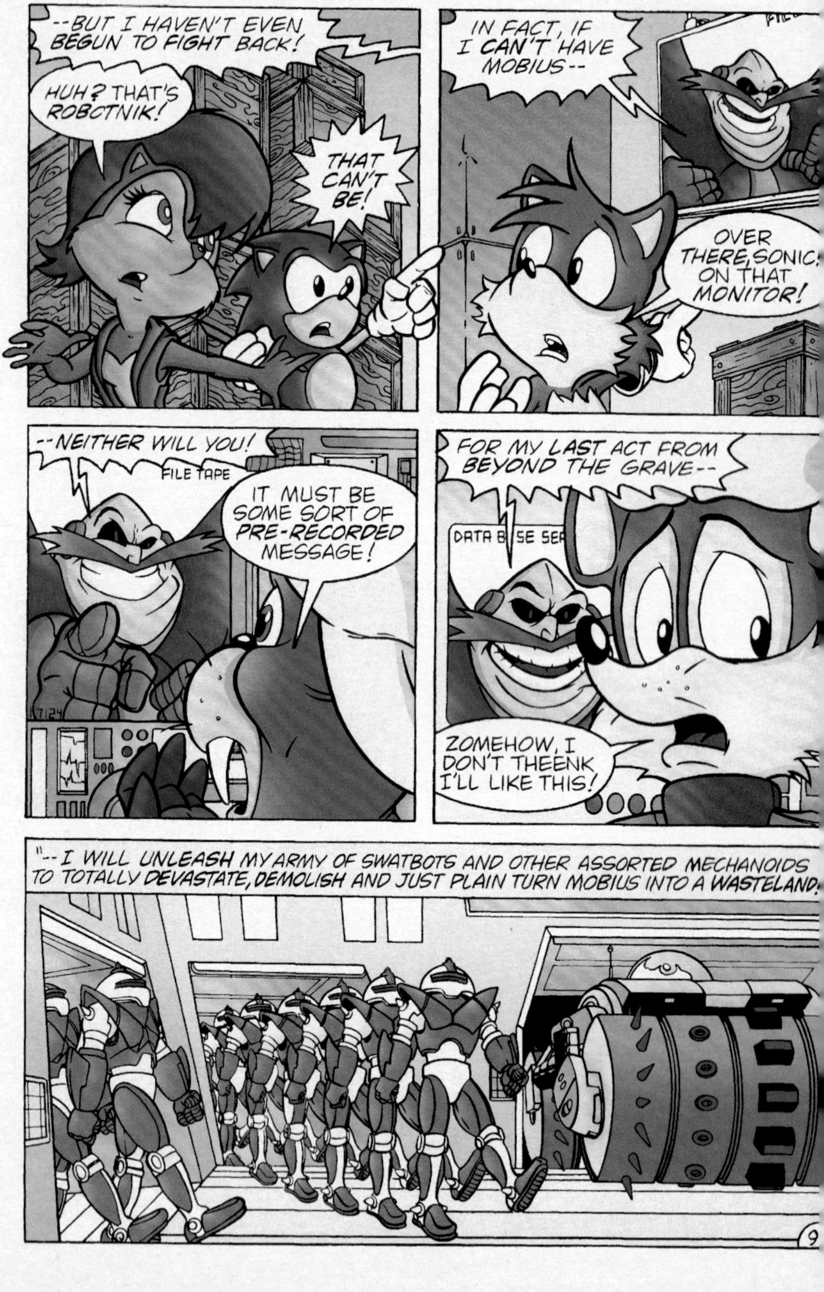
--BUT I HAVEN'T EVEN BEGUN TO FIGHT BACK!
HUH? THAT'S ROBOTNIK!
THAT CAN'T BE!
IN FACT, IF I CAN'T HAVE MOBIUS--
OVER THERE, SONIC! ON THAT MONITOR!
--NEITHER WILL YOU!
FILE TAPE
IT MUST BE SOME SORT OF PRE-RECORDED MESSAGE!
FOR MY LAST ACT FROM BEYOND THE GRAVE--
ZOMEHOW, I DON'T THEENK I'LL LIKE THIS!
"--I WILL UNLEASH MY ARMY OF SWATBOTS AND OTHER ASSORTED MECHANOIDS TO TOTALLY DEVASTATE, DEMOLISH AND JUST PLAIN TURN MOBIUS INTO A WASTELAND.

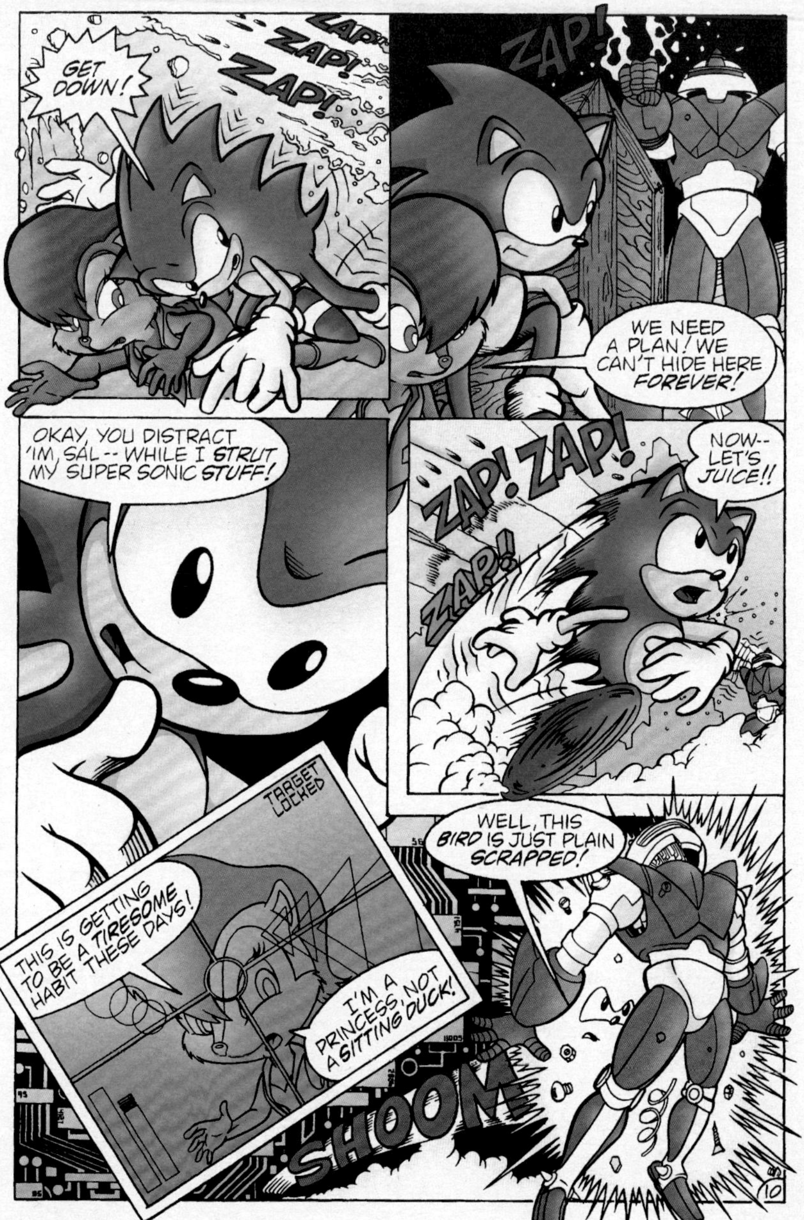
GET DOWN!
ZAP! ZAP! ZAP!
ZAP!
WE NEED A PLAN! WE CAN'T HIDE HERE FOREVER!
OKAY, YOU DISTRACT 'IM, SAL -- WHILE I STRUT MY SUPER SONIC STUFF!
ZAP! ZAP! ZAP!
NOW-- LET'S JUICE!!
TARGET LOCKED
THIS IS GETTING TO BE A TIRESOME HABIT THESE DAYS!
I'M A PRINCESS, NOT A SITTING DUCK!
WELL, THIS BIRD IS JUST PLAIN SCRAPPED!
SHOOOM!

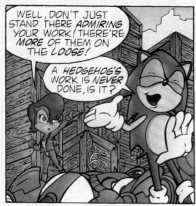

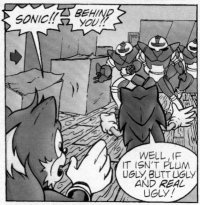

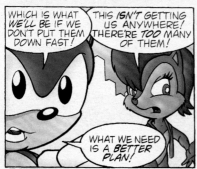

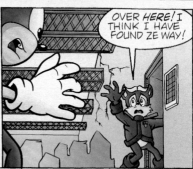

WELL, DON'T JUST STAND THERE ADMIRING YOUR WORK! THERE'RE MORE OF THEM ON THE LOOSE!
A HEDGEHOG'S WORK IS NEVER DONE, IS IT?
SONIC!!
BEHIND YOU!!
WELL, IF IT ISN'T PLUM UGLY, BUTT UGLY AND REAL UGLY!
WHICH IS WHAT WE'LL BE IF WE DON'T PUT THEM DOWN FAST!
THIS ISN'T GETTING US ANYWHERE! THERE'RE TOO MANY OF THEM!
WHAT WE NEED IS A BETTER PLAN!
OVER HERE! I THINK I HAVE FOUND ZE WAY!
ATTENTION! OPERATION: WASTELAND SHALL NOW
COMMENCE! ATTENTION! OPERATION: WASTELAND
MON DIEU!!

END PART 2

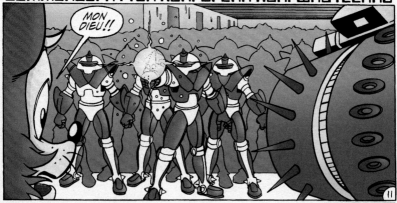

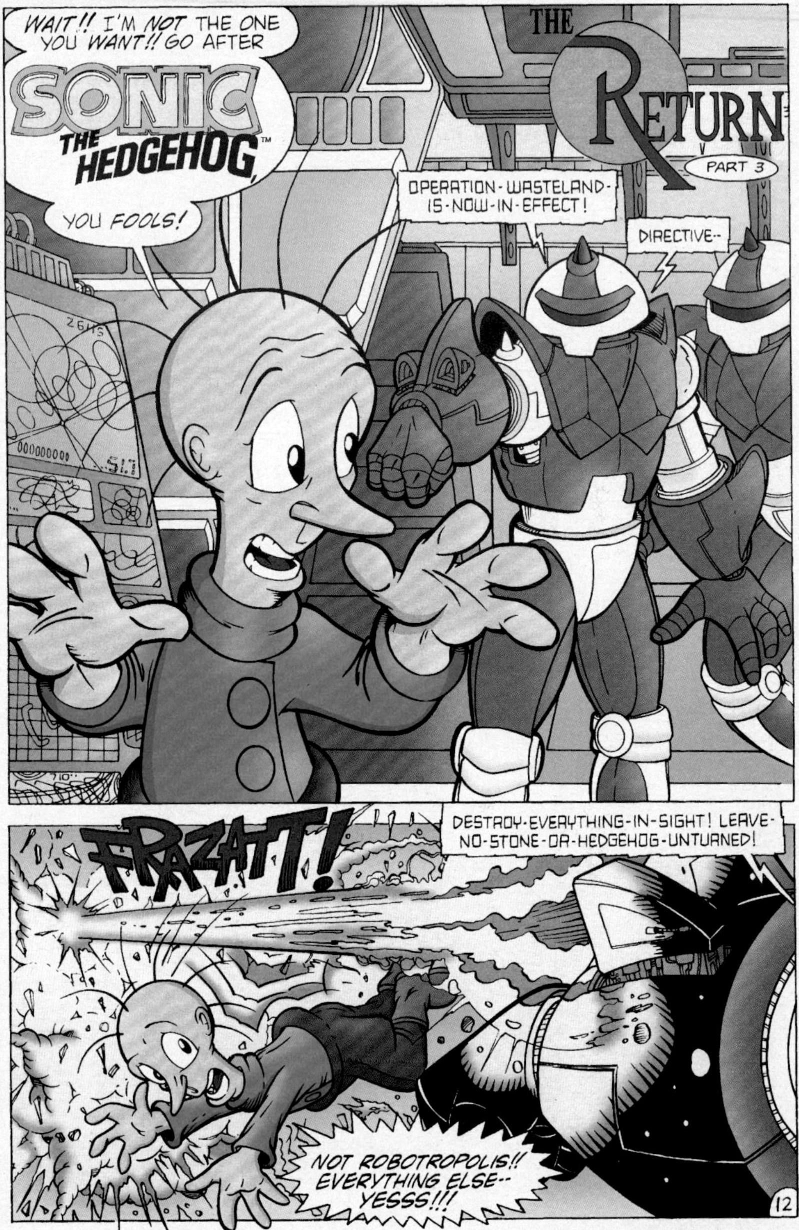
WAIT!! I'M NOT THE ONE YOU WANT!! GO AFTER
SONIC THE HEDGEHOG™,
YOU FOOLS!
THE RETURN
PART 3
OPERATION-WASTELAND-IS-NOW-IN-EFFECT!
DIRECTIVE--
FRAZATT!
DESTROY-EVERYTHING-IN-SIGHT! LEAVE-NO-STONE-OR-HEDGEHOG-UNTURNED!
NOT ROBOTROPOLIS!! EVERYTHING ELSE-- YESSS!!!

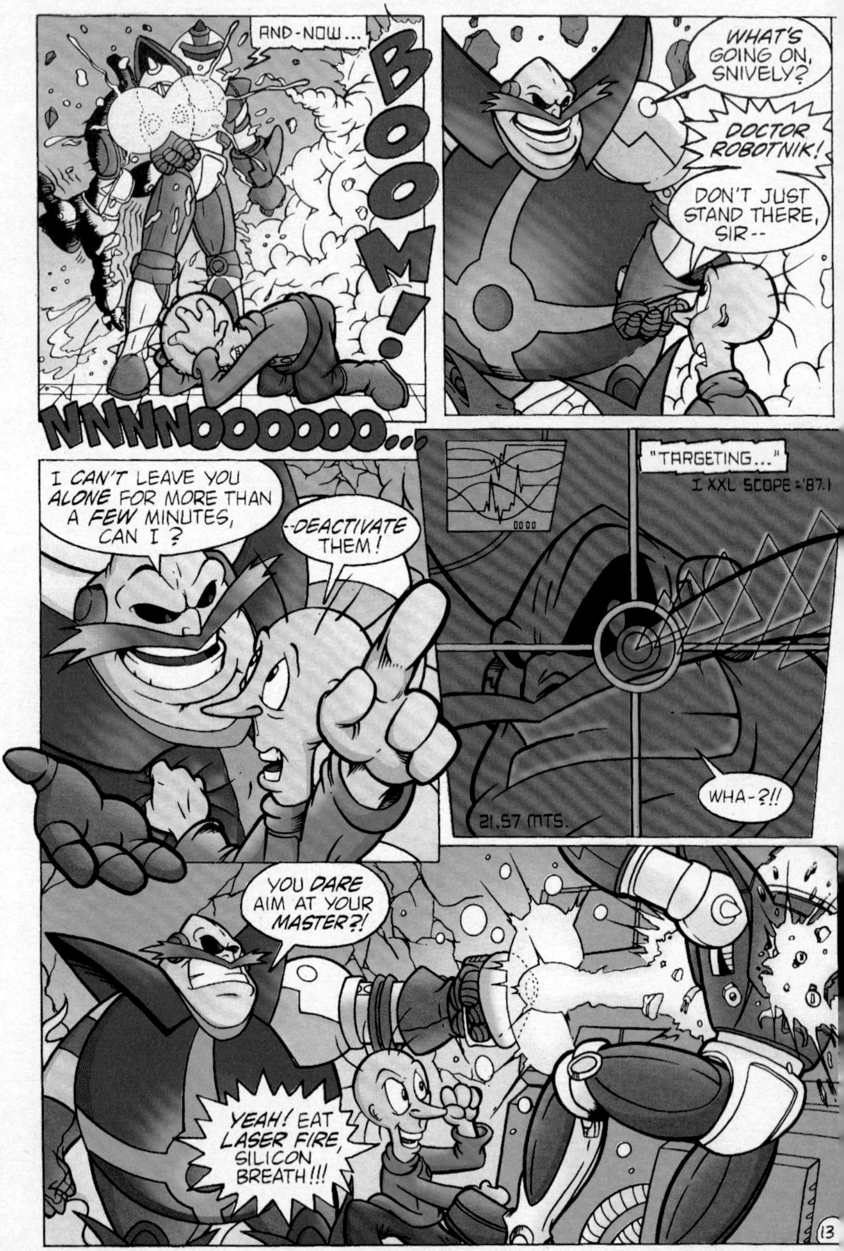
AND-NOW...
BOOOM!
NNNNOOOOOOO...
WHAT'S GOING ON, SNIVELY?
DOCTOR ROBOTNIK!
DON'T JUST STAND THERE, SIR --
I CAN'T LEAVE YOU ALONE FOR MORE THAN A FEW MINUTES, CAN I ?
--DEACTIVATE THEM!
"TARGETING..."
I XXL SCOPE ='87.1
21.57 MTS.
WHA-?!!
YOU DARE AIM AT YOUR MASTER?!
YEAH! EAT LASER FIRE, SILICON BREATH!!!

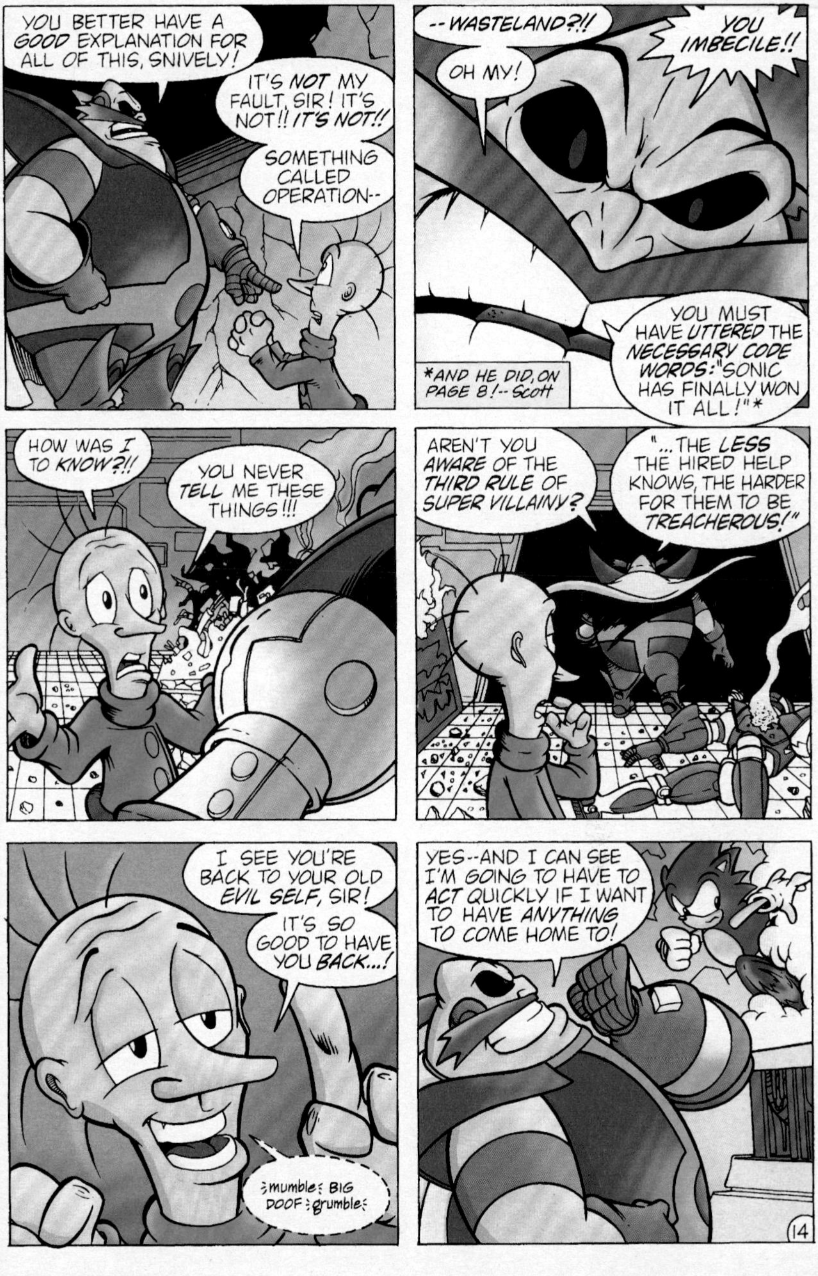
YOU BETTER HAVE A GOOD EXPLANATION FOR ALL OF THIS, SNIVELY!
IT'S NOT MY FAULT, SIR! IT'S NOT!! IT'S NOT!!
SOMETHING CALLED OPERATION--
--WASTELAND?!!
OH MY!
YOU IMBECILE!!
YOU MUST HAVE UTTERED THE NECESSARY CODE WORDS: "SONIC HAS FINALLY WON IT ALL!"*
*AND HE DID, ON PAGE 8! -- Scott
HOW WAS I TO KNOW?!!
YOU NEVER TELL ME THESE THINGS!!!
AREN'T YOU AWARE OF THE THIRD RULE OF SUPER VILLAINY?
"...THE LESS THE HIRED HELP KNOWS, THE HARDER FOR THEM TO BE TREACHEROUS!"
I SEE YOU'RE BACK TO YOUR OLD EVIL SELF, SIR!
IT'S SO GOOD TO HAVE YOU BACK...!
mumble BIG DOOF grumble
YES--AND I CAN SEE I'M GOING TO HAVE TO ACT QUICKLY IF I WANT TO HAVE ANYTHING TO COME HOME TO!

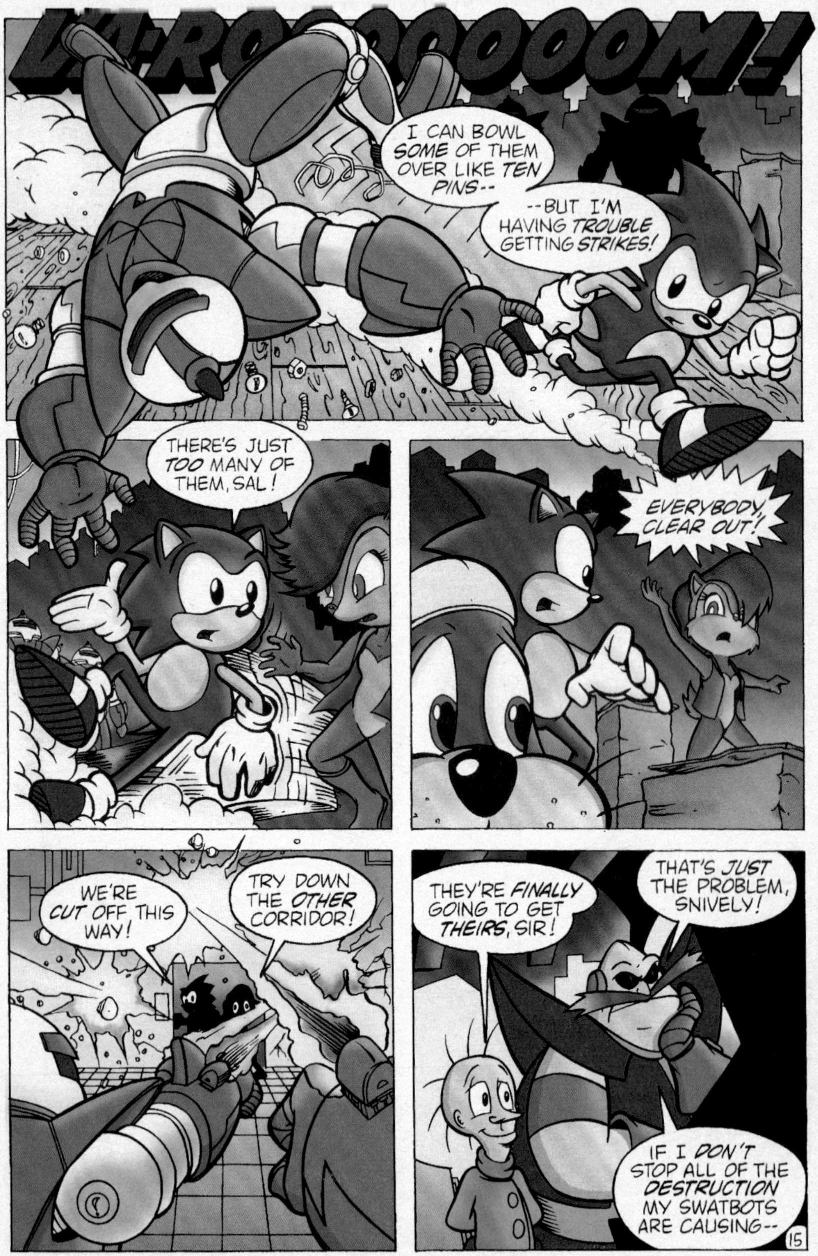
KA-ROOOOOOOM!
I CAN BOWL SOME OF THEM OVER LIKE TEN PINS--
--BUT I'M HAVING TROUBLE GETTING STRIKES!
THERE'S JUST TOO MANY OF THEM, SAL!
EVERYBODY, CLEAR OUT!
WE'RE CUT OFF THIS WAY!
TRY DOWN THE OTHER CORRIDOR!
THEY'RE FINALLY GOING TO GET THEIRS, SIR!
THAT'S JUST THE PROBLEM, SNIVELY!
IF I DON'T STOP ALL OF THE DESTRUCTION MY SWATBOTS ARE CAUSING--
15

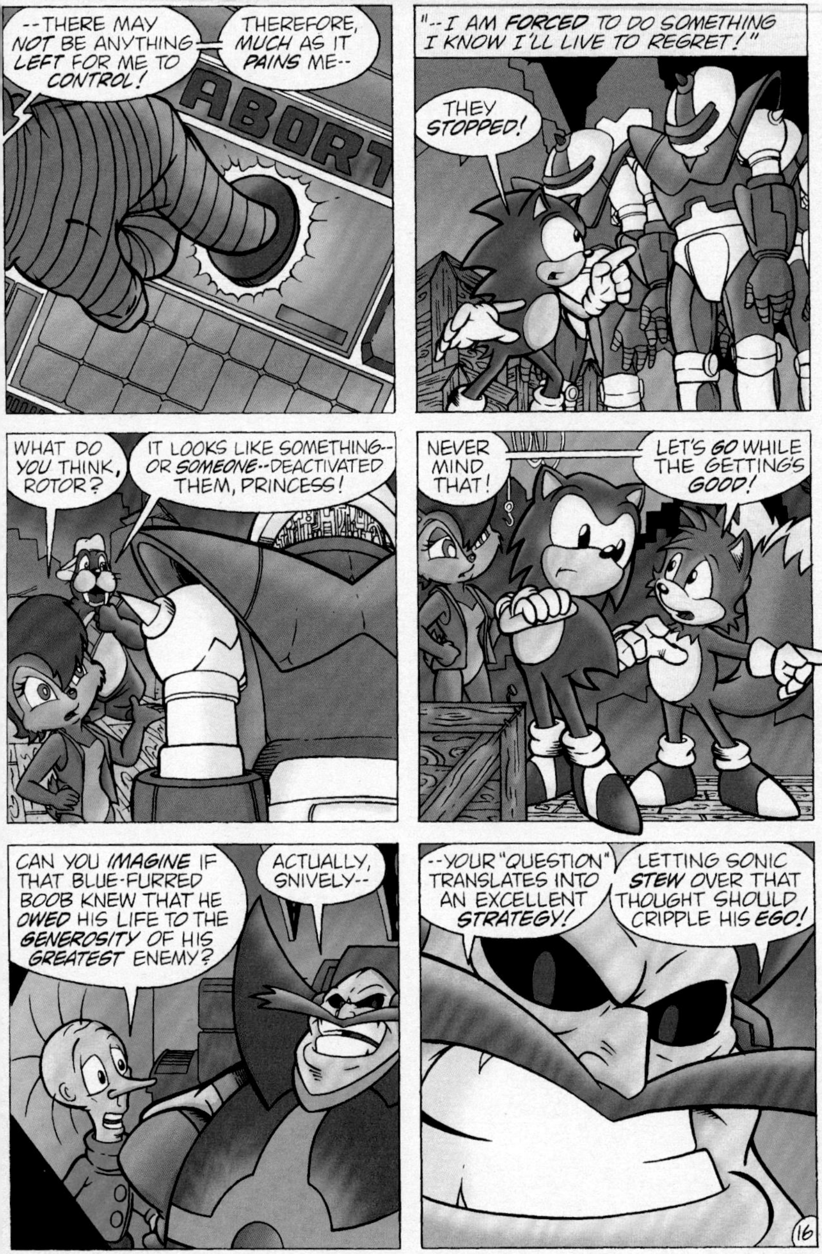
--THERE MAY NOT BE ANYTHING LEFT FOR ME TO CONTROL!
THEREFORE, MUCH AS IT PAINS ME--
ABORT
"--I AM FORCED TO DO SOMETHING I KNOW I'LL LIVE TO REGRET!"
THEY STOPPED!
WHAT DO YOU THINK, ROTOR?
IT LOOKS LIKE SOMETHING--OR SOMEONE--DEACTIVATED THEM, PRINCESS!
NEVER MIND THAT!
LET'S GO WHILE THE GETTING'S GOOD!
CAN YOU IMAGINE IF THAT BLUE-FURRED BOOB KNEW THAT HE OWED HIS LIFE TO THE GENEROSITY OF HIS GREATEST ENEMY?
ACTUALLY, SNIVELY--
--YOUR "QUESTION" TRANSLATES INTO AN EXCELLENT STRATEGY!
LETTING SONIC STEW OVER THAT THOUGHT SHOULD CRIPPLE HIS EGO!
16

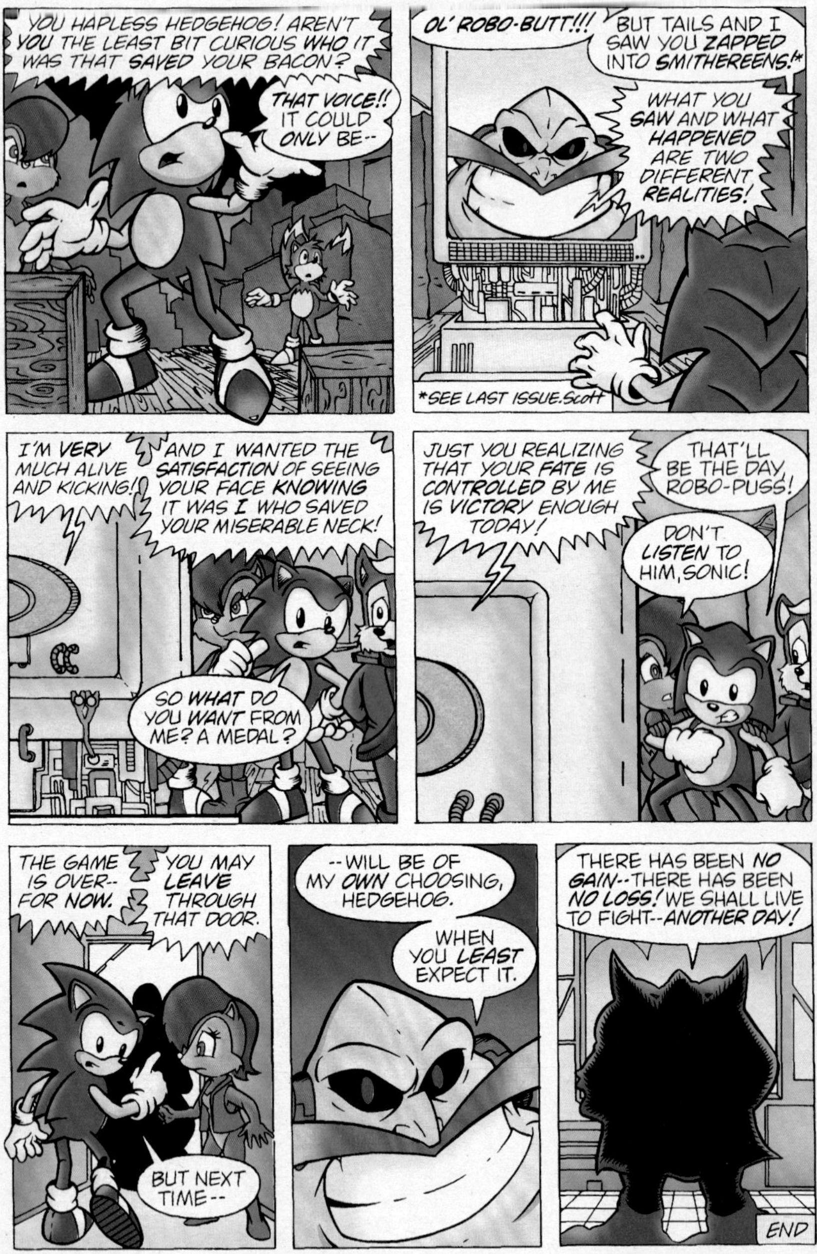
YOU HAPLESS HEDGEHOG! AREN'T YOU THE LEAST BIT CURIOUS WHO IT WAS THAT SAVED YOUR BACON?
THAT VOICE!! IT COULD ONLY BE--
OL' ROBO-BUTT!!!
BUT TAILS AND I SAW YOU ZAPPED INTO SMITHEREENS!*
WHAT YOU SAW AND WHAT HAPPENED ARE TWO DIFFERENT REALITIES!
*SEE LAST ISSUE. Scott
I'M VERY MUCH ALIVE AND KICKING!
AND I WANTED THE SATISFACTION OF SEEING YOUR FACE KNOWING IT WAS I WHO SAVED YOUR MISERABLE NECK!
SO WHAT DO YOU WANT FROM ME? A MEDAL?
JUST YOU REALIZING THAT YOUR FATE IS CONTROLLED BY ME IS VICTORY ENOUGH TODAY!
THAT'LL BE THE DAY, ROBO-PUSS!
DON'T LISTEN TO HIM, SONIC!
THE GAME IS OVER-- FOR NOW.
YOU MAY LEAVE THROUGH THAT DOOR.
BUT NEXT TIME--
--WILL BE OF MY OWN CHOOSING, HEDGEHOG.
WHEN YOU LEAST EXPECT IT.
THERE HAS BEEN NO GAIN--THERE HAS BEEN NO LOSS! WE SHALL LIVE TO FIGHT--ANOTHER DAY!
END

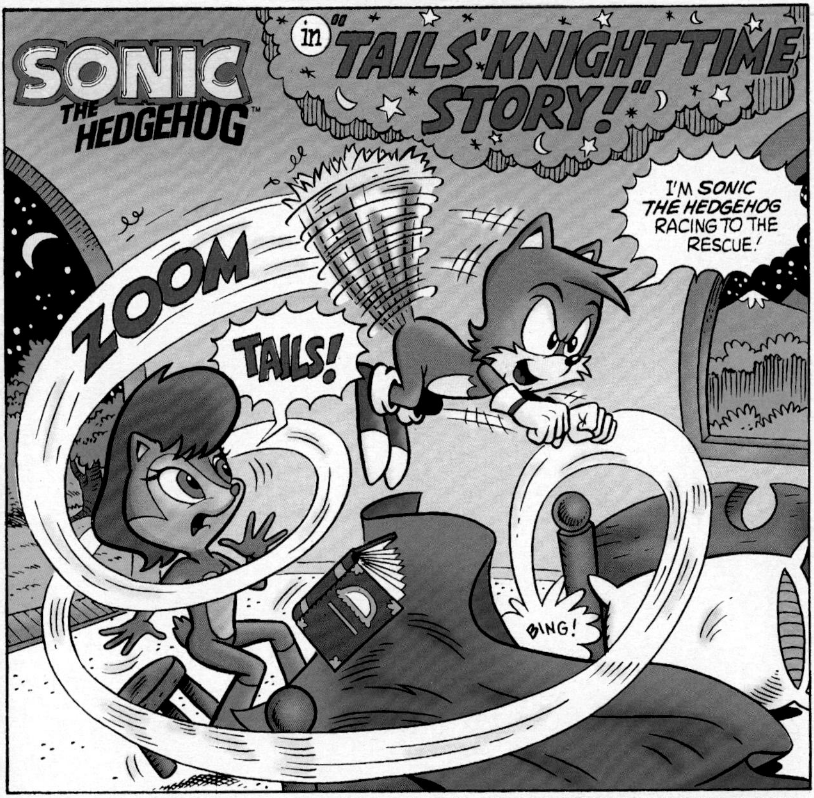
SONIC THE HEDGEHOG™
in "TAILS' KNIGHT TIME STORY!"
ZOOM
TAILS!
I'M SONIC THE HEDGEHOG RACING TO THE RESCUE!
BING!

SCRIPT: ANGELO DECESARE PENCILS: DAVE MANAK INKS: JON DAGASTINO LETTERS: BILL YOSHIDA

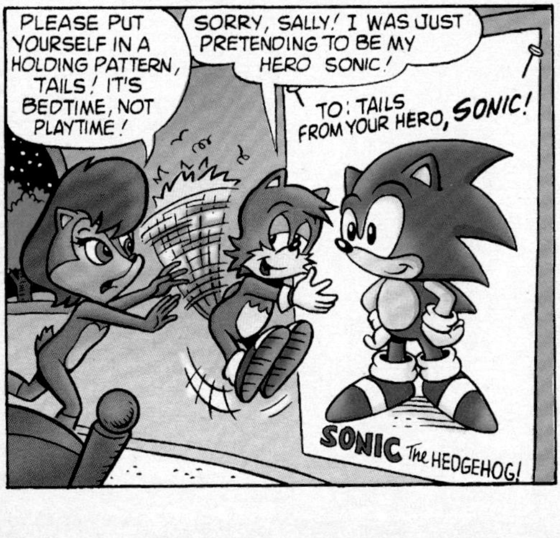
PLEASE PUT YOURSELF IN A HOLDING PATTERN, TAILS! IT'S BEDTIME, NOT PLAYTIME!
SORRY, SALLY! I WAS JUST PRETENDING TO BE MY HERO SONIC!
TO: TAILS FROM YOUR HERO, SONIC!
SONIC The HEDGEHOG!

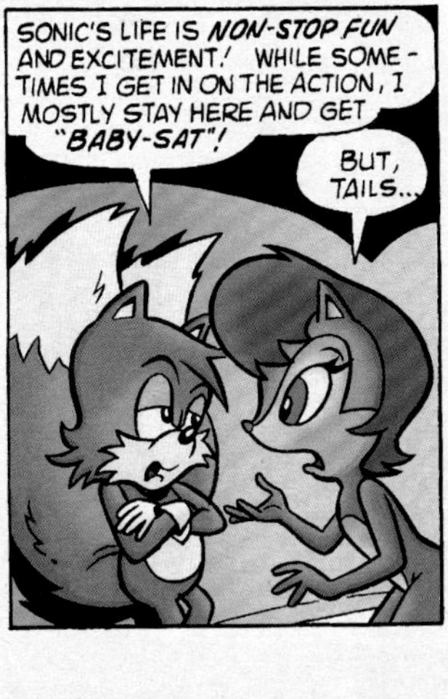
SONIC'S LIFE IS NON-STOP FUN AND EXCITEMENT! WHILE SOMETIMES I GET IN ON THE ACTION, I MOSTLY STAY HERE AND GET "BABY-SAT"!
BUT, TAILS...

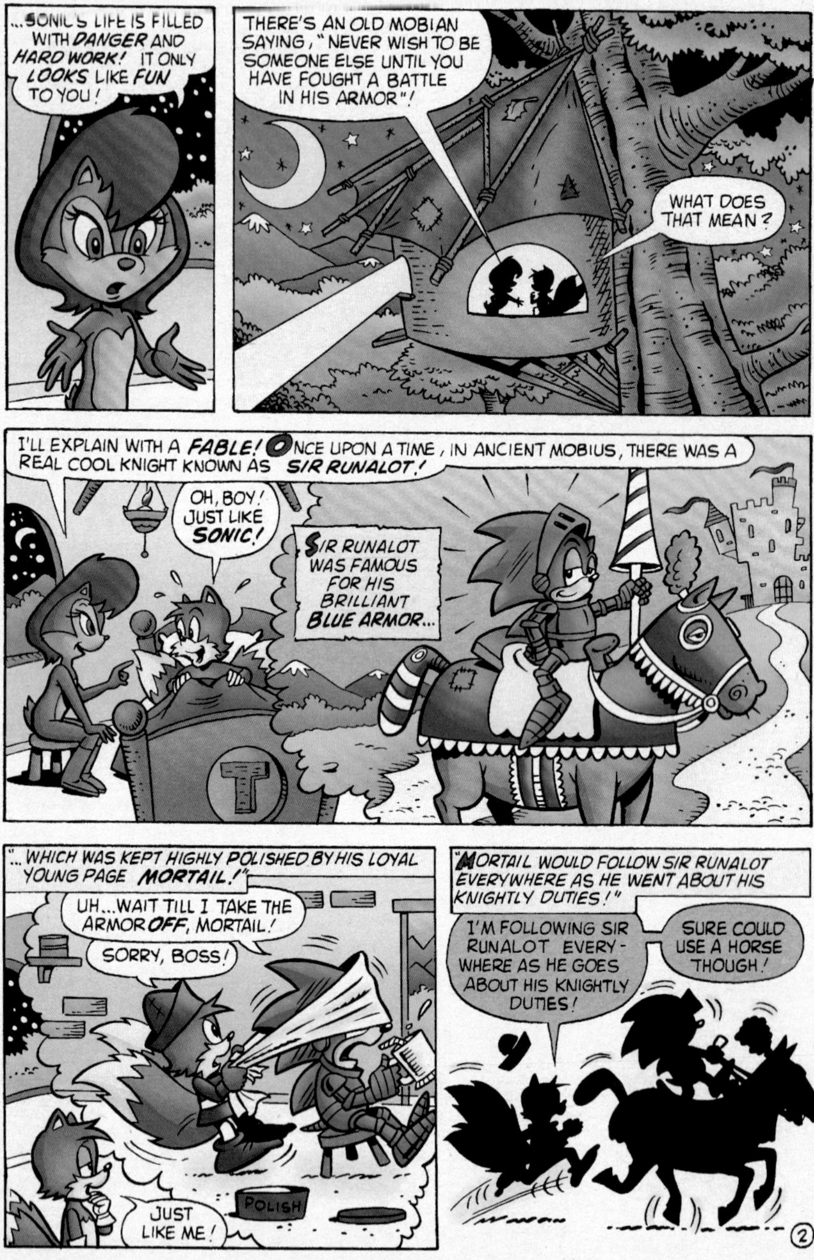
...SONIC'S LIFE IS FILLED WITH DANGER AND HARD WORK! IT ONLY LOOKS LIKE FUN TO YOU!
THERE'S AN OLD MOBIAN SAYING, "NEVER WISH TO BE SOMEONE ELSE UNTIL YOU HAVE FOUGHT A BATTLE IN HIS ARMOR"!
WHAT DOES THAT MEAN?
I'LL EXPLAIN WITH A FABLE! ONCE UPON A TIME, IN ANCIENT MOBIUS, THERE WAS A REAL COOL KNIGHT KNOWN AS SIR RUNALOT!
OH, BOY! JUST LIKE SONIC!
SIR RUNALOT WAS FAMOUS FOR HIS BRILLIANT BLUE ARMOR...
T
"...WHICH WAS KEPT HIGHLY POLISHED BY HIS LOYAL YOUNG PAGE MORTAIL!"
UH...WAIT TILL I TAKE THE ARMOR OFF, MORTAIL!
SORRY, BOSS!
POLISH
JUST LIKE ME!
"MORTAIL WOULD FOLLOW SIR RUNALOT EVERYWHERE AS HE WENT ABOUT HIS KNIGHTLY DUTIES!"
I'M FOLLOWING SIR RUNALOT EVERY-WHERE AS HE GOES ABOUT HIS KNIGHTLY DUTIES!
SURE COULD USE A HORSE THOUGH!

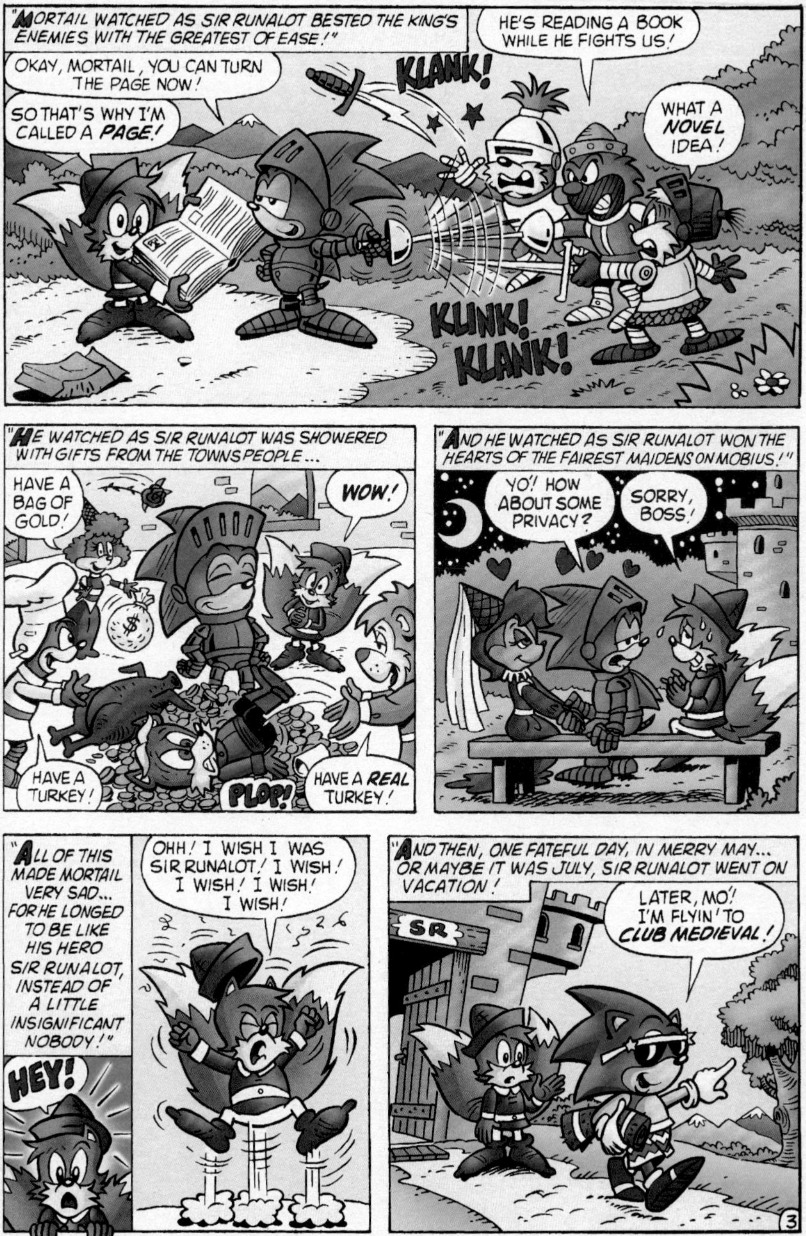
"MORTAIL WATCHED AS SIR RUNALOT BESTED THE KING'S ENEMIES WITH THE GREATEST OF EASE!"
HE'S READING A BOOK WHILE HE FIGHTS US!
OKAY, MORTAIL, YOU CAN TURN THE PAGE NOW!
KLANK!
SO THAT'S WHY I'M CALLED A PAGE!
WHAT A NOVEL IDEA!
KLINK! KLANK!
"HE WATCHED AS SIR RUNALOT WAS SHOWERED WITH GIFTS FROM THE TOWNSPEOPLE...
HAVE A BAG OF GOLD!
WOW!
HAVE A TURKEY!
PLOP!
HAVE A REAL TURKEY!
"AND HE WATCHED AS SIR RUNALOT WON THE HEARTS OF THE FAIREST MAIDENS ON MOBIUS!"
YO! HOW ABOUT SOME PRIVACY?
SORRY, BOSS!
"ALL OF THIS MADE MORTAIL VERY SAD... FOR HE LONGED TO BE LIKE HIS HERO SIR RUNALOT, INSTEAD OF A LITTLE INSIGNIFICANT NOBODY!"
HEY!
OHH! I WISH I WAS SIR RUNALOT! I WISH! I WISH! I WISH! I WISH!
"AND THEN, ONE FATEFUL DAY, IN MERRY MAY... OR MAYBE IT WAS JULY, SIR RUNALOT WENT ON VACATION!
SR
LATER, MO! I'M FLYIN' TO CLUB MEDIEVAL!
3

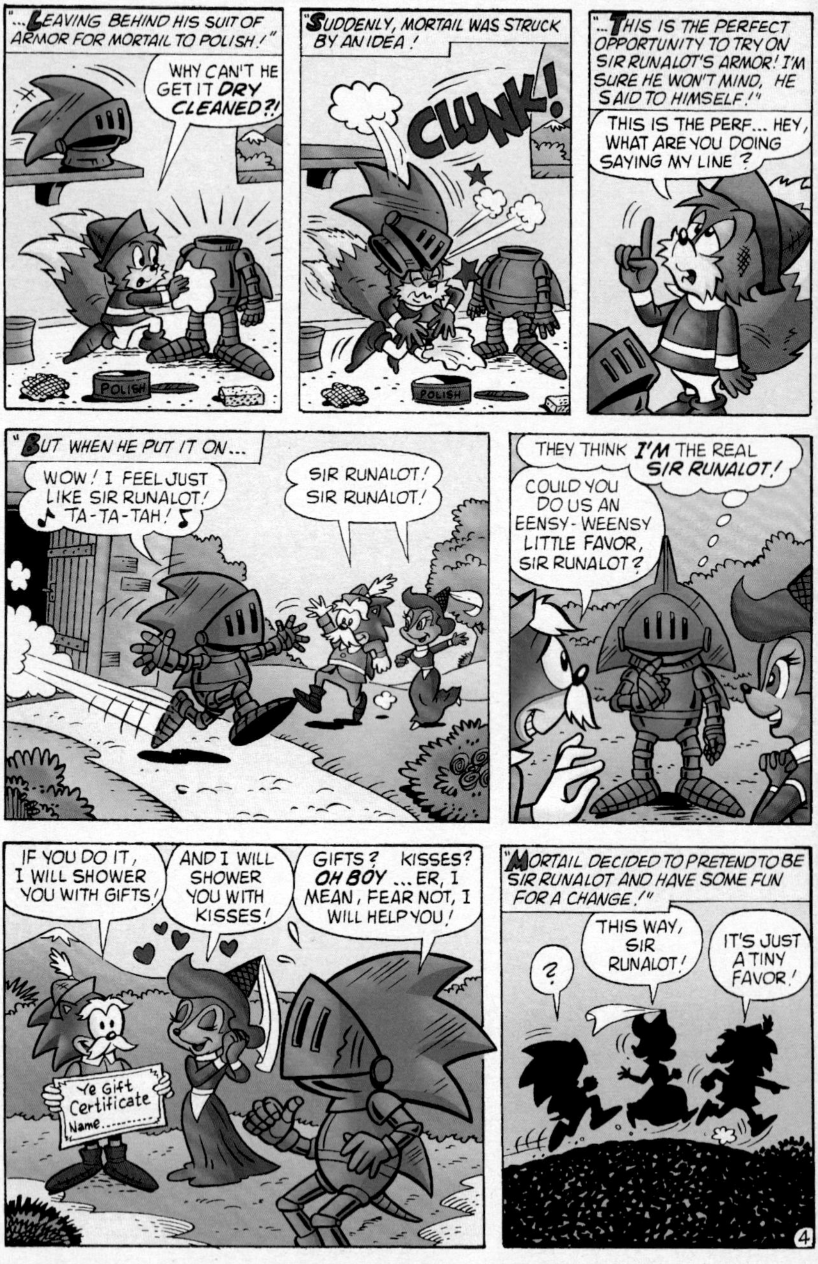

"...LEAVING BEHIND HIS SUIT OF ARMOR FOR MORTAIL TO POLISH!"
WHY CAN'T HE GET IT DRY CLEANED?!
POLISH
"SUDDENLY, MORTAIL WAS STRUCK BY AN IDEA!
CLUNK!
POLISH
"...THIS IS THE PERFECT OPPORTUNITY TO TRY ON SIR RUNALOT'S ARMOR! I'M SURE HE WON'T MIND, HE SAID TO HIMSELF!"
THIS IS THE PERF... HEY, WHAT ARE YOU DOING SAYING MY LINE?
"BUT WHEN HE PUT IT ON...
WOW! I FEEL JUST LIKE SIR RUNALOT! ♪ TA-TA-TAH! ♫
SIR RUNALOT! SIR RUNALOT!
THEY THINK I'M THE REAL SIR RUNALOT!
COULD YOU DO US AN EENSY-WEENSY LITTLE FAVOR, SIR RUNALOT?
IF YOU DO IT, I WILL SHOWER YOU WITH GIFTS!
AND I WILL SHOWER YOU WITH KISSES!
GIFTS? KISSES? OH BOY ...ER, I MEAN, FEAR NOT, I WILL HELP YOU!
Ye Gift Certificate Name.........
"MORTAIL DECIDED TO PRETEND TO BE SIR RUNALOT AND HAVE SOME FUN FOR A CHANGE!"
?
THIS WAY, SIR RUNALOT!
IT'S JUST A TINY FAVOR!

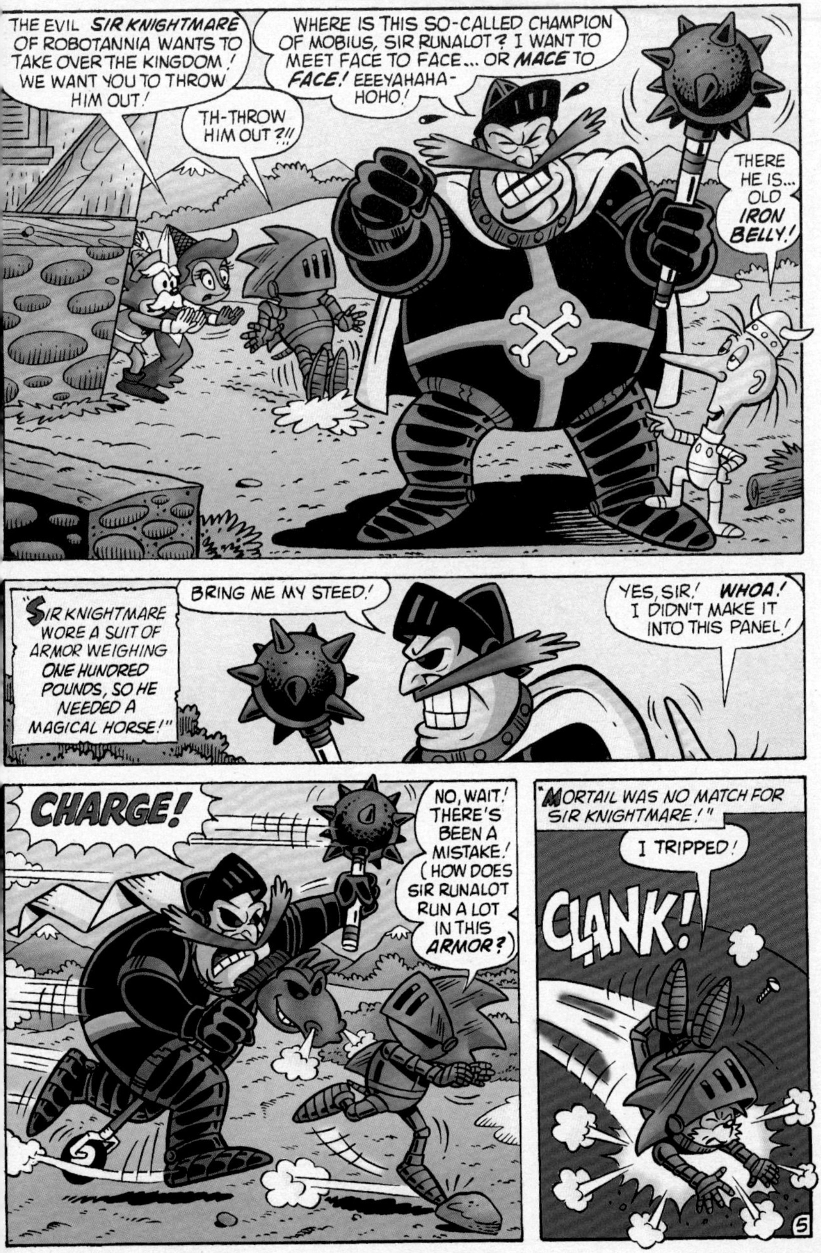
THE EVIL SIR KNIGHTMARE OF ROBOTANNIA WANTS TO TAKE OVER THE KINGDOM! WE WANT YOU TO THROW HIM OUT!
TH-THROW HIM OUT?!!
WHERE IS THIS SO-CALLED CHAMPION OF MOBIUS, SIR RUNALOT? I WANT TO MEET FACE TO FACE... OR MACE TO FACE! EEEYAHAHA-HOHO!
THERE HE IS... OLD IRON BELLY!
"SIR KNIGHTMARE WORE A SUIT OF ARMOR WEIGHING ONE HUNDRED POUNDS, SO HE NEEDED A MAGICAL HORSE!"
BRING ME MY STEED!
YES, SIR! WHOA! I DIDN'T MAKE IT INTO THIS PANEL!
CHARGE!
NO, WAIT! THERE'S BEEN A MISTAKE! (HOW DOES SIR RUNALOT RUN A LOT IN THIS ARMOR?)
"MORTAIL WAS NO MATCH FOR SIR KNIGHTMARE!"
I TRIPPED!
CLANK!

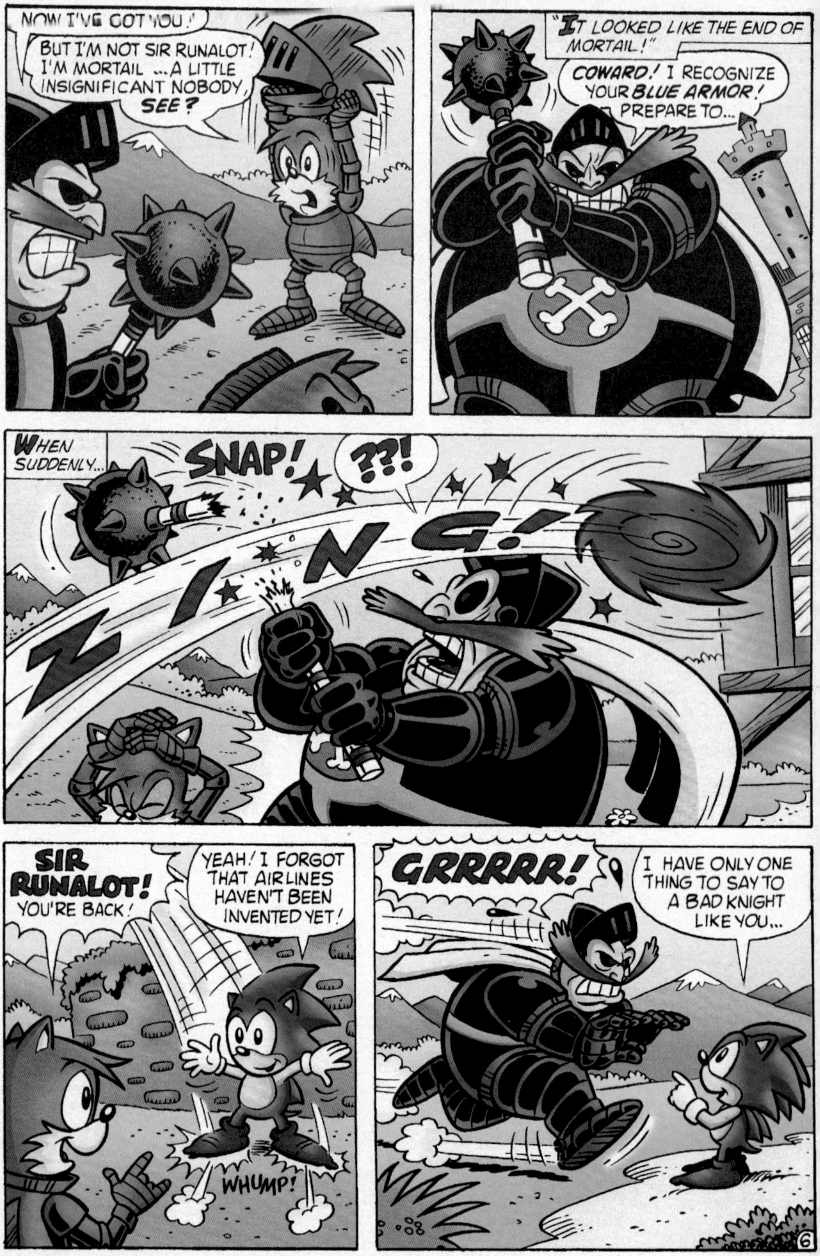
NOW I'VE GOT YOU!
BUT I'M NOT SIR RUNALOT! I'M MORTAIL ...A LITTLE INSIGNIFICANT NOBODY, SEE?
"IT LOOKED LIKE THE END OF MORTAIL!"
COWARD! I RECOGNIZE YOUR BLUE ARMOR! PREPARE TO...
WHEN SUDDENLY...
SNAP!
??!
Z I N G!
SIR RUNALOT! YOU'RE BACK!
YEAH! I FORGOT THAT AIRLINES HAVEN'T BEEN INVENTED YET!
WHUMP!
GRRRRRR!
I HAVE ONLY ONE THING TO SAY TO A BAD KNIGHT LIKE YOU...
6

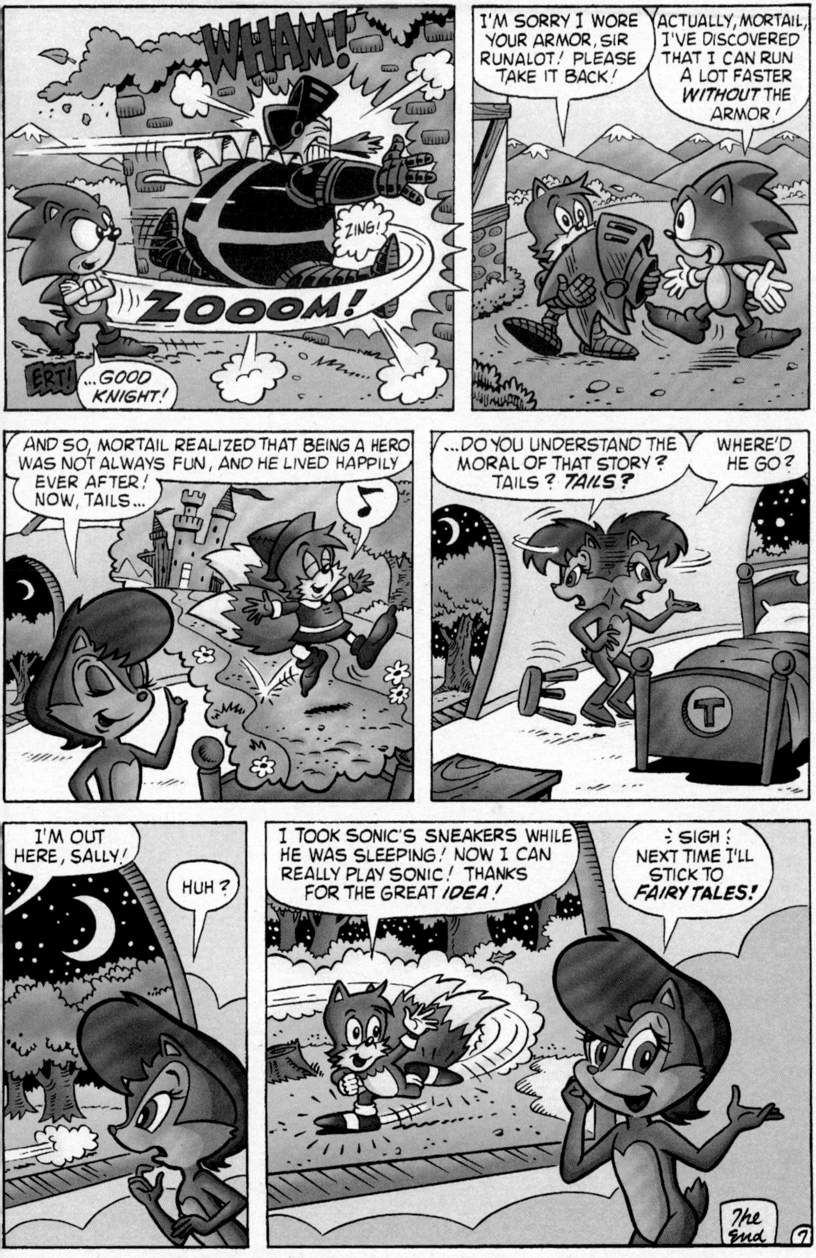
WHAM!
ZING!
ZOOOM!
ERT!
...GOOD KNIGHT!
I'M SORRY I WORE YOUR ARMOR, SIR RUNALOT! PLEASE TAKE IT BACK!
ACTUALLY, MORTAIL, I'VE DISCOVERED THAT I CAN RUN A LOT FASTER *WITHOUT* THE ARMOR!
AND SO, MORTAIL REALIZED THAT BEING A HERO WAS NOT ALWAYS FUN, AND HE LIVED HAPPILY EVER AFTER! NOW, TAILS...
...DO YOU UNDERSTAND THE MORAL OF THAT STORY? TAILS? *TAILS?*
WHERE'D HE GO?
T
I'M OUT HERE, SALLY!
HUH?
I TOOK SONIC'S SNEAKERS WHILE HE WAS SLEEPING! NOW I CAN REALLY PLAY SONIC! THANKS FOR THE GREAT *IDEA!*
:SIGH: NEXT TIME I'LL STICK TO *FAIRY TALES!*
The End

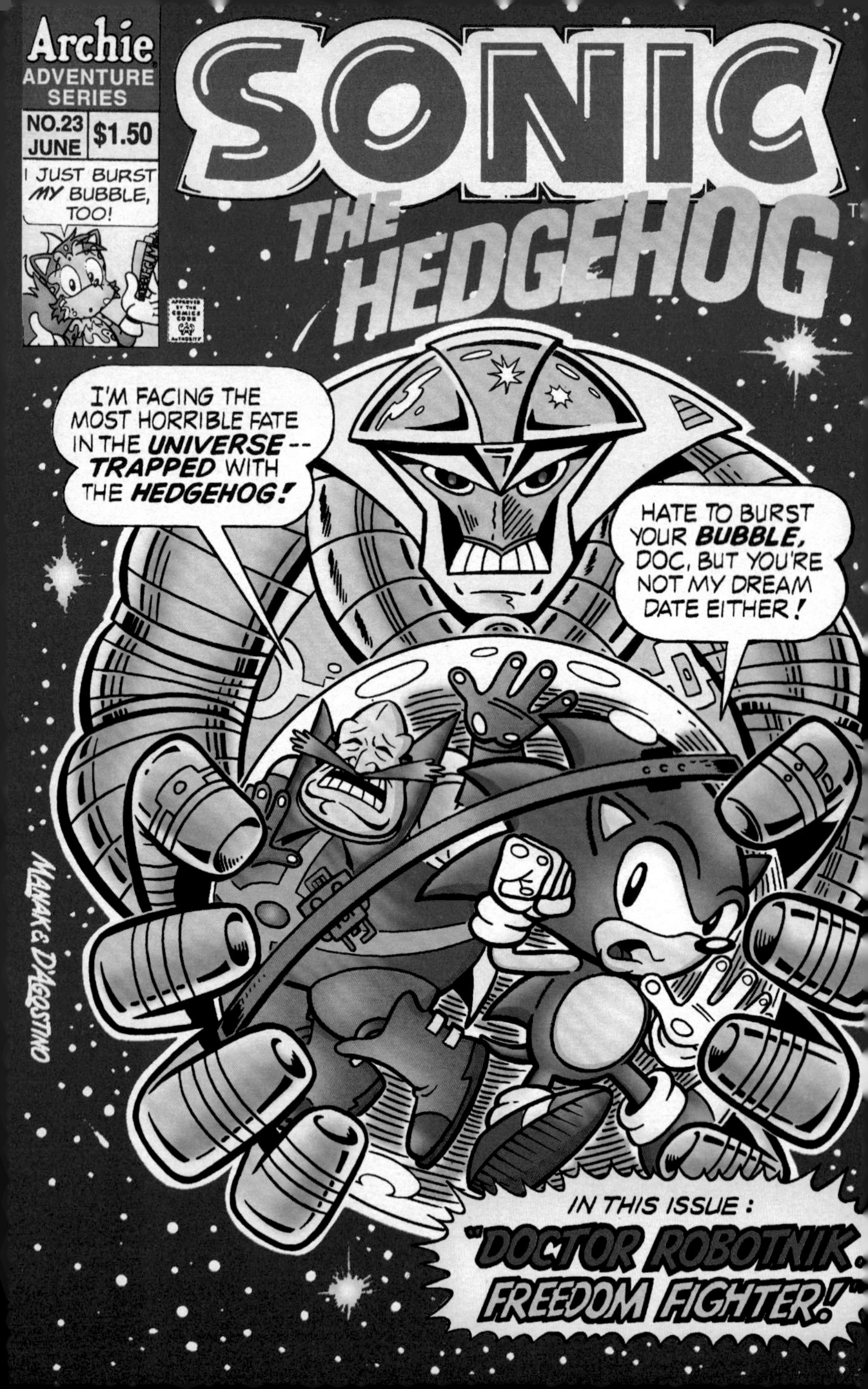
Archie ADVENTURE SERIES
NO.23 JUNE $1.50
SONIC THE HEDGEHOG
I JUST BURST MY BUBBLE, TOO!
I'M FACING THE MOST HORRIBLE FATE IN THE UNIVERSE -- TRAPPED WITH THE HEDGEHOG!
HATE TO BURST YOUR BUBBLE, DOC, BUT YOU'RE NOT MY DREAM DATE EITHER!
MANAK & D'AGOSTINO
IN THIS ISSUE:
"DOCTOR ROBOTNIK... FREEDOM FIGHTER!"

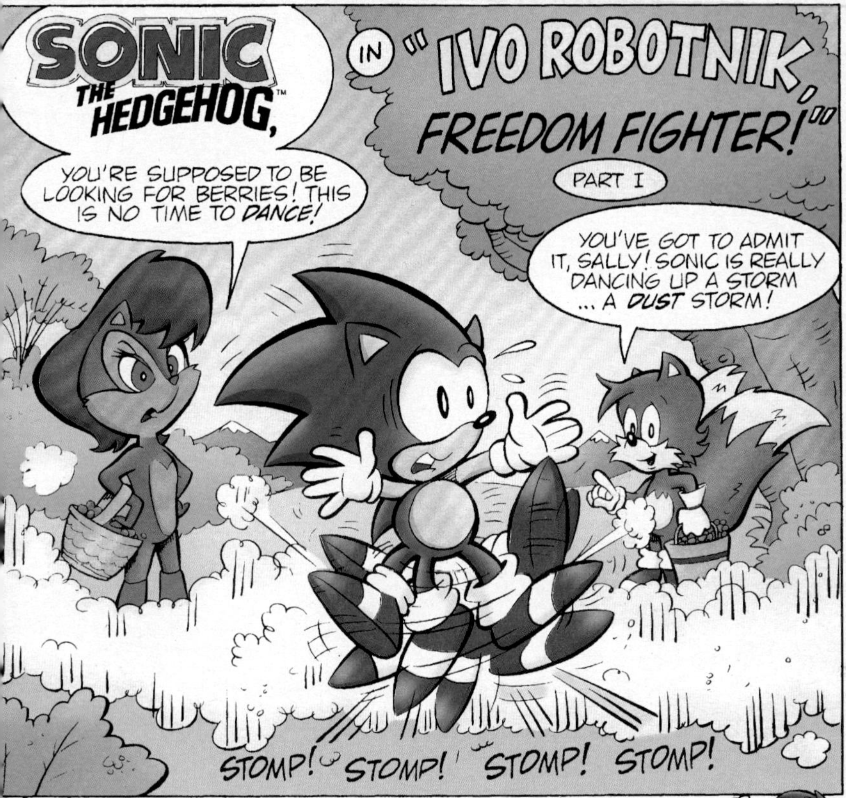
SONIC THE HEDGEHOG™,
IN "IVO ROBOTNIK, FREEDOM FIGHTER!"
PART I
YOU'RE SUPPOSED TO BE LOOKING FOR BERRIES! THIS IS NO TIME TO DANCE!
YOU'VE GOT TO ADMIT IT, SALLY! SONIC IS REALLY DANCING UP A STORM ... A DUST STORM!
STOMP! STOMP! STOMP! STOMP!

SCRIPT: ANGELO DECESARE PENCILS: DAVE MANAK INKS: RICH KOSLOWSKI LETTERS: MINDY EISMAN COLORS: BARRY GROSSMAN EDITOR: SCOTT FULOP MANAGING EDITOR: VICTOR GORELICK EDITOR-IN-CHIEF: RICHARD GOLDWATER

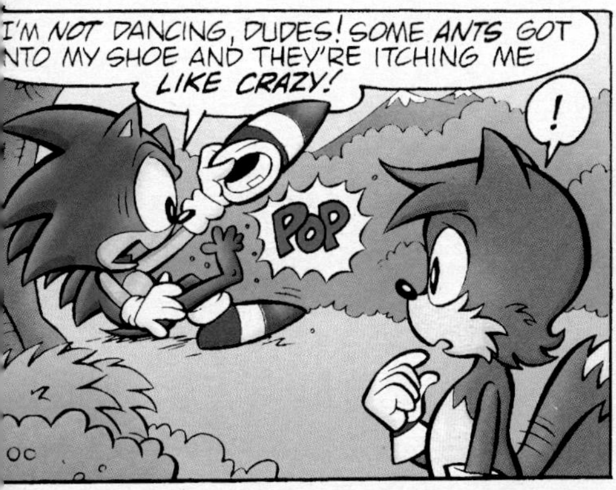
I'M NOT DANCING, DUDES! SOME ANTS GOT INTO MY SHOE AND THEY'RE ITCHING ME LIKE CRAZY!
!
POP

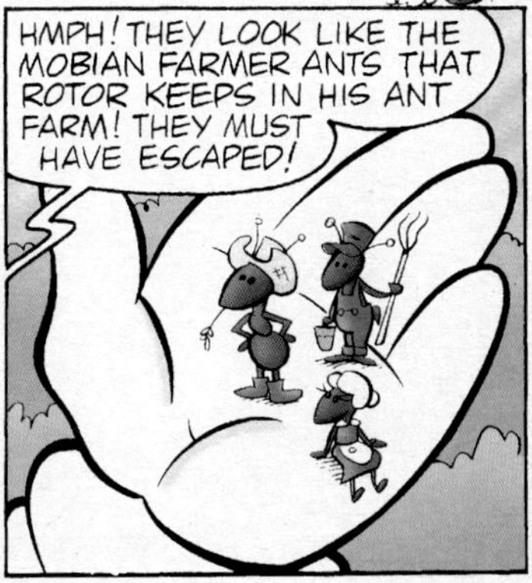
HMPH! THEY LOOK LIKE THE MOBIAN FARMER ANTS THAT ROTOR KEEPS IN HIS ANT FARM! THEY MUST HAVE ESCAPED!

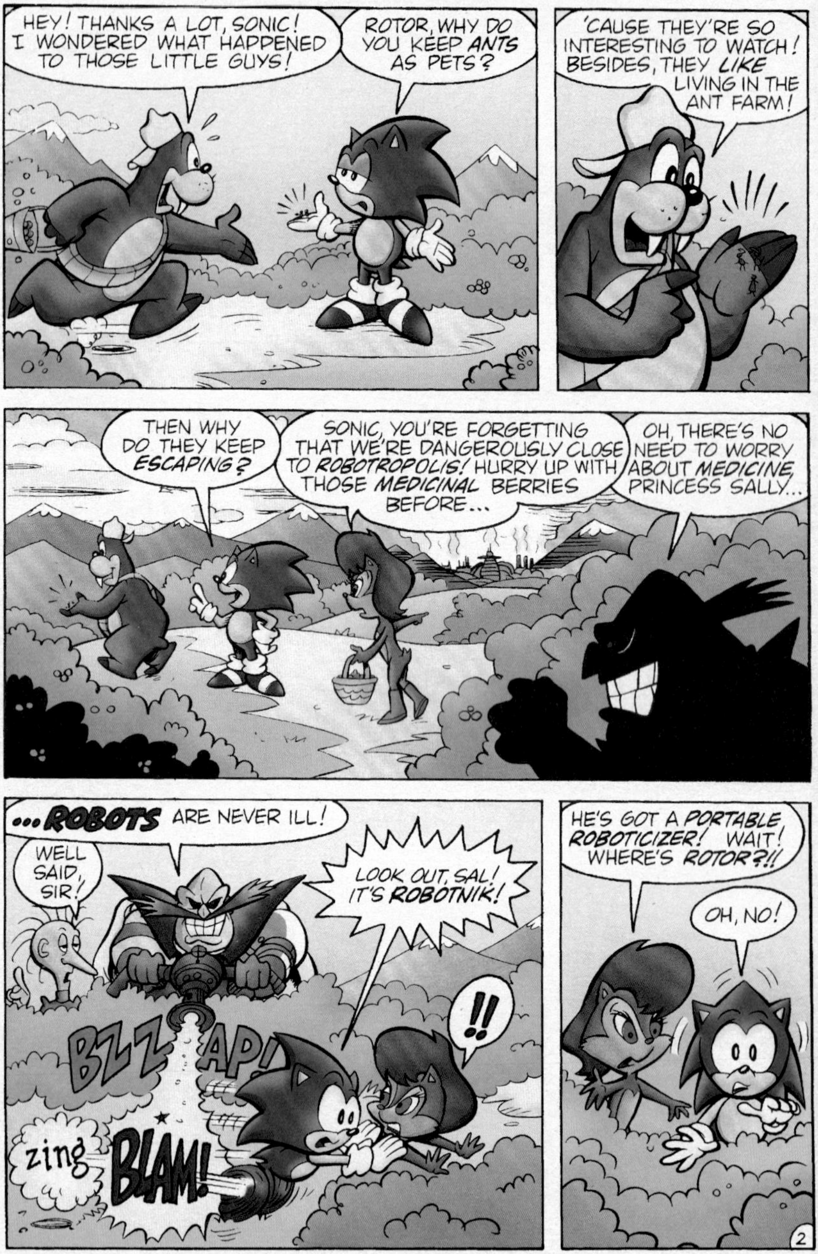

HEY! THANKS A LOT, SONIC! I WONDERED WHAT HAPPENED TO THOSE LITTLE GUYS!
ROTOR, WHY DO YOU KEEP ANTS AS PETS?
'CAUSE THEY'RE SO INTERESTING TO WATCH! BESIDES, THEY LIKE LIVING IN THE ANT FARM!
THEN WHY DO THEY KEEP ESCAPING?
SONIC, YOU'RE FORGETTING THAT WE'RE DANGEROUSLY CLOSE TO ROBOTROPOLIS! HURRY UP WITH THOSE MEDICINAL BERRIES BEFORE...
OH, THERE'S NO NEED TO WORRY ABOUT MEDICINE, PRINCESS SALLY...
...ROBOTS ARE NEVER ILL!
WELL SAID, SIR!
LOOK OUT, SAL! IT'S ROBOTNIK!
!!
BZZAP!
zing
BLAM!
HE'S GOT A PORTABLE ROBOTICIZER! WAIT! WHERE'S ROTOR?!!
OH, NO!

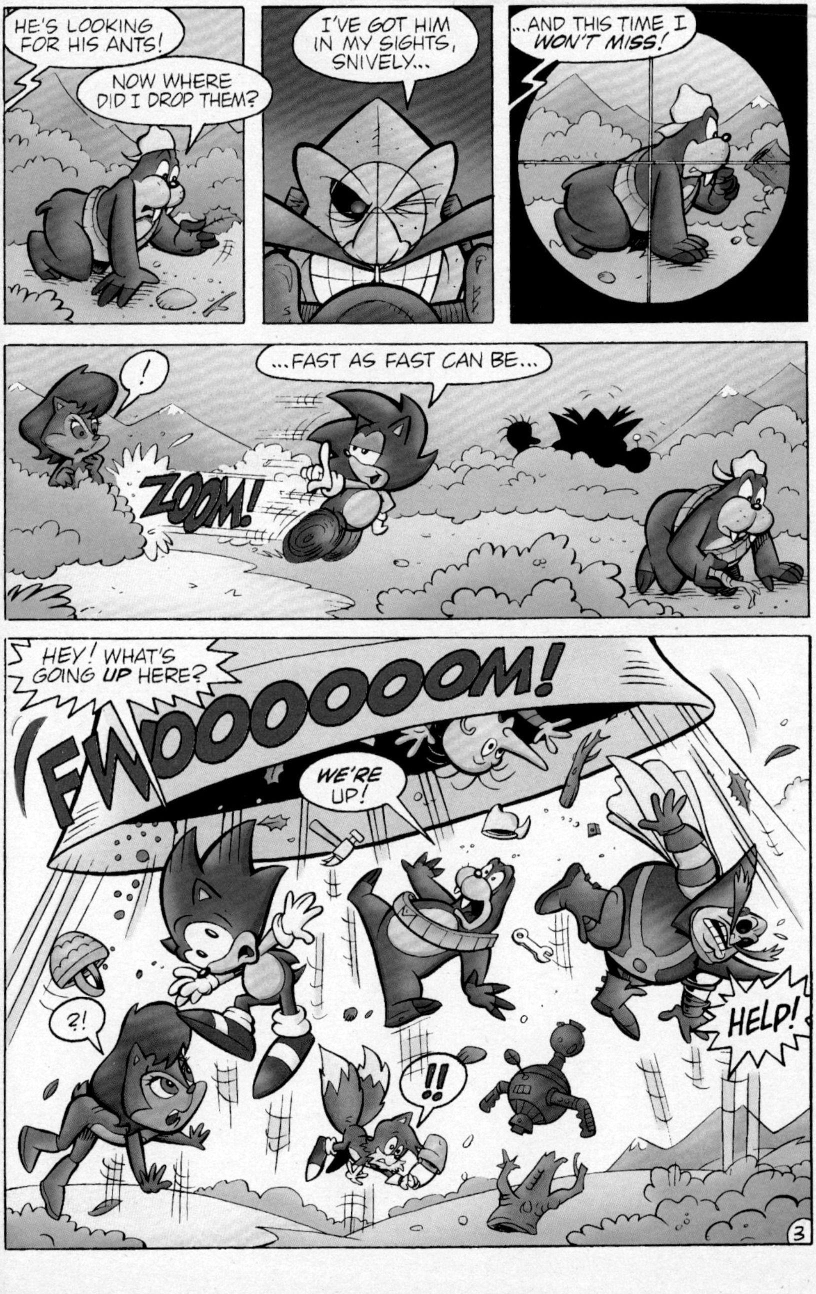
HE'S LOOKING FOR HIS ANTS!
NOW WHERE DID I DROP THEM?
I'VE GOT HIM IN MY SIGHTS, SNIVELY...
...AND THIS TIME I WON'T MISS!
!
...FAST AS FAST CAN BE...
ZOOM!
HEY! WHAT'S GOING UP HERE?
FWOOOOOOOM!
WE'RE UP!
?!
!!
HELP!

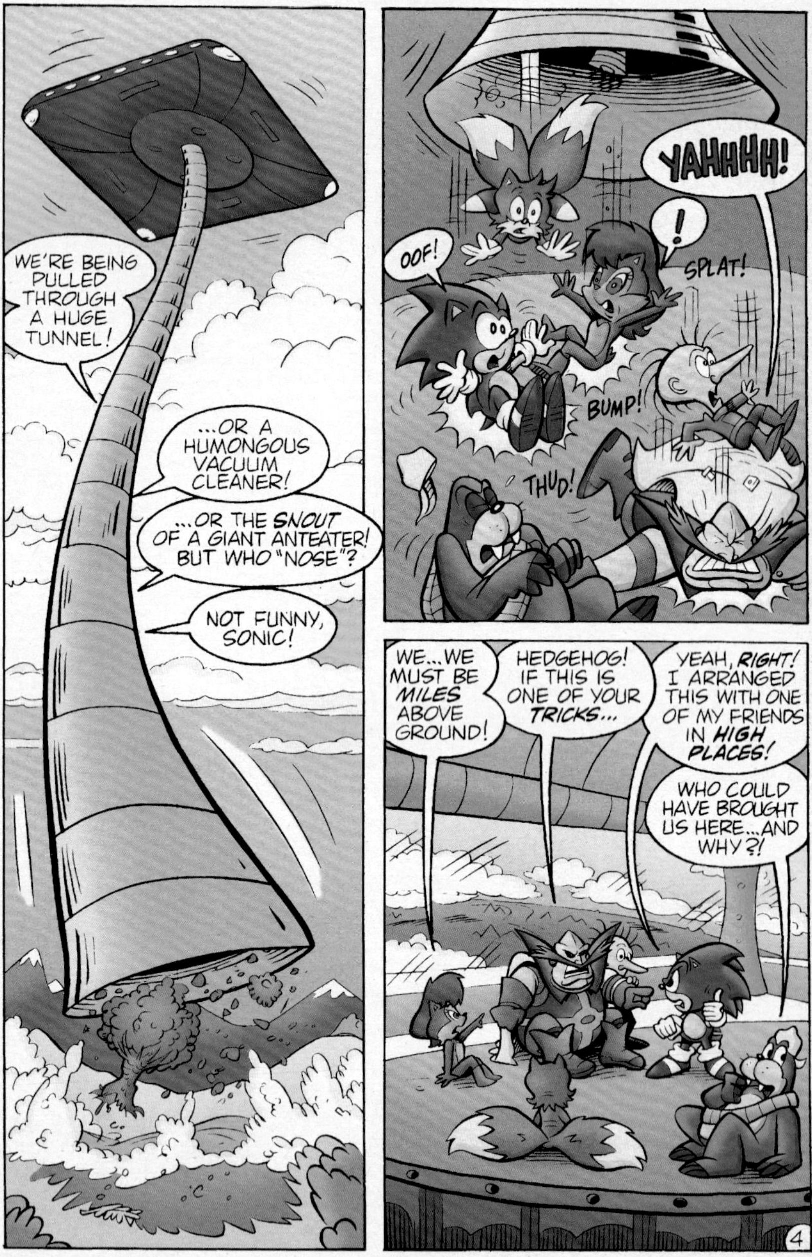

WE'RE BEING PULLED THROUGH A HUGE TUNNEL!
...OR A HUMONGOUS VACUUM CLEANER!
...OR THE SNOUT OF A GIANT ANTEATER! BUT WHO "NOSE"?
NOT FUNNY, SONIC!
YAHHHH!
!
OOF!
SPLAT!
BUMP!
THUD!
WE...WE MUST BE MILES ABOVE GROUND!
HEDGEHOG! IF THIS IS ONE OF YOUR TRICKS...
YEAH, RIGHT! I ARRANGED THIS WITH ONE OF MY FRIENDS IN HIGH PLACES!
WHO COULD HAVE BROUGHT US HERE...AND WHY?!

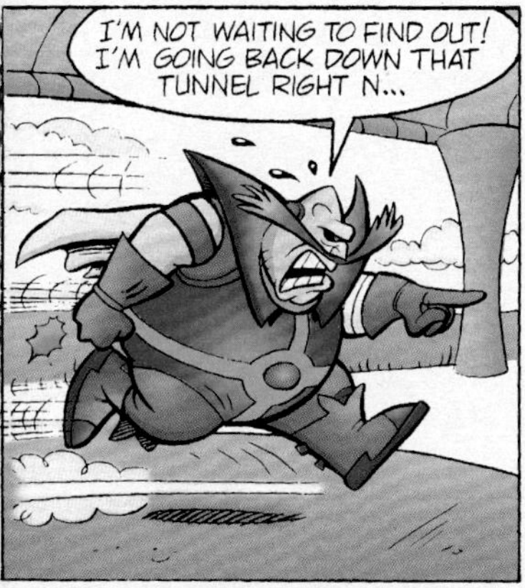
I'M NOT WAITING TO FIND OUT! I'M GOING BACK DOWN THAT TUNNEL RIGHT N...

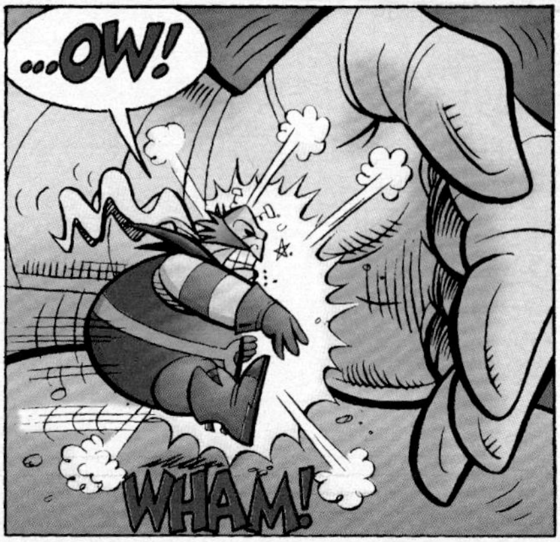
...OW!
WHAM!

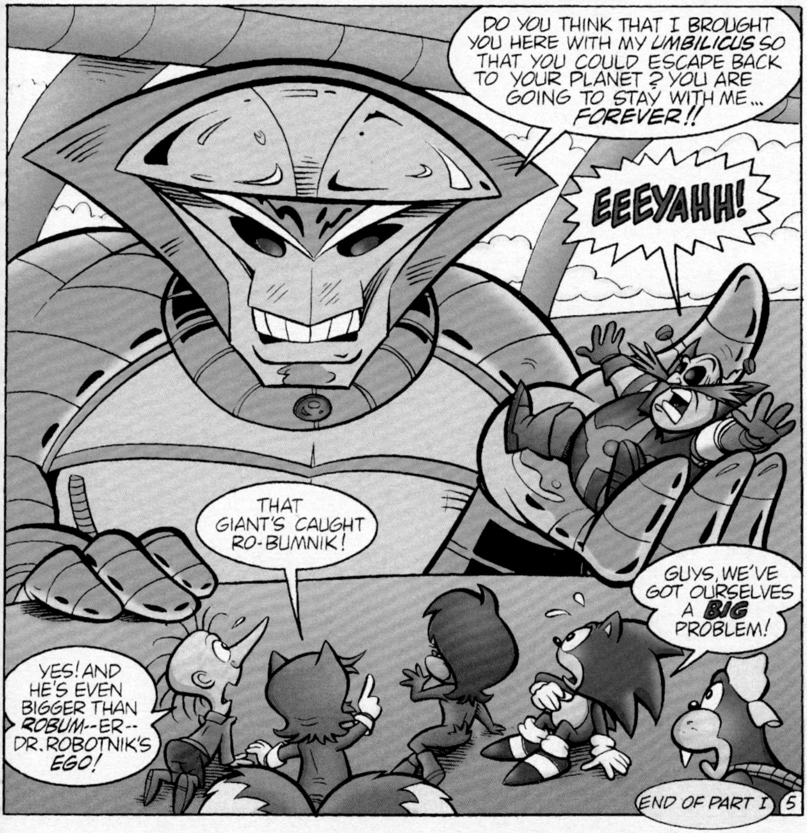
DO YOU THINK THAT I BROUGHT YOU HERE WITH MY UMBILICUS SO THAT YOU COULD ESCAPE BACK TO YOUR PLANET? YOU ARE GOING TO STAY WITH ME... FOREVER!!
EEEYAHH!
THAT GIANT'S CAUGHT RO-BUMNIK!
GUYS, WE'VE GOT OURSELVES A BIG PROBLEM!
YES! AND HE'S EVEN BIGGER THAN ROBUM--ER--DR. ROBOTNIK'S EGO!
END OF PART I

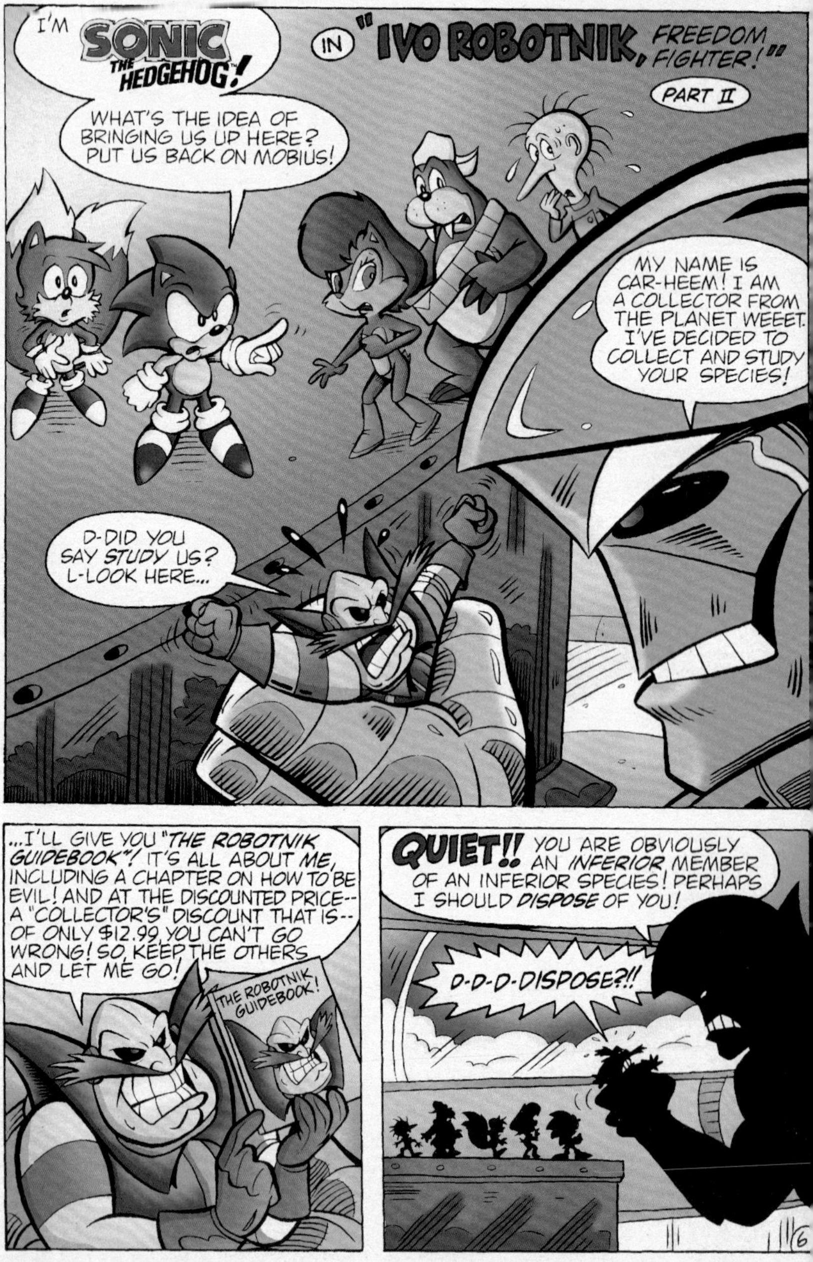
I'M SONIC THE HEDGEHOG!
IN "IVO ROBOTNIK, FREEDOM FIGHTER!"
PART II
WHAT'S THE IDEA OF BRINGING US UP HERE? PUT US BACK ON MOBIUS!
MY NAME IS CAR-HEEM! I AM A COLLECTOR FROM THE PLANET WEEET. I'VE DECIDED TO COLLECT AND STUDY YOUR SPECIES!
D-DID YOU SAY STUDY US? L-LOOK HERE...
...I'LL GIVE YOU "THE ROBOTNIK GUIDEBOOK"! IT'S ALL ABOUT ME, INCLUDING A CHAPTER ON HOW TO BE EVIL! AND AT THE DISCOUNTED PRICE-- A "COLLECTOR'S" DISCOUNT THAT IS-- OF ONLY $12.99, YOU CAN'T GO WRONG! SO, KEEP THE OTHERS AND LET ME GO!
THE ROBOTNIK GUIDEBOOK!
QUIET!! YOU ARE OBVIOUSLY AN INFERIOR MEMBER OF AN INFERIOR SPECIES! PERHAPS I SHOULD DISPOSE OF YOU!
D-D-D-DISPOSE?!!
6

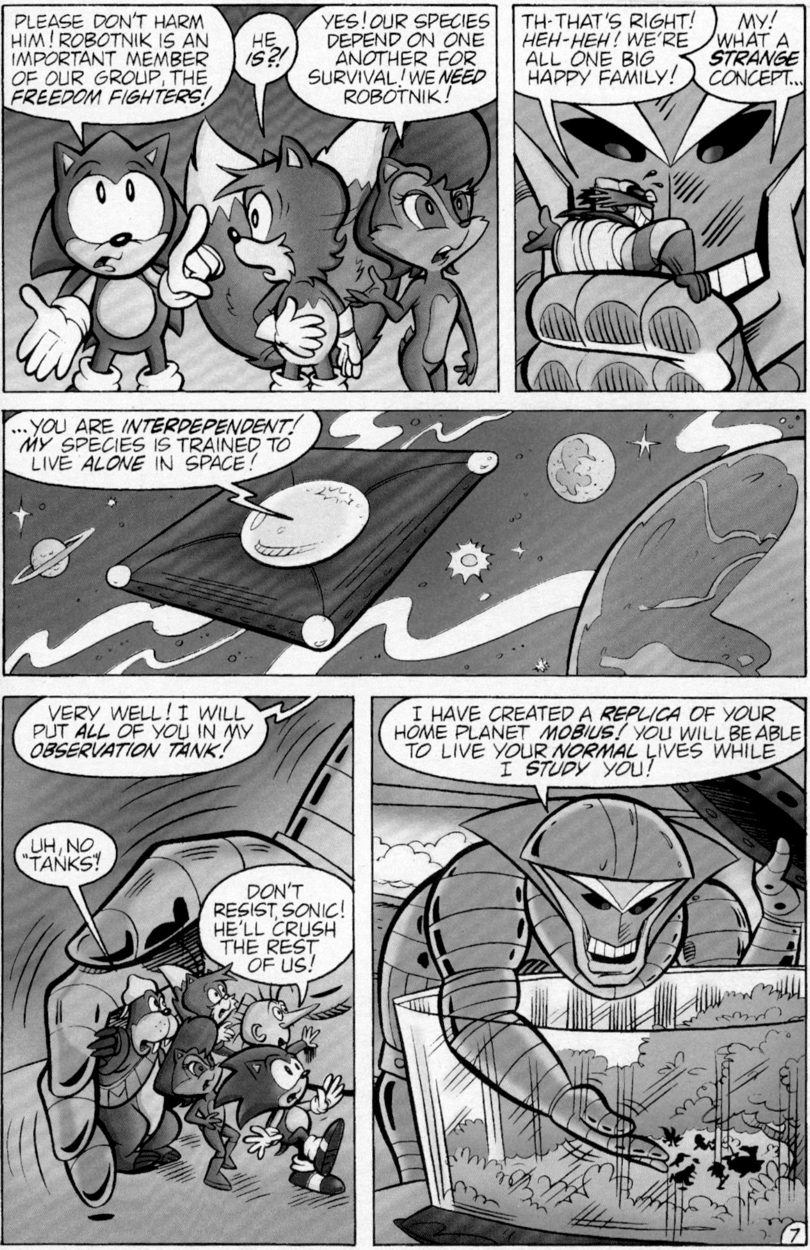
PLEASE DON'T HARM HIM! ROBOTNIK IS AN IMPORTANT MEMBER OF OUR GROUP, THE FREEDOM FIGHTERS!
HE IS?!
YES! OUR SPECIES DEPEND ON ONE ANOTHER FOR SURVIVAL! WE NEED ROBOTNIK!
TH-THAT'S RIGHT! HEH-HEH! WE'RE ALL ONE BIG HAPPY FAMILY!
MY! WHAT A STRANGE CONCEPT...
...YOU ARE INTERDEPENDENT! MY SPECIES IS TRAINED TO LIVE ALONE IN SPACE!
VERY WELL! I WILL PUT ALL OF YOU IN MY OBSERVATION TANK!
UH, NO "TANKS"!
DON'T RESIST, SONIC! HE'LL CRUSH THE REST OF US!
I HAVE CREATED A REPLICA OF YOUR HOME PLANET MOBIUS! YOU WILL BE ABLE TO LIVE YOUR NORMAL LIVES WHILE I STUDY YOU!

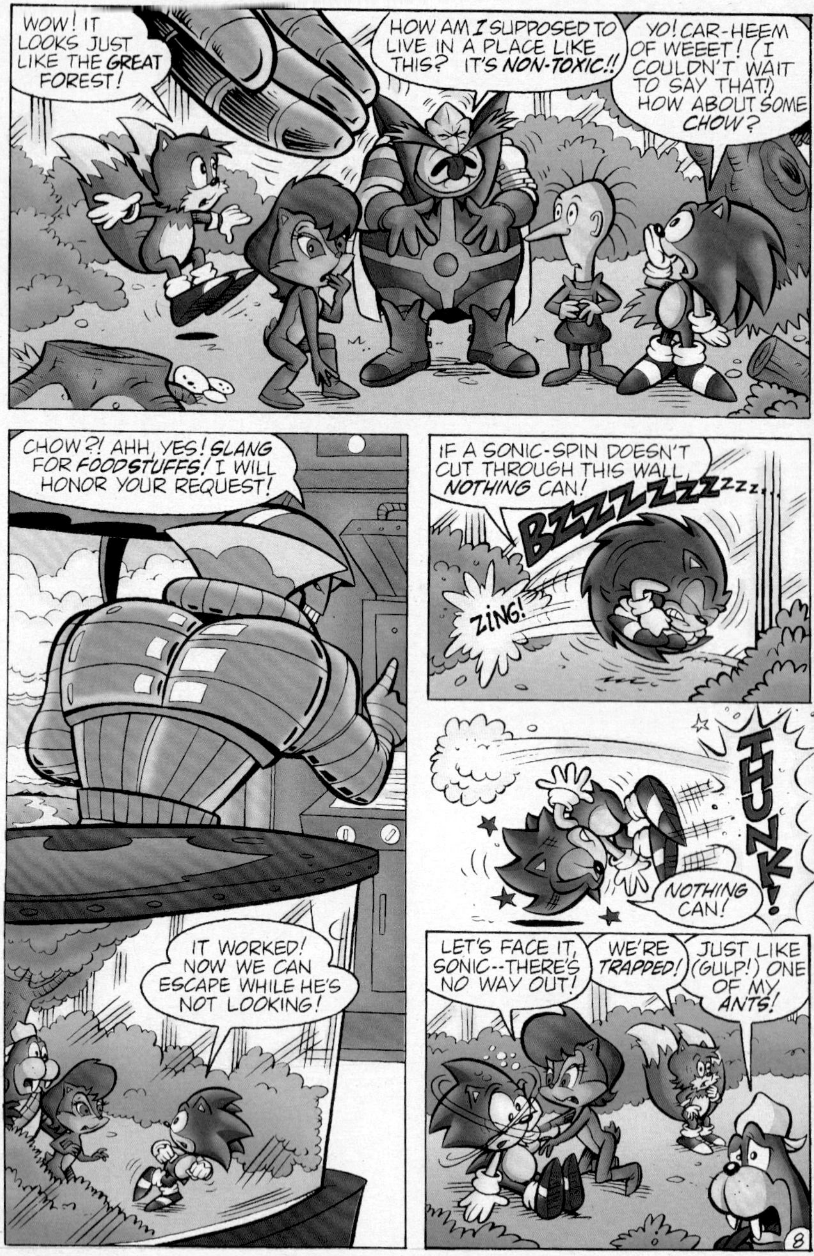
WOW! IT LOOKS JUST LIKE THE GREAT FOREST!
HOW AM I SUPPOSED TO LIVE IN A PLACE LIKE THIS? IT'S NON-TOXIC!!
YO! CAR-HEEM OF WEEET! (I COULDN'T WAIT TO SAY THAT!) HOW ABOUT SOME CHOW?
CHOW?! AHH, YES! SLANG FOR FOODSTUFFS! I WILL HONOR YOUR REQUEST!
IT WORKED! NOW WE CAN ESCAPE WHILE HE'S NOT LOOKING!
IF A SONIC-SPIN DOESN'T CUT THROUGH THIS WALL, NOTHING CAN!
BZZZZZZZzzz
ZING!
THUNK!
NOTHING CAN!
LET'S FACE IT, SONIC--THERE'S NO WAY OUT!
WE'RE TRAPPED!
JUST LIKE (GULP!) ONE OF MY ANTS!
8

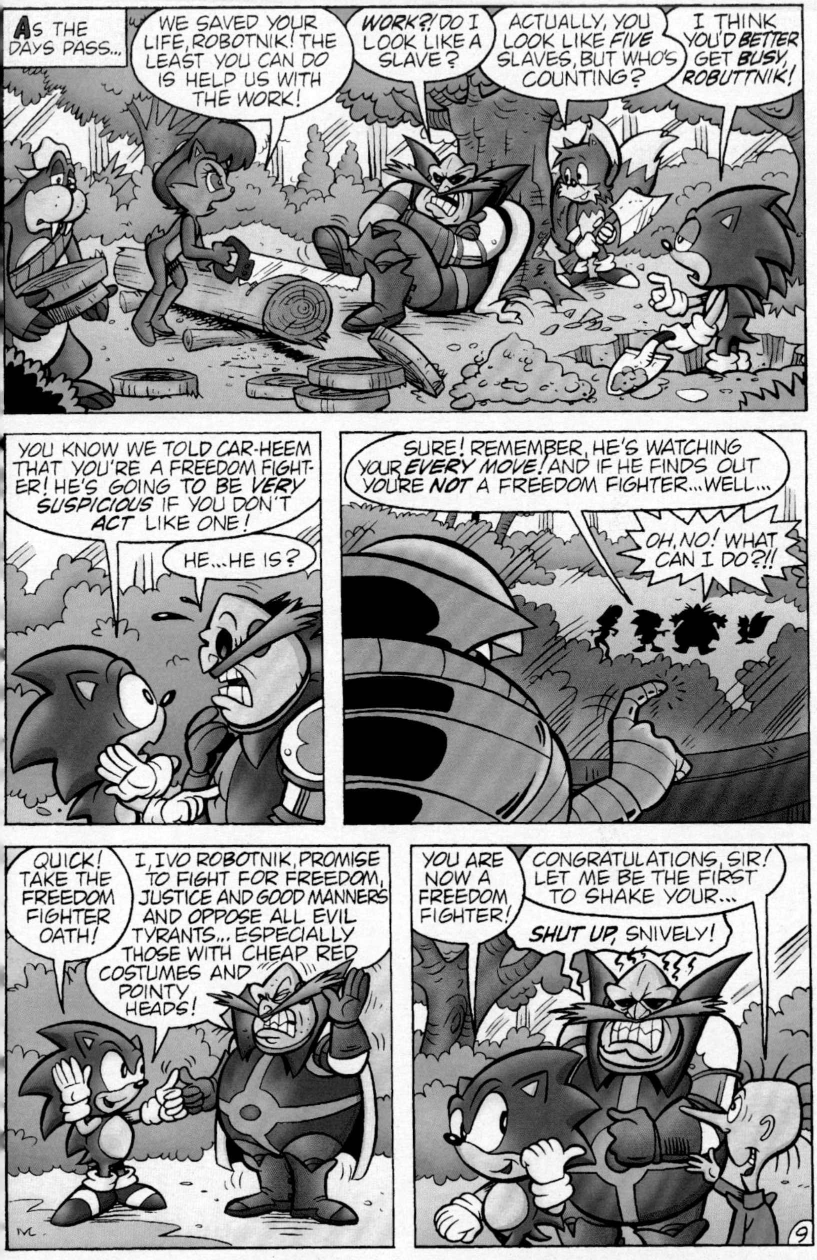

AS THE DAYS PASS...
WE SAVED YOUR LIFE, ROBOTNIK! THE LEAST YOU CAN DO IS HELP US WITH THE WORK!
WORK?! DO I LOOK LIKE A SLAVE?
ACTUALLY, YOU LOOK LIKE FIVE SLAVES, BUT WHO'S COUNTING?
I THINK YOU'D BETTER GET BUSY, ROBUTTNIK!
YOU KNOW WE TOLD CAR-HEEM THAT YOU'RE A FREEDOM FIGHTER! HE'S GOING TO BE VERY SUSPICIOUS IF YOU DON'T ACT LIKE ONE!
HE...HE IS?
SURE! REMEMBER, HE'S WATCHING YOUR EVERY MOVE! AND IF HE FINDS OUT YOU'RE NOT A FREEDOM FIGHTER...WELL...
OH, NO! WHAT CAN I DO?!!
QUICK! TAKE THE FREEDOM FIGHTER OATH!
I, IVO ROBOTNIK, PROMISE TO FIGHT FOR FREEDOM, JUSTICE AND GOOD MANNERS AND OPPOSE ALL EVIL TYRANTS... ESPECIALLY THOSE WITH CHEAP RED COSTUMES AND POINTY HEADS!
YOU ARE NOW A FREEDOM FIGHTER!
CONGRATULATIONS, SIR! LET ME BE THE FIRST TO SHAKE YOUR...
SHUT UP, SNIVELY!
9

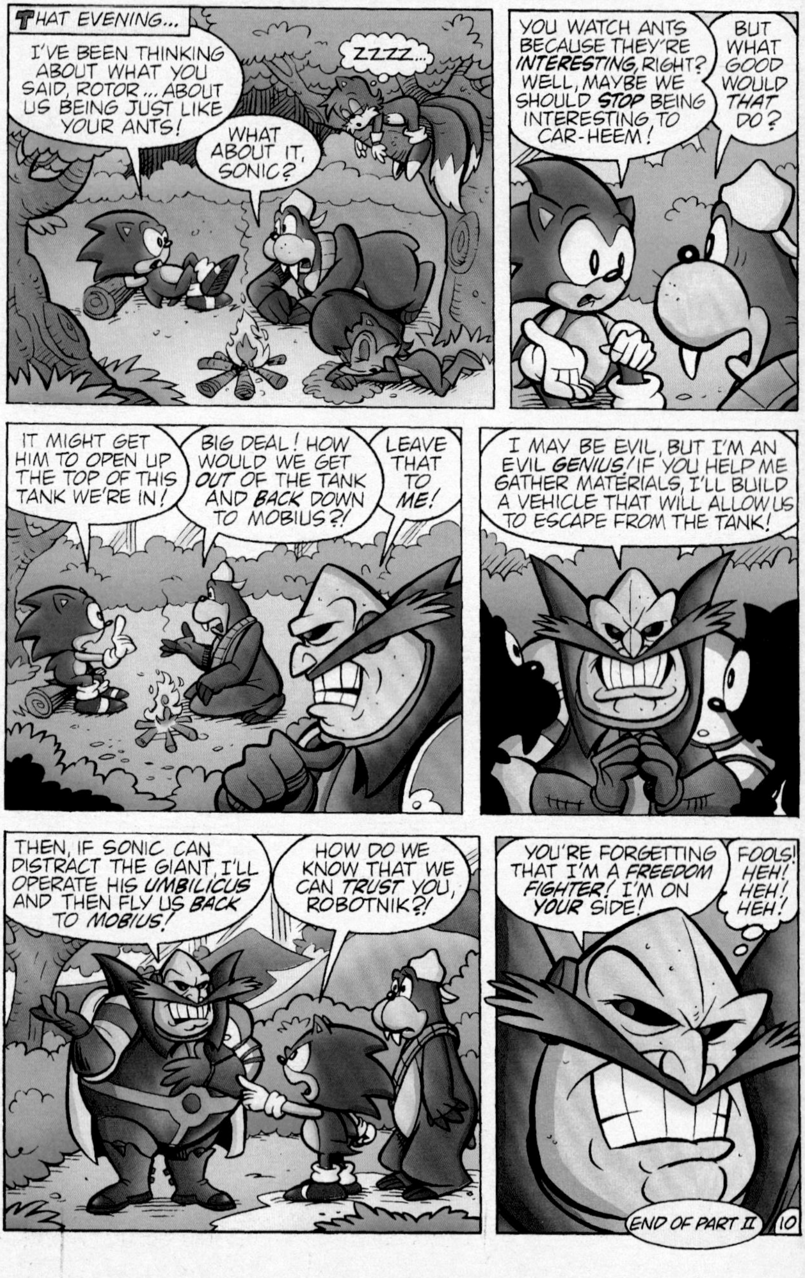
THAT EVENING...
I'VE BEEN THINKING ABOUT WHAT YOU SAID, ROTOR ... ABOUT US BEING JUST LIKE YOUR ANTS!
ZZZZ...
WHAT ABOUT IT, SONIC?
YOU WATCH ANTS BECAUSE THEY'RE INTERESTING, RIGHT? WELL, MAYBE WE SHOULD STOP BEING INTERESTING TO CAR-HEEM!
BUT WHAT GOOD WOULD THAT DO?
IT MIGHT GET HIM TO OPEN UP THE TOP OF THIS TANK WE'RE IN!
BIG DEAL! HOW WOULD WE GET OUT OF THE TANK AND BACK DOWN TO MOBIUS?!
LEAVE THAT TO ME!
I MAY BE EVIL, BUT I'M AN EVIL GENIUS! IF YOU HELP ME GATHER MATERIALS, I'LL BUILD A VEHICLE THAT WILL ALLOW US TO ESCAPE FROM THE TANK!
THEN, IF SONIC CAN DISTRACT THE GIANT, I'LL OPERATE HIS UMBILICUS AND THEN FLY US BACK TO MOBIUS!
HOW DO WE KNOW THAT WE CAN TRUST YOU, ROBOTNIK?!
YOU'RE FORGETTING THAT I'M A FREEDOM FIGHTER! I'M ON YOUR SIDE!
FOOLS! HEH! HEH! HEH!
END OF PART II

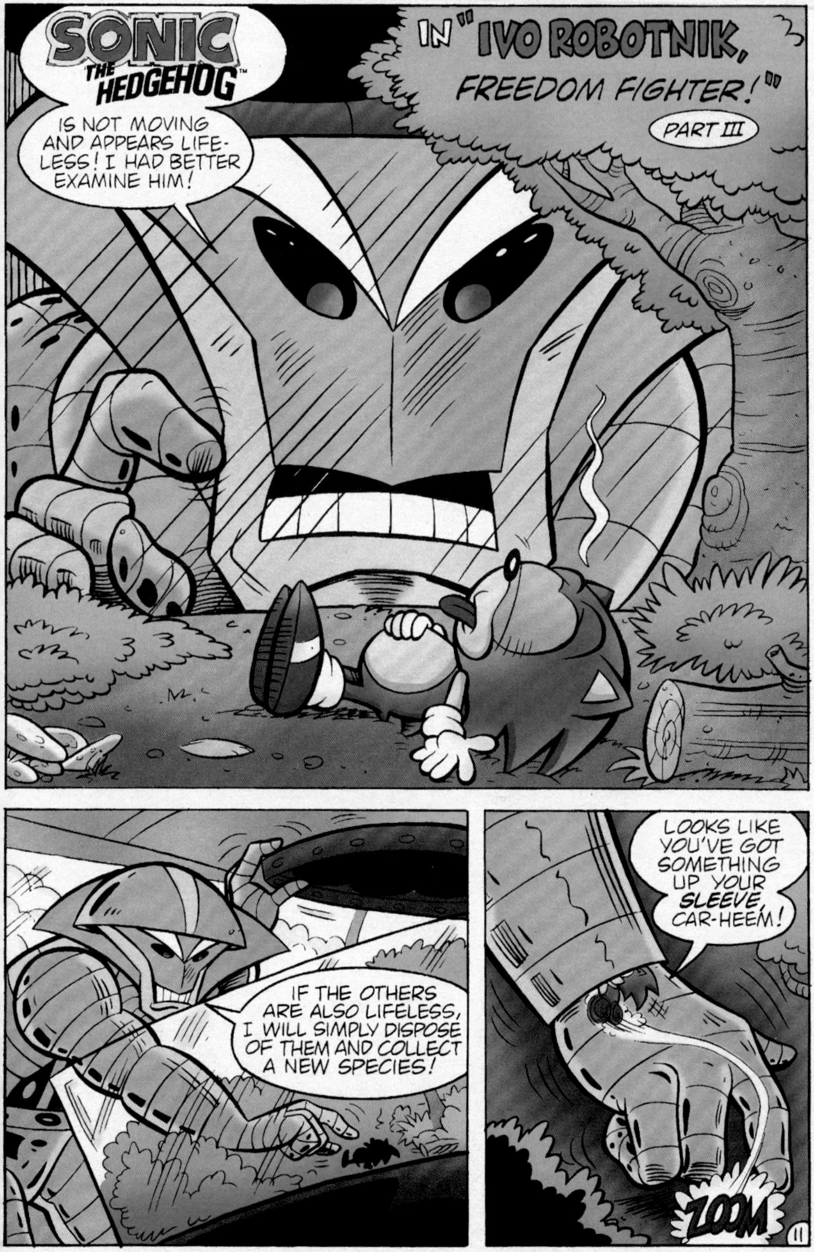
SONIC THE HEDGEHOG™
IN "IVO ROBOTNIK, FREEDOM FIGHTER!"
PART III
IS NOT MOVING AND APPEARS LIFELESS! I HAD BETTER EXAMINE HIM!
IF THE OTHERS ARE ALSO LIFELESS, I WILL SIMPLY DISPOSE OF THEM AND COLLECT A NEW SPECIES!
LOOKS LIKE YOU'VE GOT SOMETHING UP YOUR SLEEVE, CAR-HEEM!
ZOOM
11

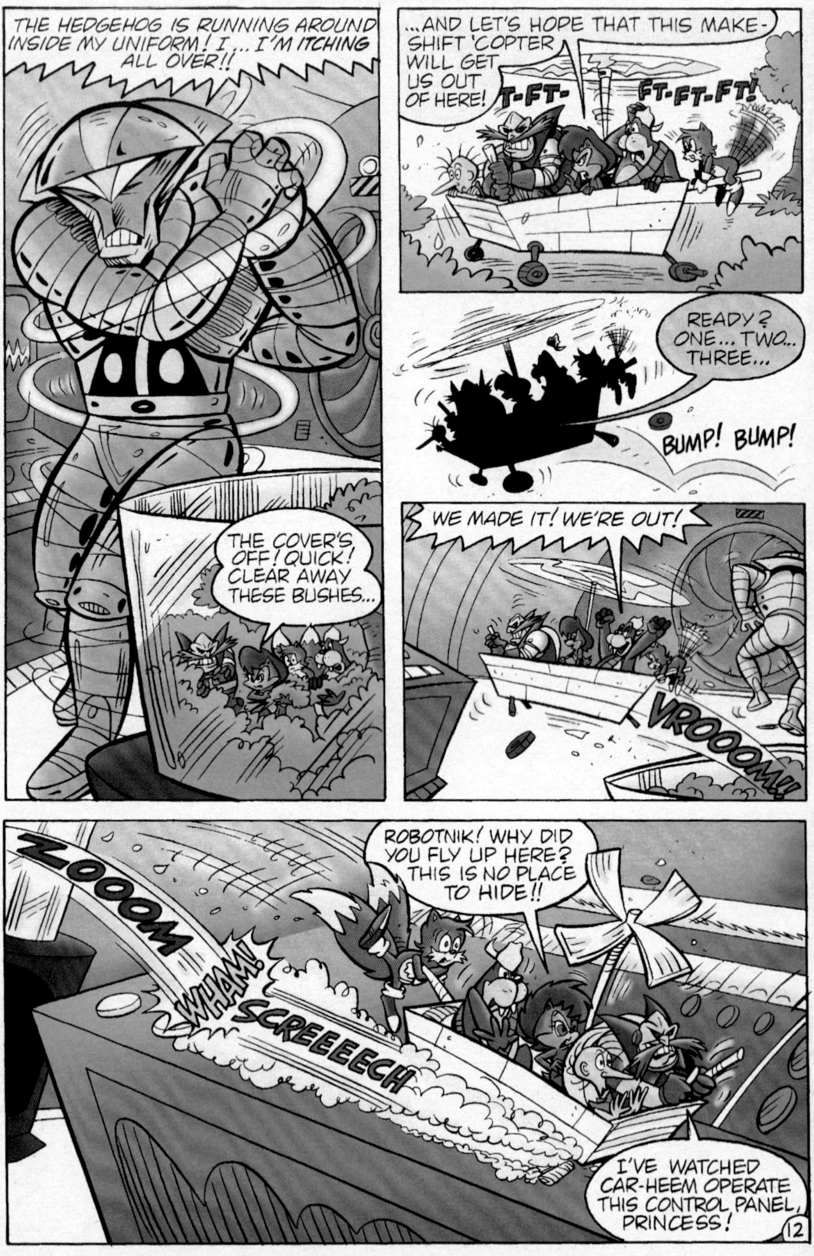
THE HEDGEHOG IS RUNNING AROUND INSIDE MY UNIFORM! I... I'M ITCHING ALL OVER!!
THE COVER'S OFF! QUICK! CLEAR AWAY THESE BUSHES...
...AND LET'S HOPE THAT THIS MAKE-SHIFT 'COPTER WILL GET US OUT OF HERE!
T-FT-
FT-FT-FT!
READY? ONE... TWO... THREE...
BUMP! BUMP!
WE MADE IT! WE'RE OUT!
VROOOOM!!
ZOOOM
WHAM!
SCREEEECH
ROBOTNIK! WHY DID YOU FLY UP HERE? THIS IS NO PLACE TO HIDE!!
I'VE WATCHED CAR-HEEM OPERATE THIS CONTROL PANEL, PRINCESS!

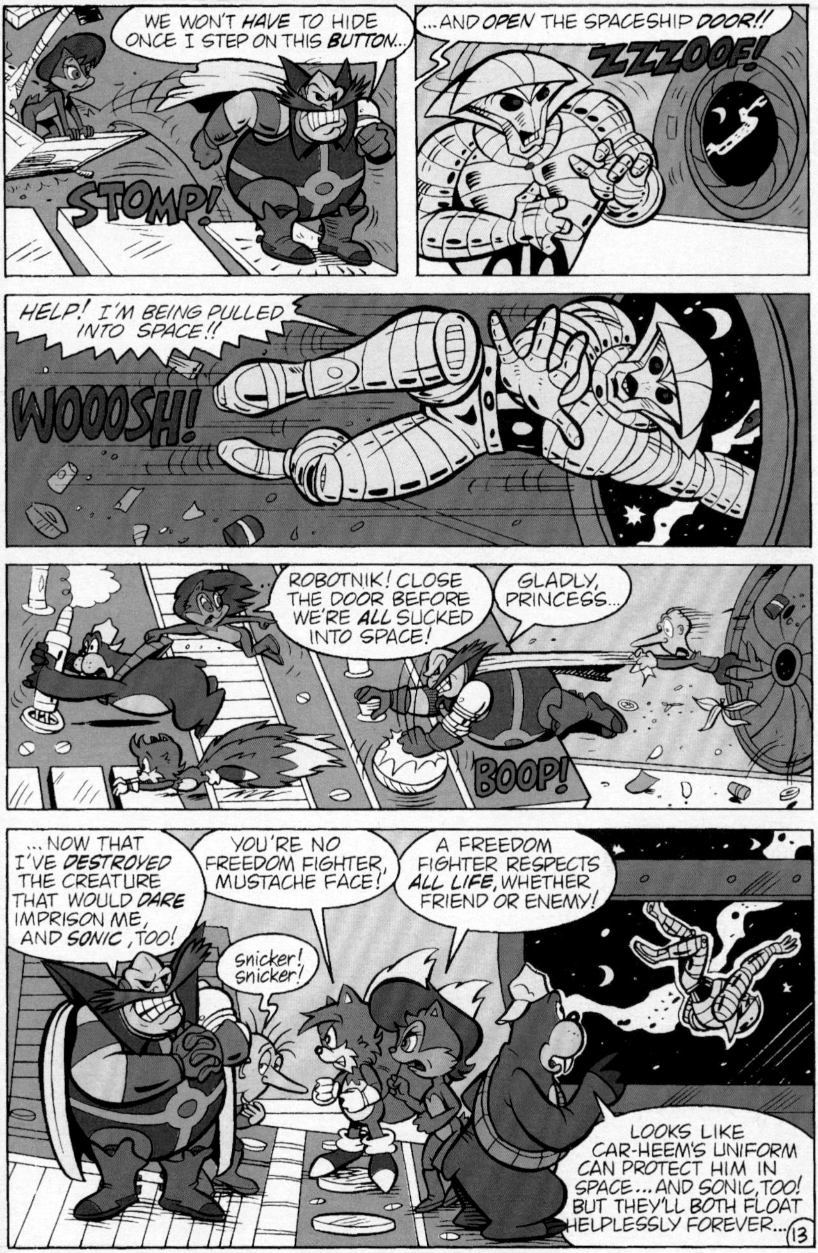
WE WON'T HAVE TO HIDE ONCE I STEP ON THIS BUTTON...
STOMP!
...AND OPEN THE SPACESHIP DOOR!!
ZZZOOF!
HELP! I'M BEING PULLED INTO SPACE!!
WOOOSH!
ROBOTNIK! CLOSE THE DOOR BEFORE WE'RE ALL SUCKED INTO SPACE!
GLADLY, PRINCESS...
BOOP!
...NOW THAT I'VE DESTROYED THE CREATURE THAT WOULD DARE IMPRISON ME, AND SONIC, TOO!
snicker! snicker!
YOU'RE NO FREEDOM FIGHTER, MUSTACHE FACE!
A FREEDOM FIGHTER RESPECTS ALL LIFE, WHETHER FRIEND OR ENEMY!
LOOKS LIKE CAR-HEEM'S UNIFORM CAN PROTECT HIM IN SPACE... AND SONIC, TOO! BUT THEY'LL BOTH FLOAT HELPLESSLY FOREVER...
13

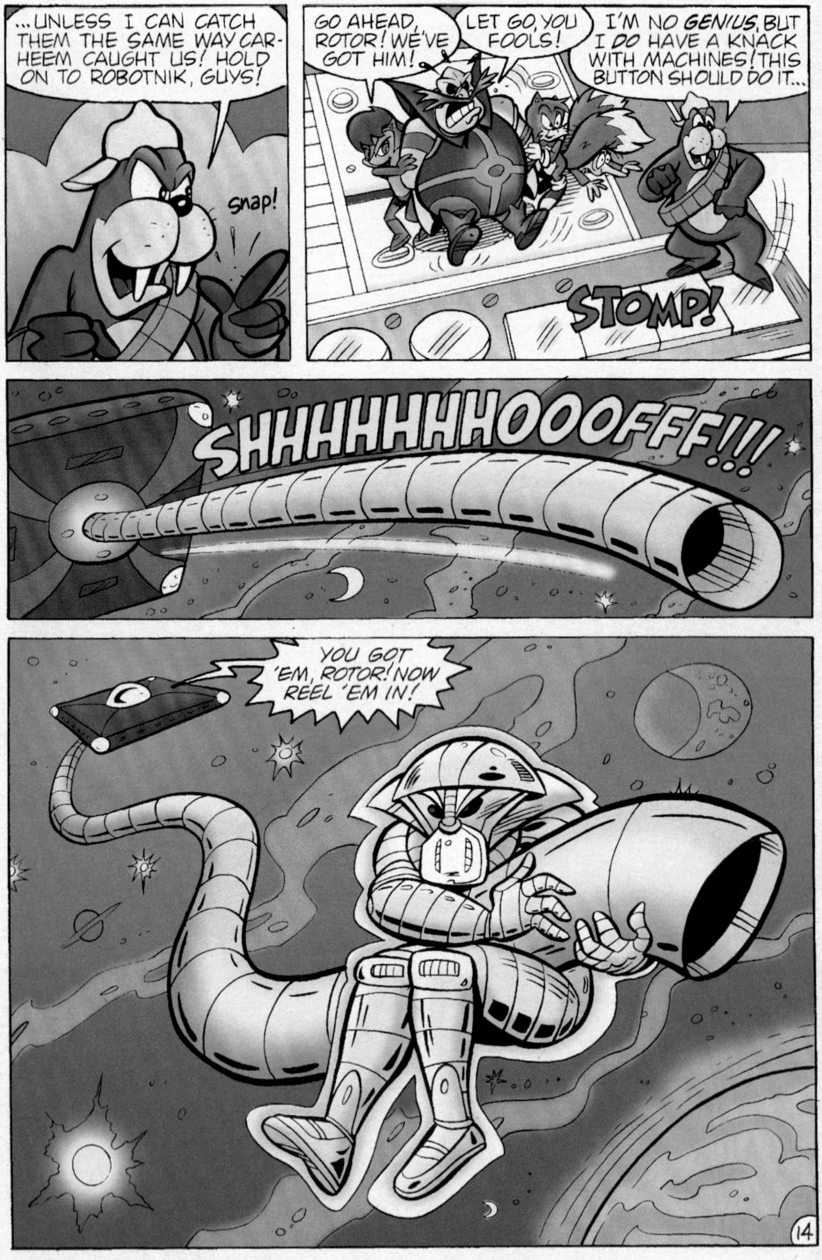
...UNLESS I CAN CATCH THEM THE SAME WAY CARHEEM CAUGHT US! HOLD ON TO ROBOTNIK, GUYS!
Snap!
GO AHEAD, ROTOR! WE'VE GOT HIM!
LET GO, YOU FOOLS!
I'M NO GENIUS, BUT I DO HAVE A KNACK WITH MACHINES! THIS BUTTON SHOULD DO IT...
STOMP!
SHHHHHHHOOOOFFF!!!
YOU GOT 'EM, ROTOR! NOW REEL 'EM IN!

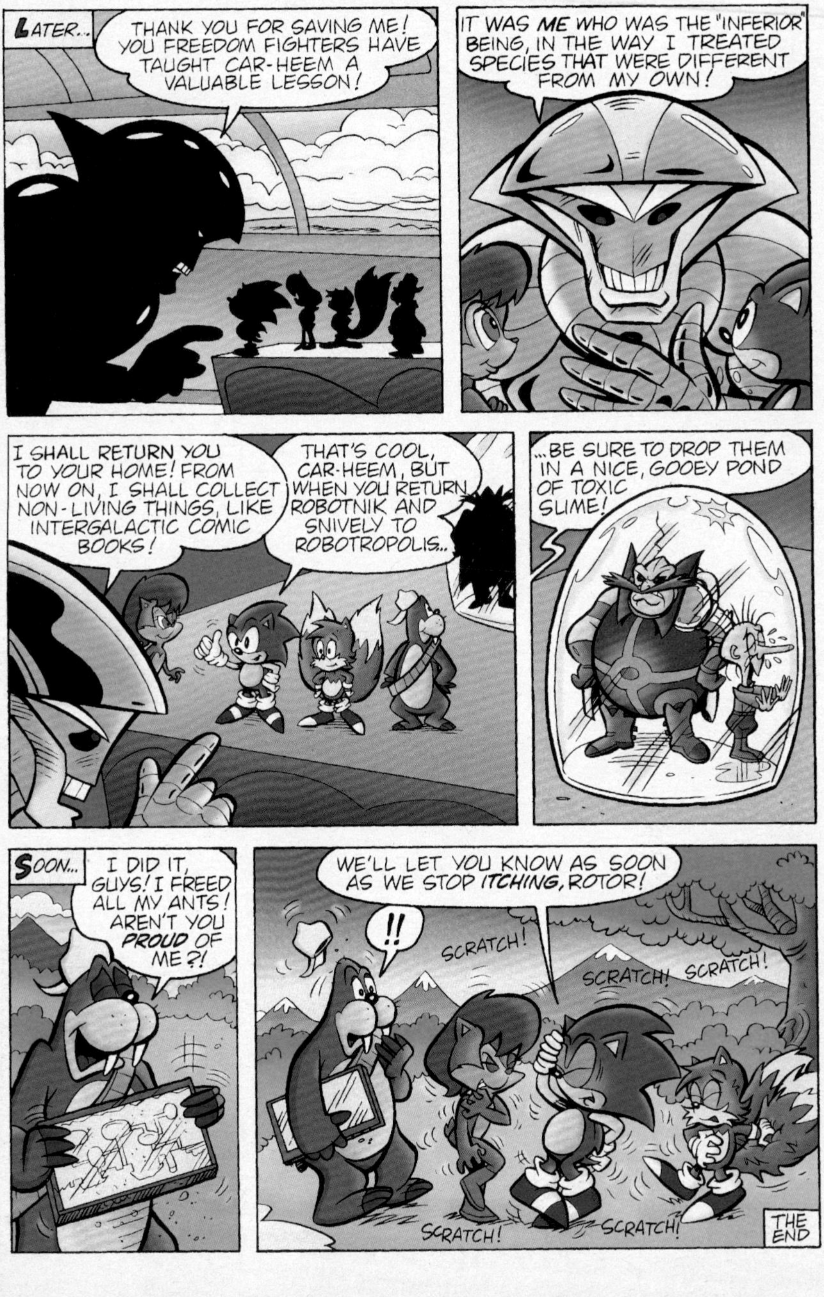
LATER...
THANK YOU FOR SAVING ME! YOU FREEDOM FIGHTERS HAVE TAUGHT CAR-HEEM A VALUABLE LESSON!
IT WAS ME WHO WAS THE "INFERIOR" BEING, IN THE WAY I TREATED SPECIES THAT WERE DIFFERENT FROM MY OWN!
I SHALL RETURN YOU TO YOUR HOME! FROM NOW ON, I SHALL COLLECT NON-LIVING THINGS, LIKE INTERGALACTIC COMIC BOOKS!
THAT'S COOL, CAR-HEEM, BUT WHEN YOU RETURN ROBOTNIK AND SNIVELY TO ROBOTROPOLIS...
...BE SURE TO DROP THEM IN A NICE, GOOEY POND OF TOXIC SLIME!
SOON...
I DID IT, GUYS! I FREED ALL MY ANTS! AREN'T YOU PROUD OF ME?!
WE'LL LET YOU KNOW AS SOON AS WE STOP ITCHING, ROTOR!
!!
SCRATCH!
SCRATCH! SCRATCH!
SCRATCH!
SCRATCH!
THE END

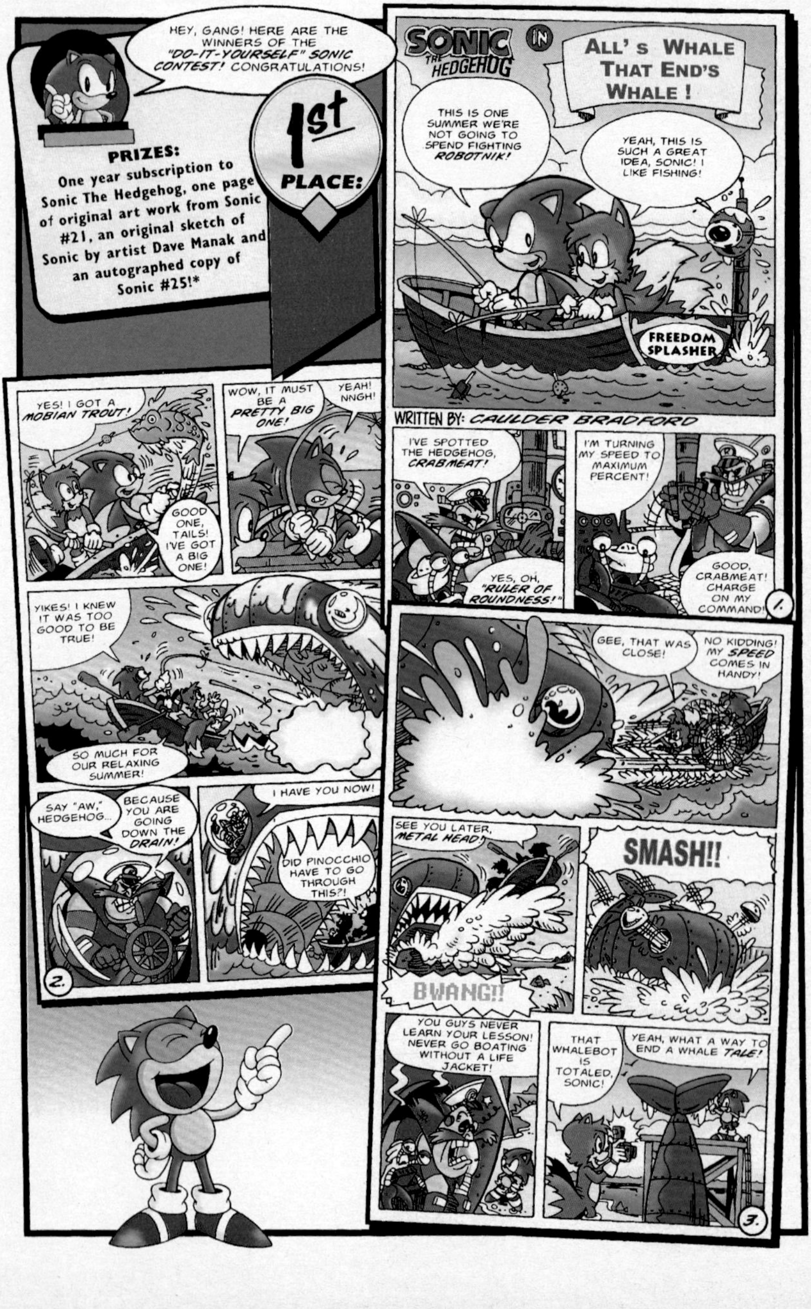
HEY, GANG! HERE ARE THE WINNERS OF THE "DO-IT-YOURSELF" SONIC CONTEST! CONGRATULATIONS!
PRIZES:
One year subscription to Sonic The Hedgehog, one page of original art work from Sonic #21, an original sketch of Sonic by artist Dave Manak and an autographed copy of Sonic #25!*
1st PLACE:
SONIC THE HEDGEHOG IN
ALL's WHALE THAT END'S WHALE !
THIS IS ONE SUMMER WE'RE NOT GOING TO SPEND FIGHTING ROBOTNIK!
YEAH, THIS IS SUCH A GREAT IDEA, SONIC! I LIKE FISHING!
FREEDOM SPLASHER
WRITTEN BY: CAULDER BRADFORD
I'VE SPOTTED THE HEDGEHOG, CRABMEAT!
YES, OH, "RULER OF ROUNDNESS!"
I'M TURNING MY SPEED TO MAXIMUM PERCENT!
GOOD, CRABMEAT! CHARGE ON MY COMMAND!
1.
YES! I GOT A MOBIAN TROUT!
GOOD ONE, TAILS! I'VE GOT A BIG ONE!
WOW, IT MUST BE A PRETTY BIG ONE!
YEAH! NNGH!
YIKES! I KNEW IT WAS TOO GOOD TO BE TRUE!
SO MUCH FOR OUR RELAXING SUMMER!
SAY "AW," HEDGEHOG...
BECAUSE YOU ARE GOING DOWN THE DRAIN!
I HAVE YOU NOW!
DID PINOCCHIO HAVE TO GO THROUGH THIS?!
2.
GEE, THAT WAS CLOSE!
NO KIDDING! MY SPEED COMES IN HANDY!
SEE YOU LATER, METAL HEAD!
BWANG!!
SMASH!!
YOU GUYS NEVER LEARN YOUR LESSON! NEVER GO BOATING WITHOUT A LIFE JACKET!
THAT WHALEBOT IS TOTALED, SONIC!
YEAH, WHAT A WAY TO END A WHALE TALE!
3.

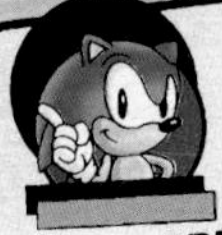

2nd PLACE:

PRIZES:

One year subscription to Sonic The Hedgehog, one page of original art work from Sonic #22 and an autographed copy of Sonic #25!*

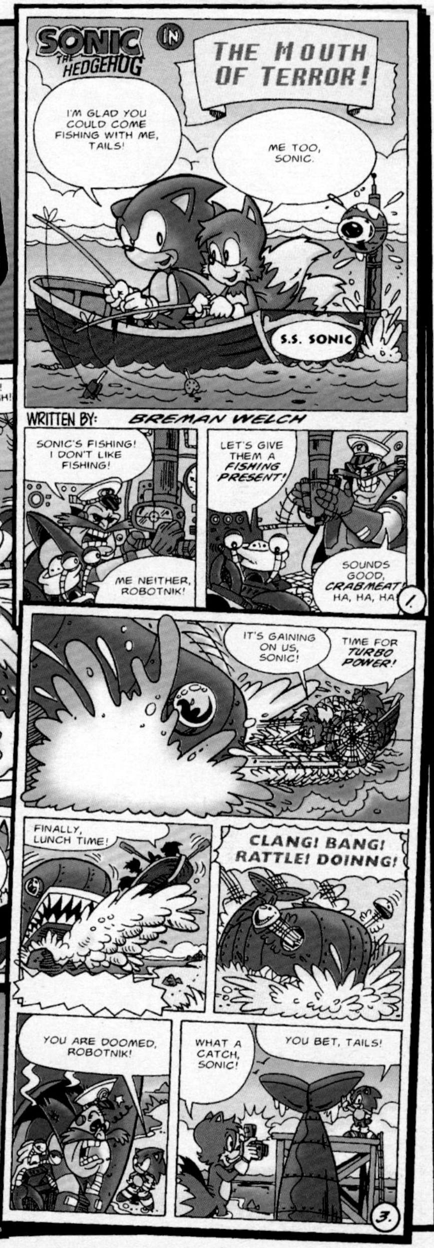
SONIC THE HEDGEHOG IN
THE MOUTH OF TERROR!
I'M GLAD YOU COULD COME FISHING WITH ME, TAILS!
ME TOO, SONIC.
S.S. SONIC
WRITTEN BY: BREMAN WELCH
SONIC'S FISHING! I DON'T LIKE FISHING!
ME NEITHER, ROBOTNIK!
LET'S GIVE THEM A FISHING PRESENT!
SOUNDS GOOD, CRABMEAT! HA, HA, HA!
1.
IT'S GAINING ON US, SONIC!
TIME FOR TURBO POWER!
FINALLY, LUNCH TIME!
CLANG! BANG! RATTLE! DOINNG!
YOU ARE DOOMED, ROBOTNIK!
WHAT A CATCH, SONIC!
YOU BET, TAILS!
3.

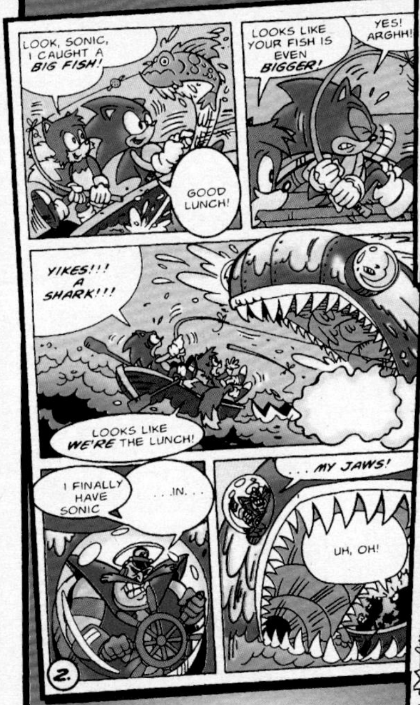
LOOK, SONIC, I CAUGHT A BIG FISH!
GOOD LUNCH!
LOOKS LIKE YOUR FISH IS EVEN BIGGER!
YES! ARGHH!
YIKES!!! A SHARK!!!
LOOKS LIKE WE'RE THE LUNCH!
I FINALLY HAVE SONIC
. . .IN. . .
. . . MY JAWS!
UH, OH!
2.

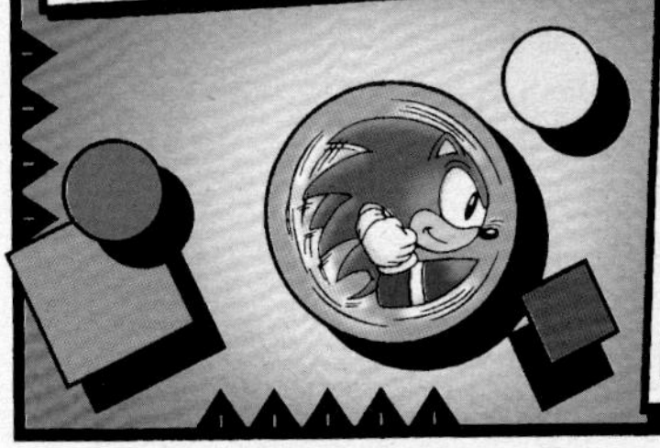

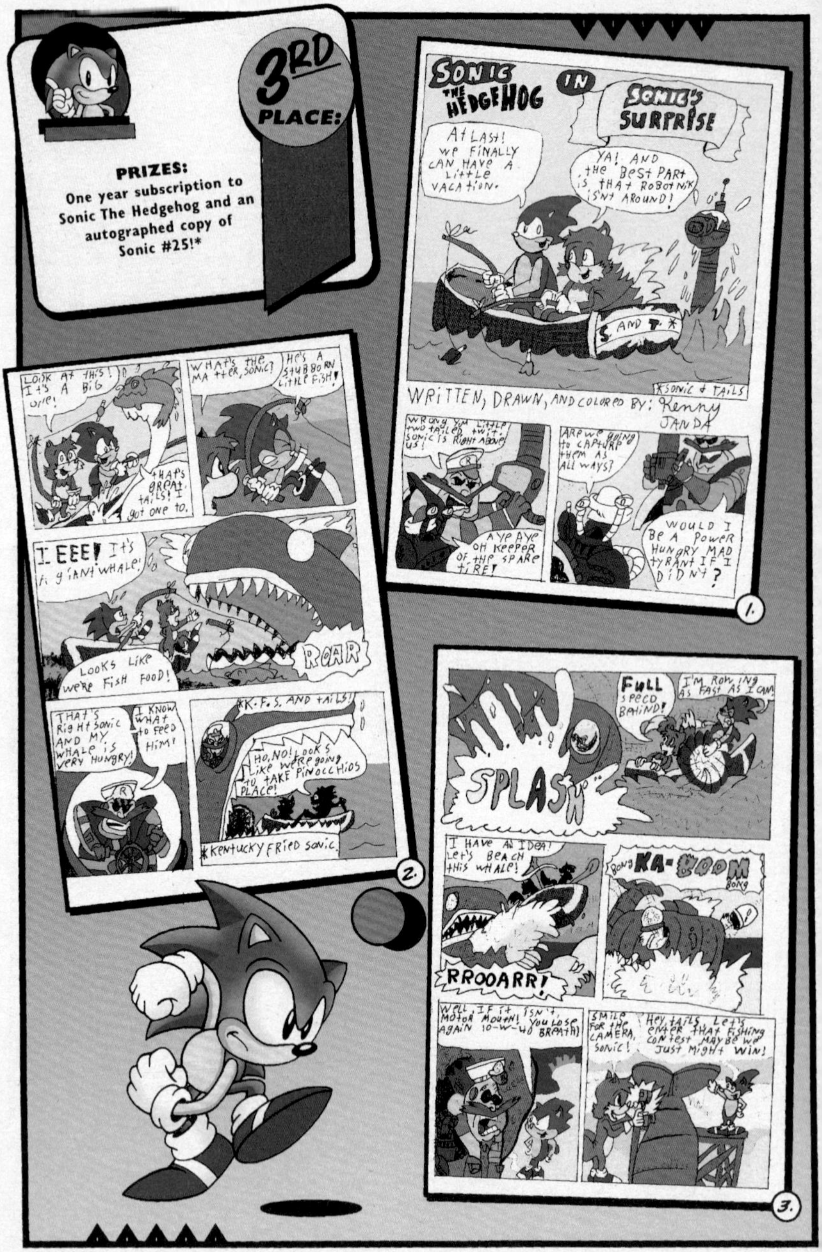
3RD PLACE:
PRIZES:
One year subscription to Sonic The Hedgehog and an autographed copy of Sonic #25!*
SONIC THE HEDGEHOG IN SONIC'S SURPRISE
AT LAST! WE FINALLY CAN HAVE A LITTLE VACATION.
YA! AND THE BEST PART IS THAT ROBOTNIK ISN'T AROUND!
S. AND T.*
*SONIC & TAILS
WRITTEN, DRAWN, AND COLORED BY: Kenny JANDA
WRONG YOU LITTLE TWO TAILED TWIT, SONIC IS RIGHT ABOVE US!
AYE AYE OH KEEPER OF THE SPARE TIRE!
ARE WE GOING TO CAPTURE THEM AS ALL WAYS?
WOULD I BE A POWER HUNGRY MAD TYRANT IF I DIDN'T?
1.
LOOK AT THIS! IT'S A BIG ONE!
THAT'S GREAT TAILS! I GOT ONE TO.
WHAT'S THE MATTER, SONIC?
HE'S A STUBBORN LITTLE FISH!
IEEE! IT'S A GIANT WHALE!
LOOKS LIKE WE'RE FISH FOOD!
ROAR
THAT'S RIGHT SONIC AND MY WHALE IS VERY HUNGRY!
I KNOW WHAT TO FEED HIM!
K.F.S. AND TAILS!
HO, NO! LOOKS LIKE WE'RE GOING TO TAKE PINOCCHIOS PLACE!
*KENTUCKY FRIED SONIC
2.
SPLASH
FULL SPEED BEHIND!
I'M ROWING AS FAST AS I CAN!
I HAVE AN IDEA! LET'S BEACH THIS WHALE!
RROOARR!
BONG KA-BOOM BONG
WELL, IF IT ISN'T MOTOR MOUTH! YOU LOSE AGAIN 10-W-40 BREATH!
SMILE FOR THE CAMERA, SONIC!
HEY, TAILS, LET'S ENTER THAT FISHING CONTEST MAYBE WE JUST MIGHT WIN!
3.

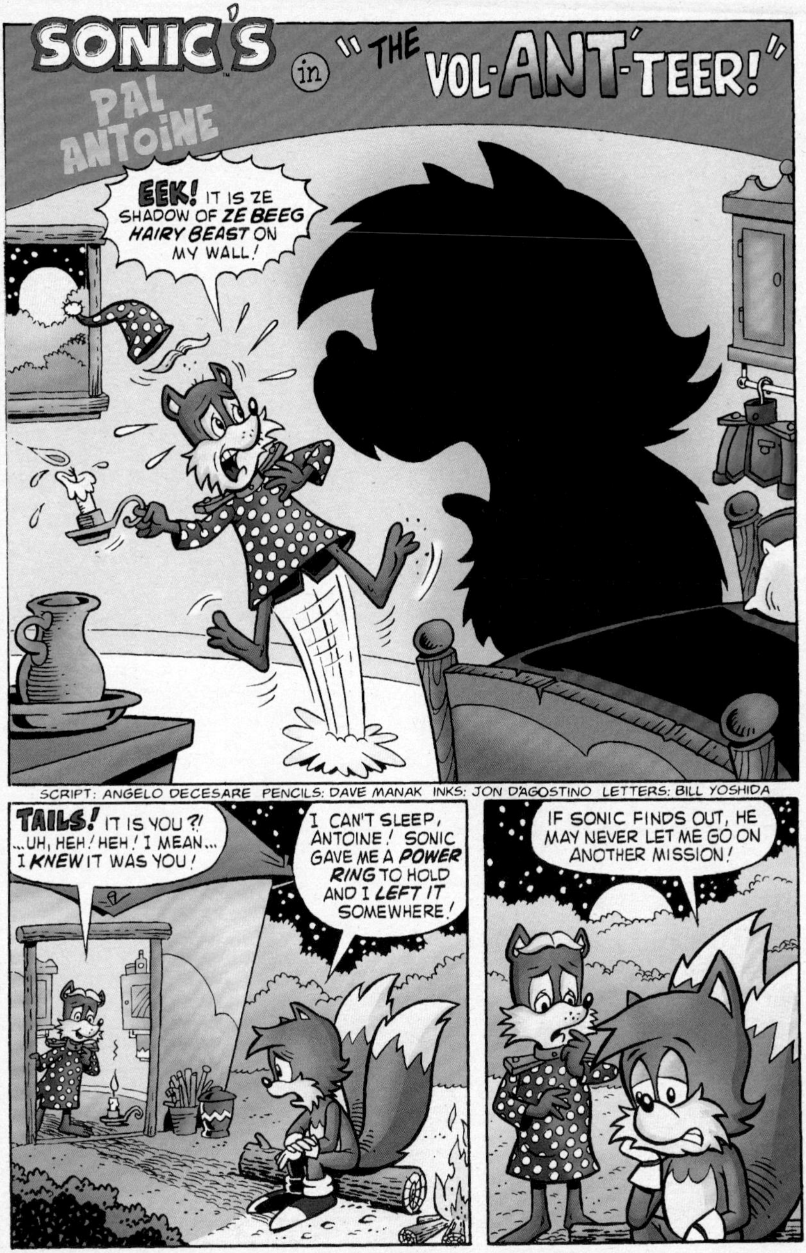
SONIC'S PAL ANTOINE in "THE VOL-ANT-TEER!"
EEK! IT IS ZE SHADOW OF ZE BEEG HAIRY BEAST ON MY WALL!
SCRIPT: ANGELO DECESARE PENCILS: DAVE MANAK INKS: JON D'AGOSTINO LETTERS: BILL YOSHIDA
TAILS! IT IS YOU?! ...UH, HEH! HEH! I MEAN... I KNEW IT WAS YOU!
I CAN'T SLEEP, ANTOINE! SONIC GAVE ME A POWER RING TO HOLD AND I LEFT IT SOMEWHERE!
IF SONIC FINDS OUT, HE MAY NEVER LET ME GO ON ANOTHER MISSION!

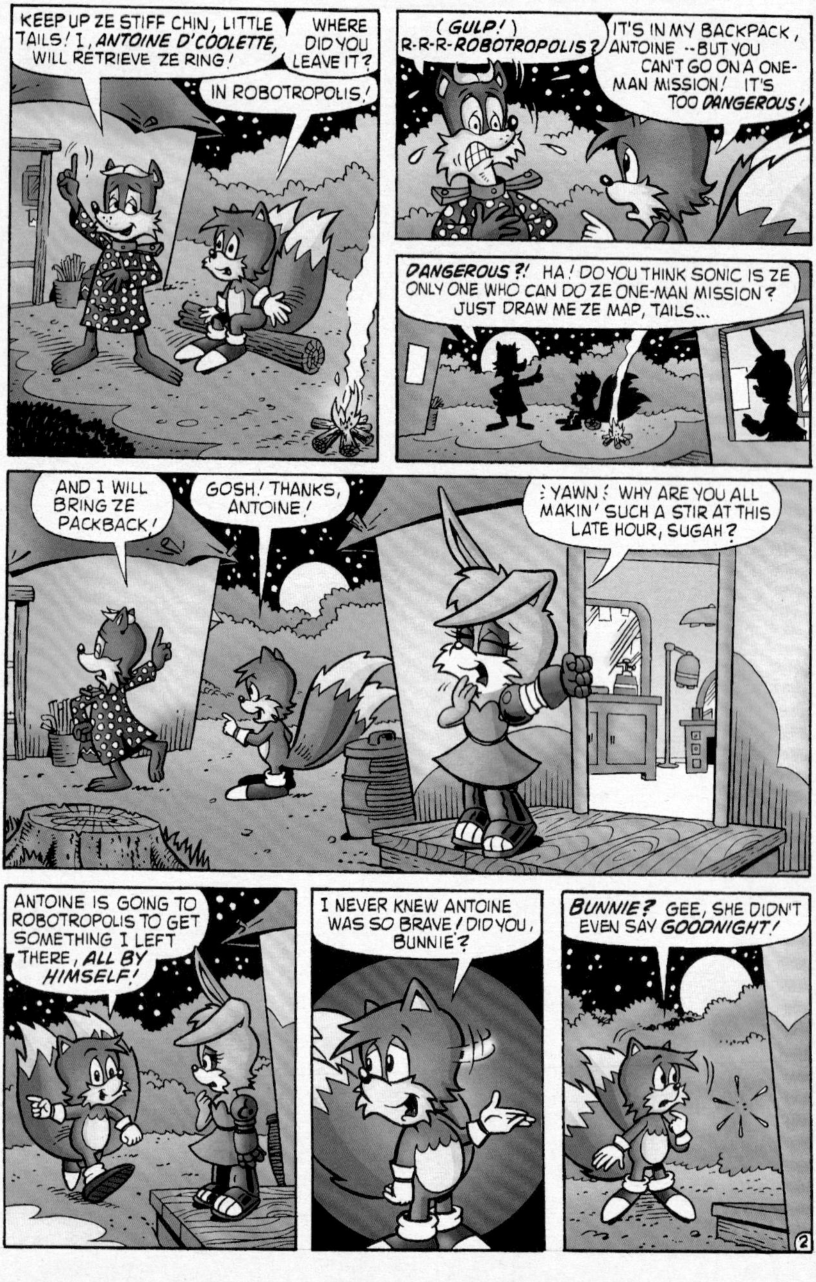
KEEP UP ZE STIFF CHIN, LITTLE TAILS! I, *ANTOINE D'COOLETTE*, WILL RETRIEVE ZE RING!
WHERE DID YOU LEAVE IT?
IN ROBOTROPOLIS!
(*GULP!*) R-R-R-*ROBOTROPOLIS?*
IT'S IN MY BACKPACK, ANTOINE --BUT YOU CAN'T GO ON A ONE-MAN MISSION! IT'S TOO *DANGEROUS!*
DANGEROUS?! HA! DO YOU THINK SONIC IS ZE ONLY ONE WHO CAN DO ZE ONE-MAN MISSION? JUST DRAW ME ZE MAP, TAILS...
AND I WILL BRING ZE PACKBACK!
GOSH! THANKS, ANTOINE!
:YAWN: WHY ARE YOU ALL MAKIN' SUCH A STIR AT THIS LATE HOUR, SUGAH?
ANTOINE IS GOING TO ROBOTROPOLIS TO GET SOMETHING I LEFT THERE, *ALL BY HIMSELF!*
I NEVER KNEW ANTOINE WAS SO BRAVE! DID YOU, BUNNIE?
BUNNIE? GEE, SHE DIDN'T EVEN SAY *GOODNIGHT!*
2

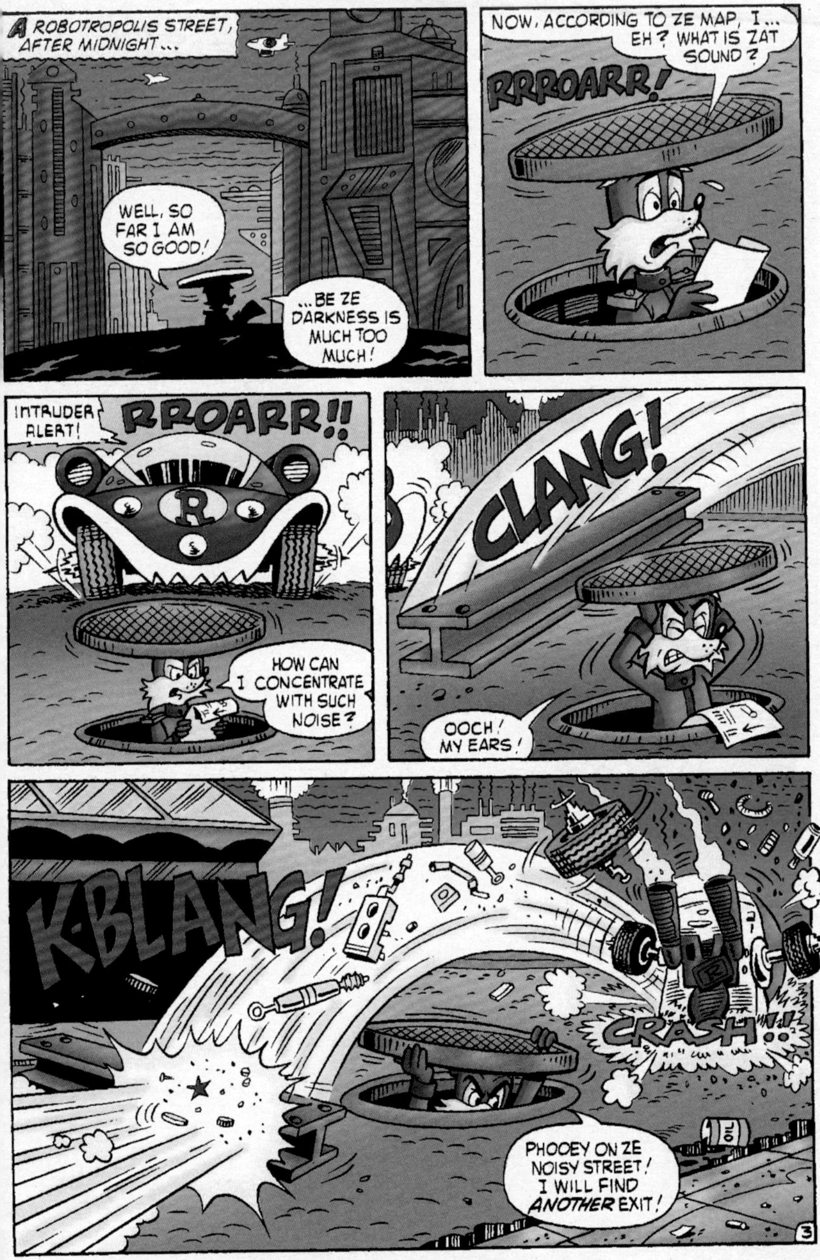

A ROBOTROPOLIS STREET, AFTER MIDNIGHT ...
WELL, SO FAR I AM SO GOOD!
...BE ZE DARKNESS IS MUCH TOO MUCH!
NOW, ACCORDING TO ZE MAP, I ... EH? WHAT IS ZAT SOUND?
RRROARR!
INTRUDER ALERT!
RRROARR!!
HOW CAN I CONCENTRATE WITH SUCH NOISE?
CLANG!
OOCH! MY EARS!
K-BLANG!
CRASH!!
OIL
PHOOEY ON ZE NOISY STREET! I WILL FIND *ANOTHER* EXIT!

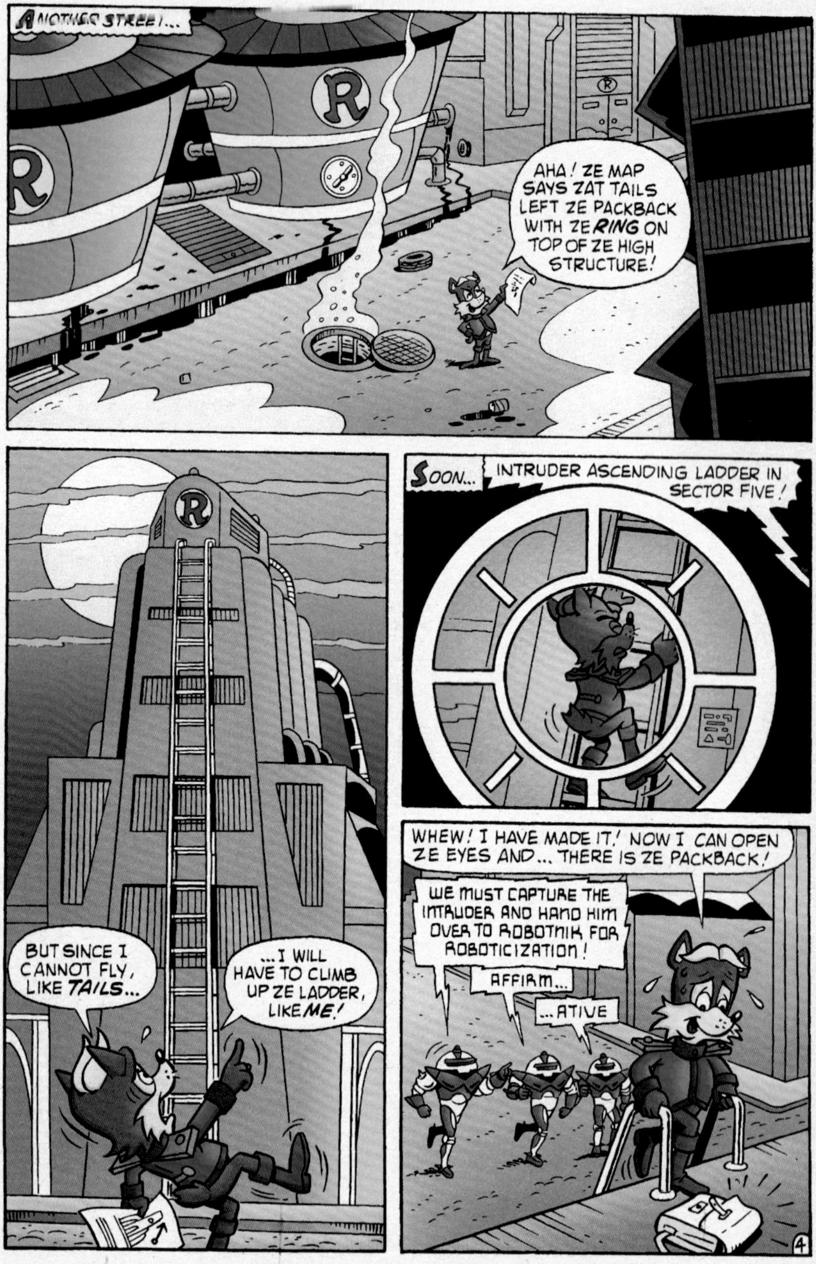
ANOTHER STREET...
AHA! ZE MAP SAYS ZAT TAILS LEFT ZE PACKBACK WITH ZE RING ON TOP OF ZE HIGH STRUCTURE!
BUT SINCE I CANNOT FLY, LIKE TAILS...
...I WILL HAVE TO CLIMB UP ZE LADDER, LIKE ME!
SOON...
INTRUDER ASCENDING LADDER IN SECTOR FIVE!
WHEW! I HAVE MADE IT! NOW I CAN OPEN ZE EYES AND... THERE IS ZE PACKBACK!
WE MUST CAPTURE THE INTRUDER AND HAND HIM OVER TO ROBOTNIK FOR ROBOTICIZATION!
AFFIRM...
...ATIVE

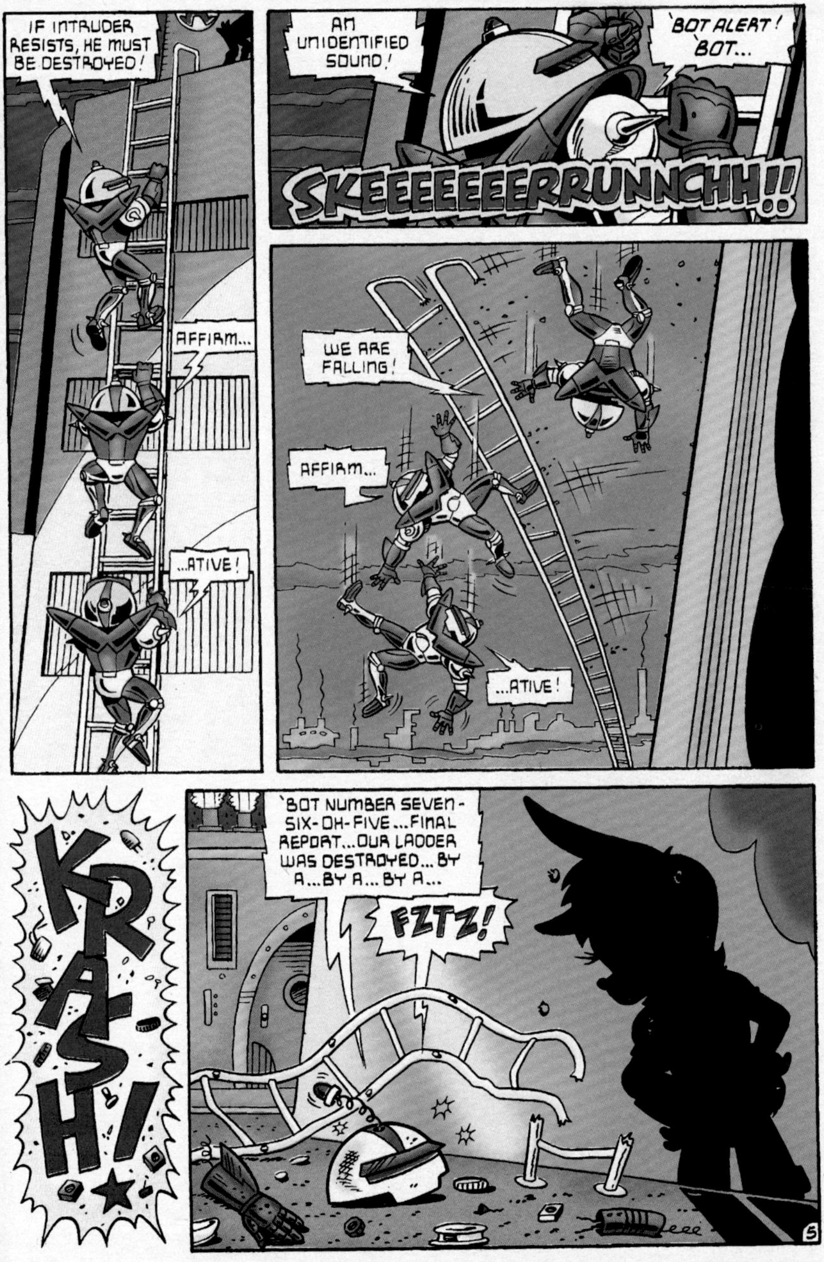
IF INTRUDER RESISTS, HE MUST BE DESTROYED!
AFFIRM...
...ATIVE!
AN UNIDENTIFIED SOUND!
`BOT ALERT! `BOT...
SKEEEEEEEERRUNNCHH!!
WE ARE FALLING!
AFFIRM...
...ATIVE!
KRASH!
`BOT NUMBER SEVEN-SIX-OH-FIVE...FINAL REPORT...OUR LADDER WAS DESTROYED... BY A...BY A...BY A...
FZTZ!
5

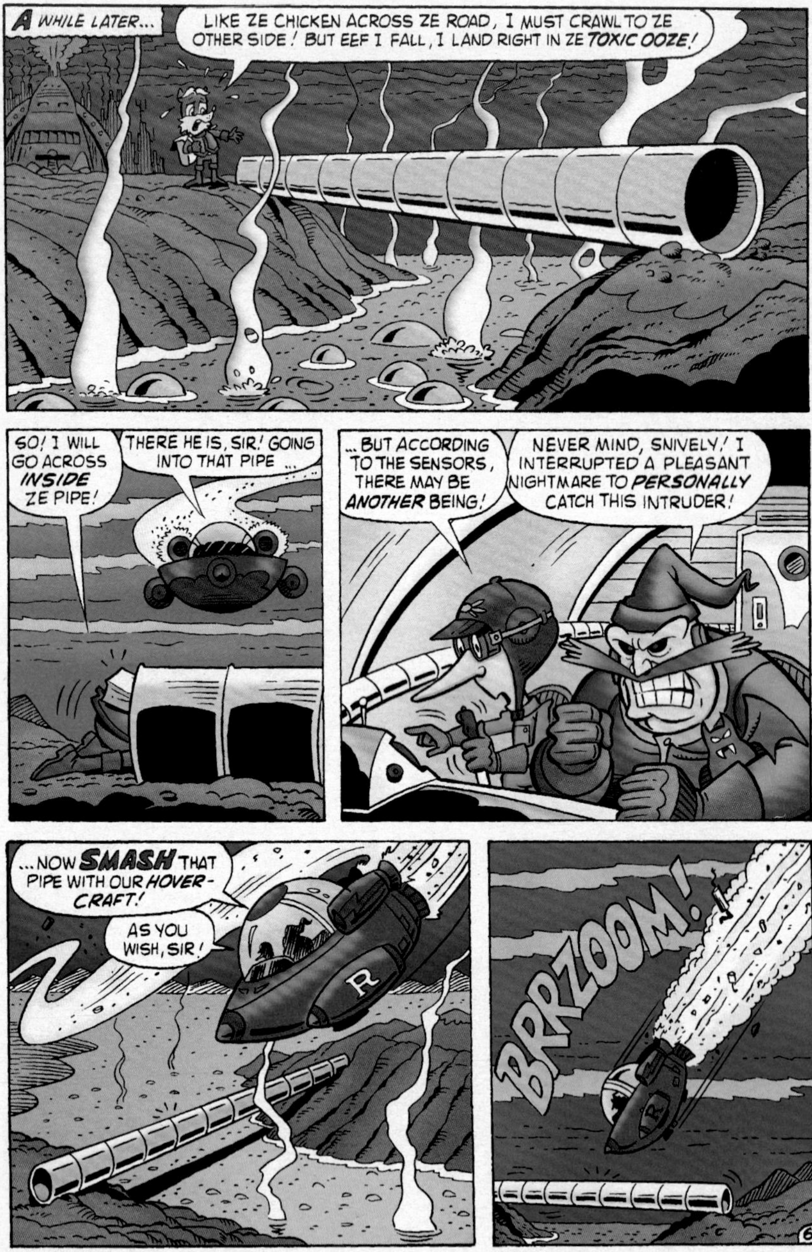
A WHILE LATER...
LIKE ZE CHICKEN ACROSS ZE ROAD, I MUST CRAWL TO ZE OTHER SIDE! BUT EEF I FALL, I LAND RIGHT IN ZE TOXIC OOZE!
SO! I WILL GO ACROSS INSIDE ZE PIPE!
THERE HE IS, SIR! GOING INTO THAT PIPE ...
...BUT ACCORDING TO THE SENSORS, THERE MAY BE ANOTHER BEING!
NEVER MIND, SNIVELY! I INTERRUPTED A PLEASANT NIGHTMARE TO PERSONALLY CATCH THIS INTRUDER!
...NOW SMASH THAT PIPE WITH OUR HOVER-CRAFT!
AS YOU WISH, SIR!
R
BRRZOOM!
R
6

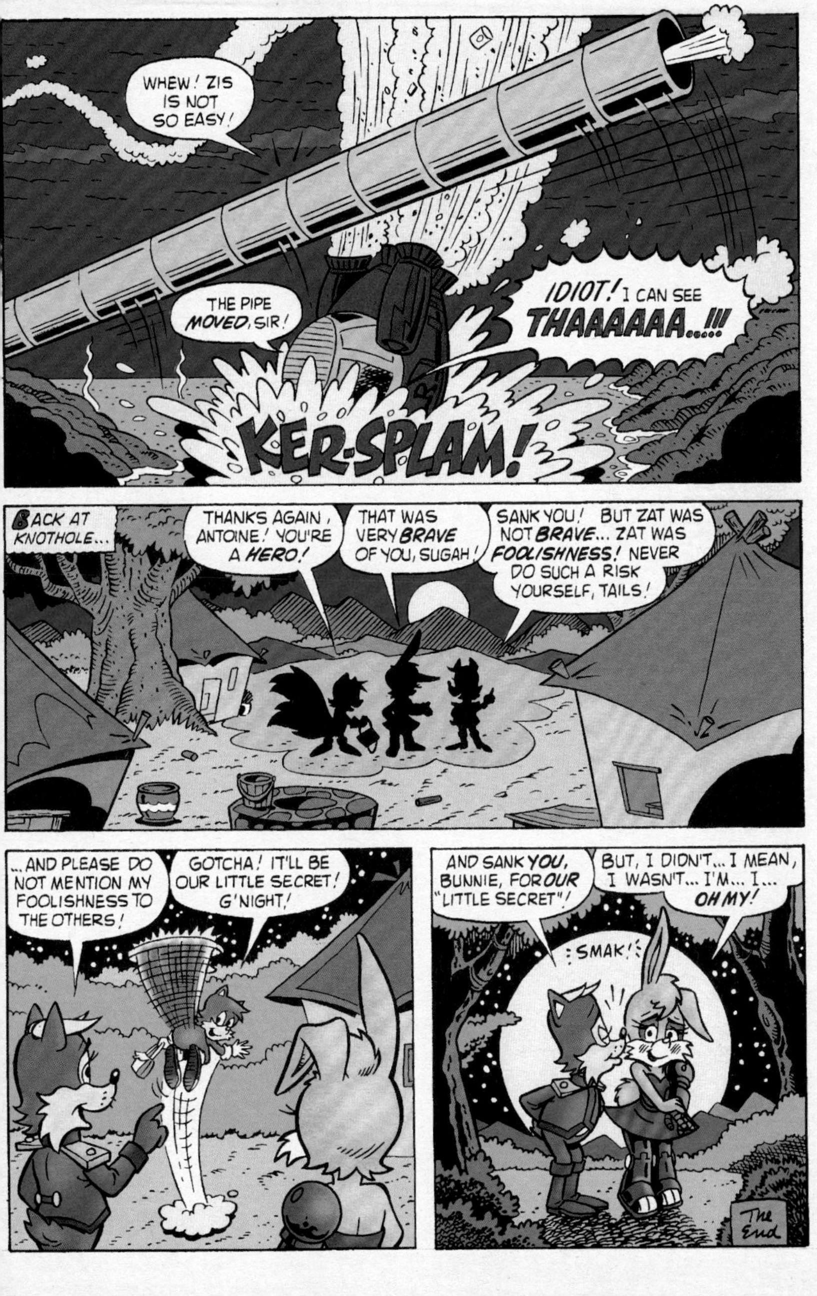
WHEW! ZIS IS NOT SO EASY!
THE PIPE MOVED, SIR!
IDIOT! I CAN SEE THAAAAAA...!!!
KER-SPLAM!
BACK AT KNOTHOLE...
THANKS AGAIN, ANTOINE! YOU'RE A HERO!
THAT WAS VERY BRAVE OF YOU, SUGAH!
SANK YOU! BUT ZAT WAS NOT BRAVE... ZAT WAS FOOLISHNESS! NEVER DO SUCH A RISK YOURSELF, TAILS!
...AND PLEASE DO NOT MENTION MY FOOLISHNESS TO THE OTHERS!
GOTCHA! IT'LL BE OUR LITTLE SECRET! G'NIGHT!
AND SANK YOU, BUNNIE, FOR OUR "LITTLE SECRET"!
SMAK!
BUT, I DIDN'T... I MEAN, I WASN'T... I'M... I... OH MY!
The End

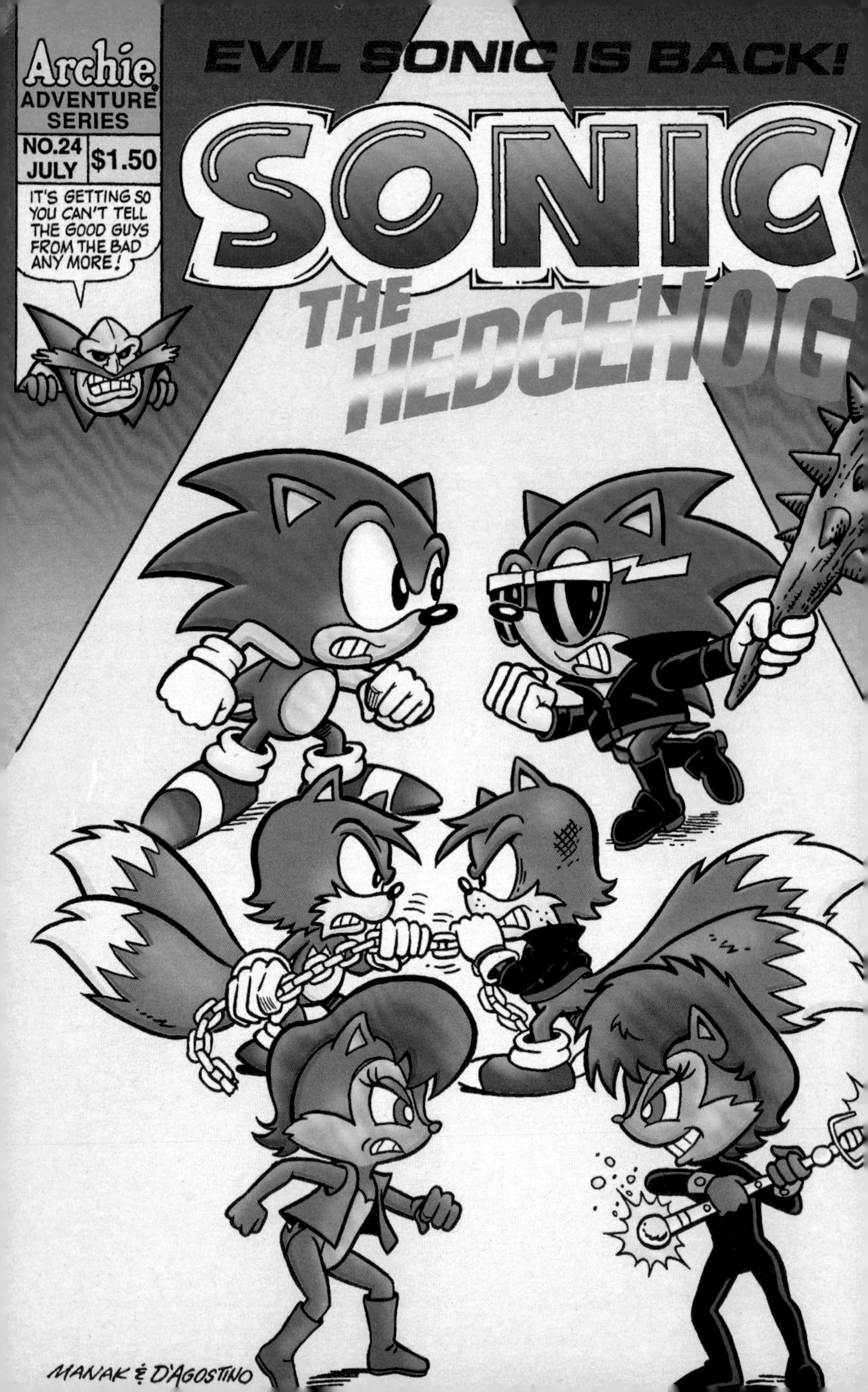

Archie ADVENTURE SERIES
NO.24 JULY
$1.50
EVIL SONIC IS BACK!
SONIC THE HEDGEHOG
IT'S GETTING SO YOU CAN'T TELL THE GOOD GUYS FROM THE BAD ANY MORE!
MANAK & D'AGOSTINO

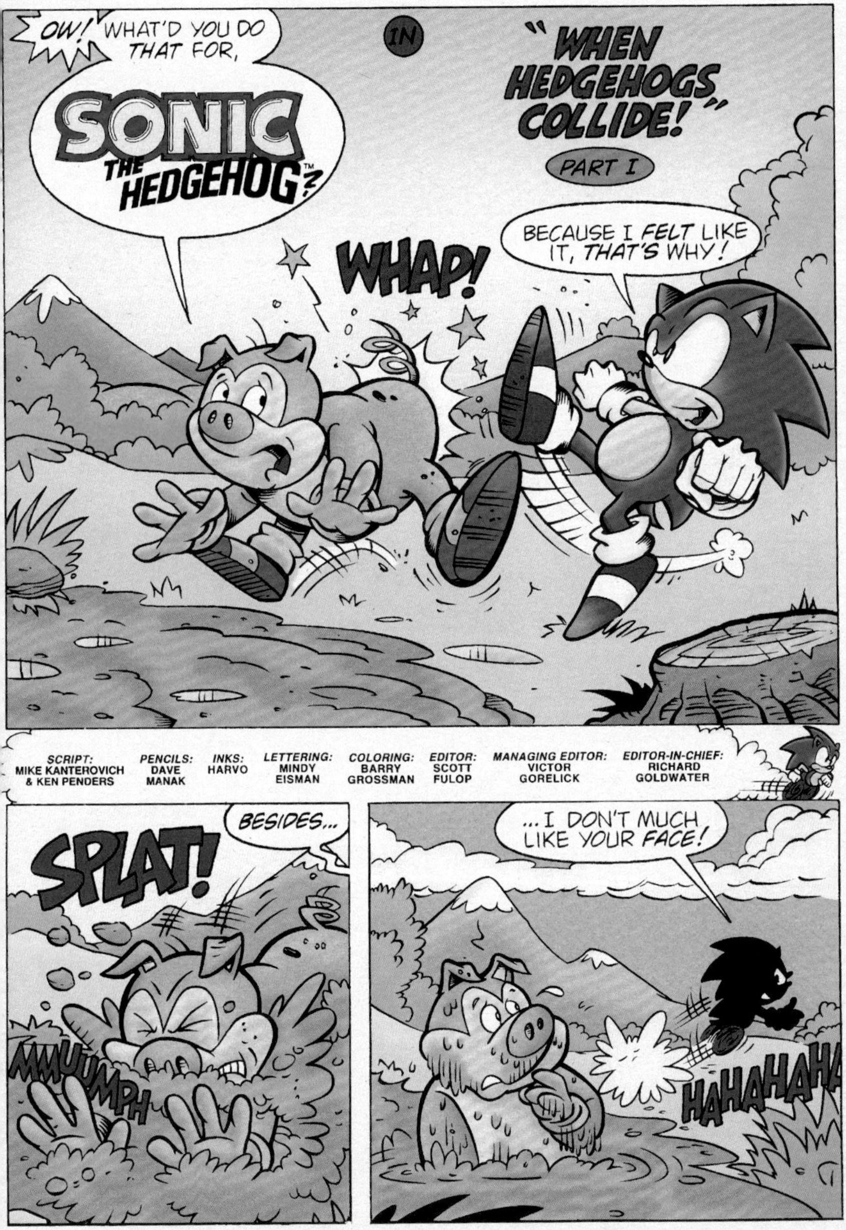
OW! WHAT'D YOU DO THAT FOR,
SONIC THE HEDGEHOG™?
IN
"WHEN HEDGEHOGS COLLIDE!"
PART I
WHAP!
BECAUSE I FELT LIKE IT, THAT'S WHY!
SCRIPT: MIKE KANTEROVICH & KEN PENDERS
PENCILS: DAVE MANAK
INKS: HARVO
LETTERING: MINDY EISMAN
COLORING: BARRY GROSSMAN
EDITOR: SCOTT FULOP
MANAGING EDITOR: VICTOR GORELICK
EDITOR-IN-CHIEF: RICHARD GOLDWATER
SPLAT!
BESIDES...
MMUUMPH
...I DON'T MUCH LIKE YOUR FACE!
HAHAHAHA

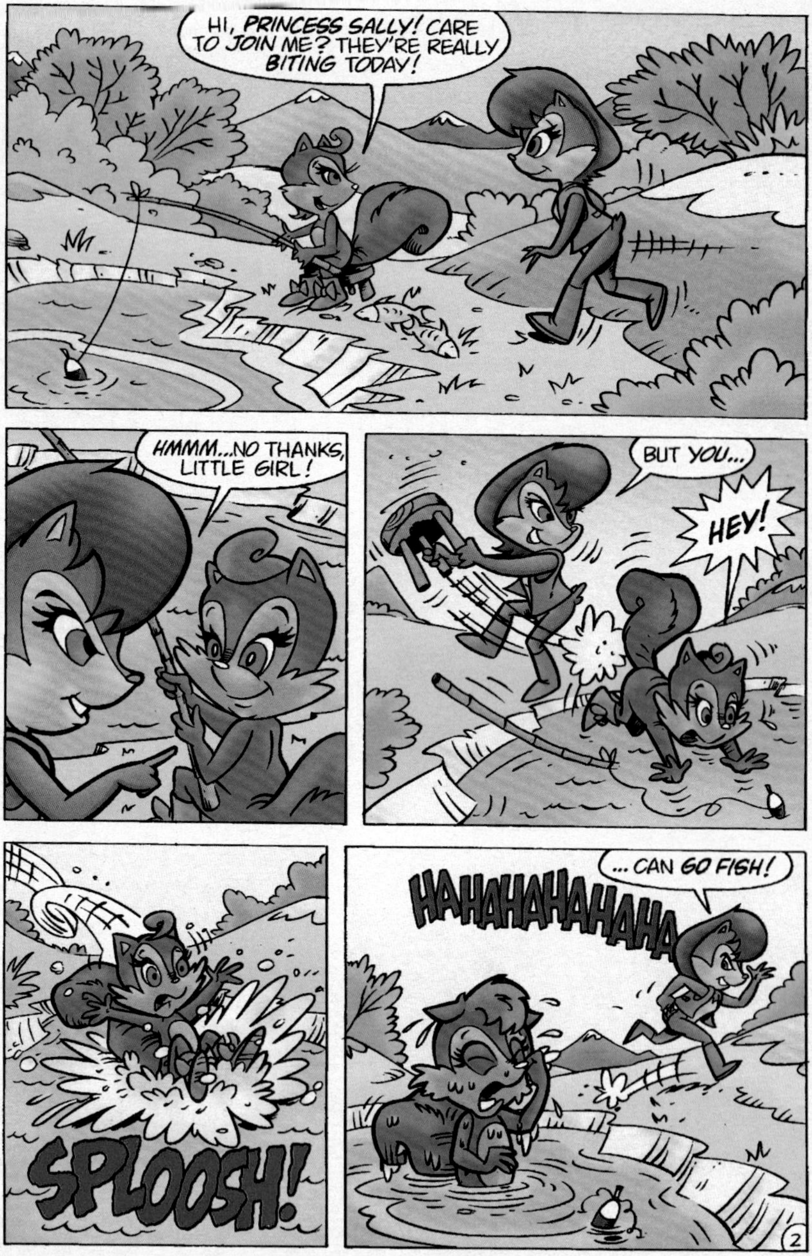
HI, PRINCESS SALLY! CARE TO JOIN ME? THEY'RE REALLY BITING TODAY!
HMMM...NO THANKS, LITTLE GIRL!
BUT YOU...
HEY!
SPLOOSH!
...CAN GO FISH!
HAHAHAHAHAHAHA

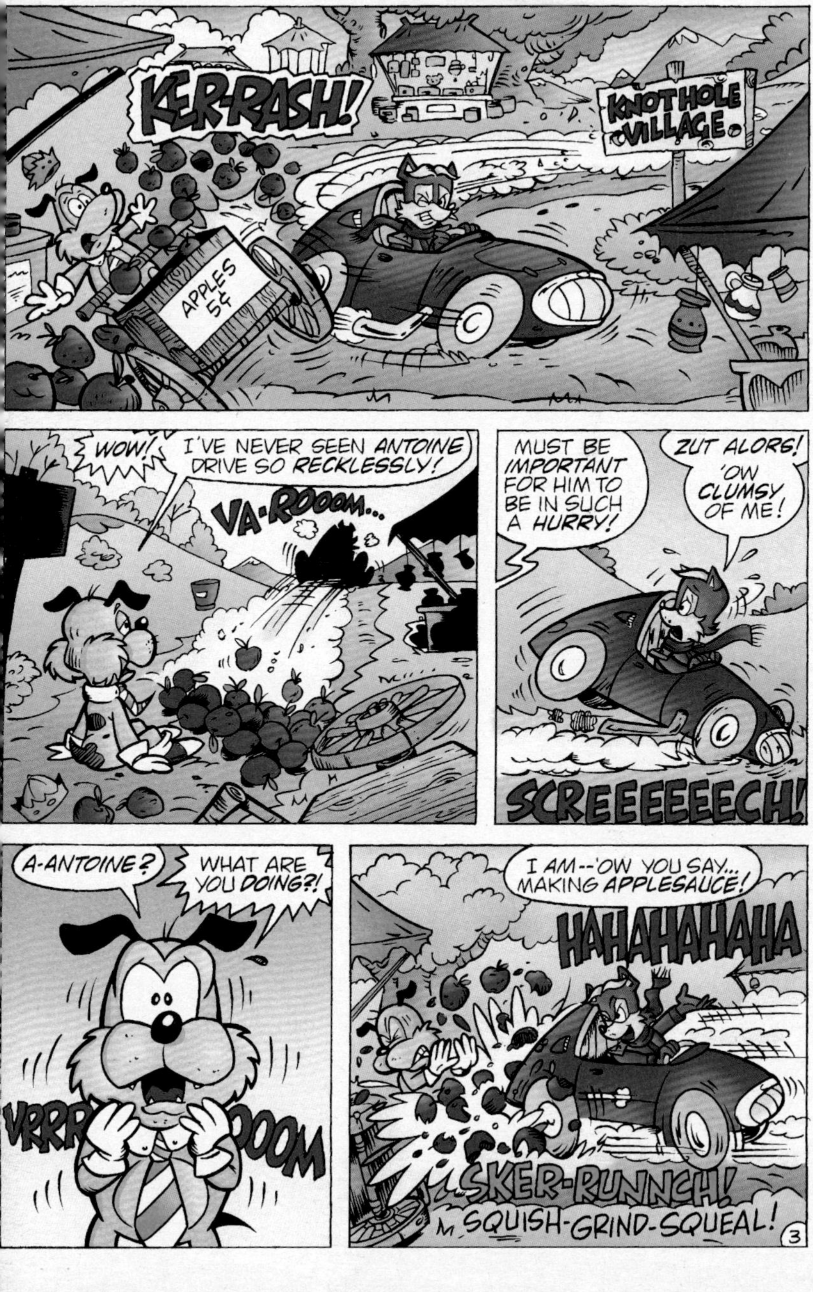
KER-RASH!
KNOTHOLE VILLAGE
APPLES 5¢
WOW!
I'VE NEVER SEEN ANTOINE DRIVE SO RECKLESSLY!
VA-ROOOM...
MUST BE IMPORTANT FOR HIM TO BE IN SUCH A HURRY!
ZUT ALORS! 'OW CLUMSY OF ME!
SCREEEEEEECH!
A-ANTOINE?
WHAT ARE YOU DOING?!
VRRR OOOM
I AM--'OW YOU SAY... MAKING APPLESAUCE!
HAHAHAHAHA
SKER-RUNNCH!
SQUISH-GRIND-SQUEAL!

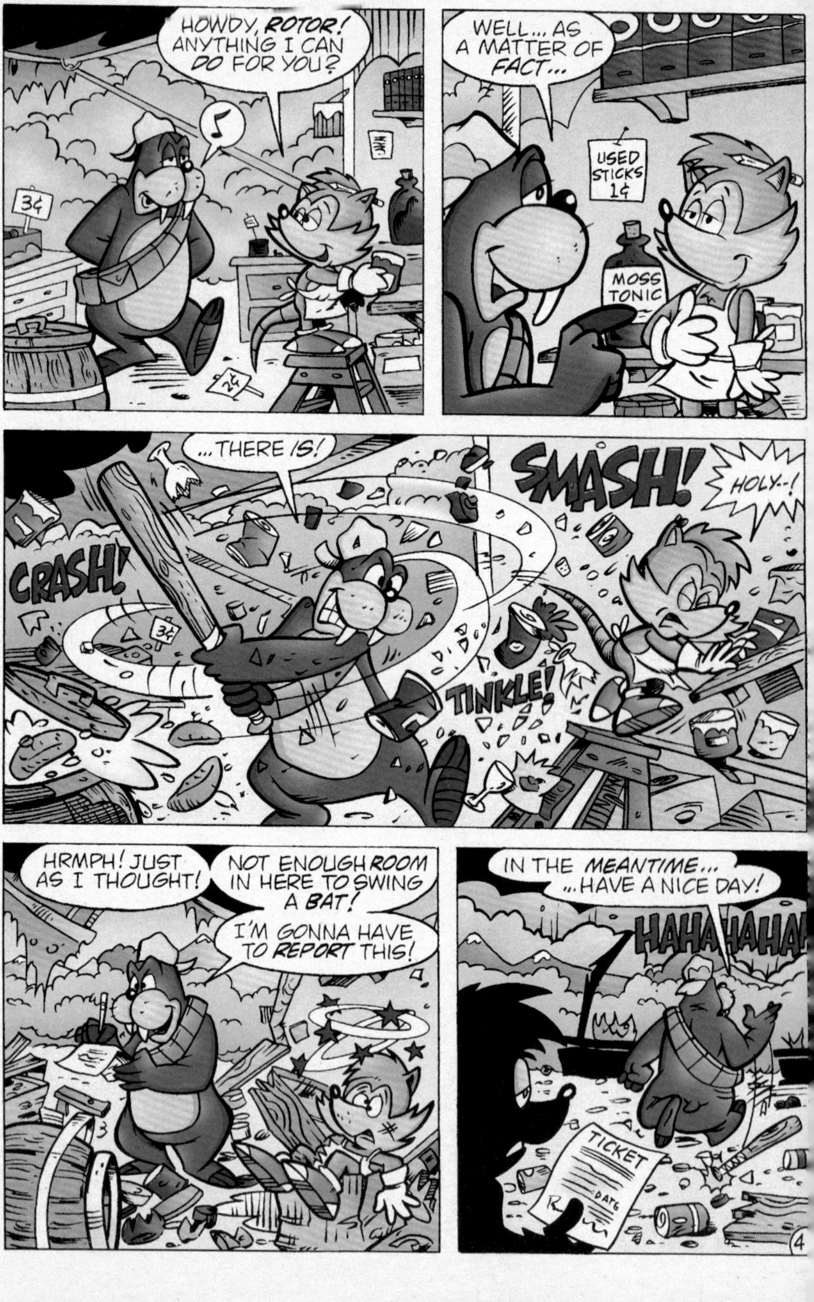
HOWDY, ROTOR! ANYTHING I CAN DO FOR YOU?
3¢
2¢
WELL... AS A MATTER OF FACT...
USED STICKS 1¢
MOSS TONIC
...THERE IS!
SMASH!
HOLY--!
CRASH!
3¢
TINKLE!
HRMPH! JUST AS I THOUGHT!
NOT ENOUGH ROOM IN HERE TO SWING A BAT!
I'M GONNA HAVE TO REPORT THIS!
IN THE MEANTIME... ...HAVE A NICE DAY!
HAHAHAHAH
TICKET
DATE

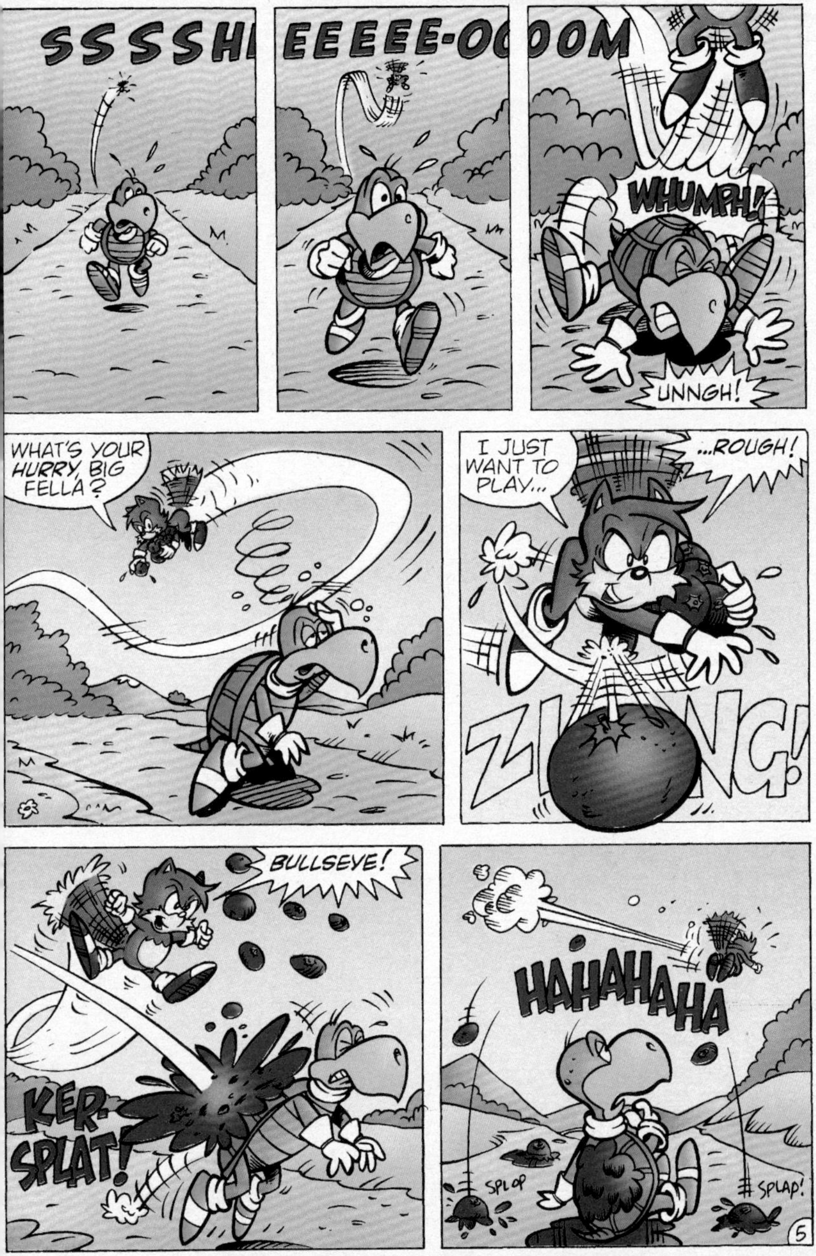

SSSSSHEEEEEE-OOOOM
WHUMPH!
UNNGH!
WHAT'S YOUR HURRY, BIG FELLA?
I JUST WANT TO PLAY...
...ROUGH!
ZING!
BULLSEYE!
KER-SPLAT!
HAHAHAHA
SPLOP
SPLAP!

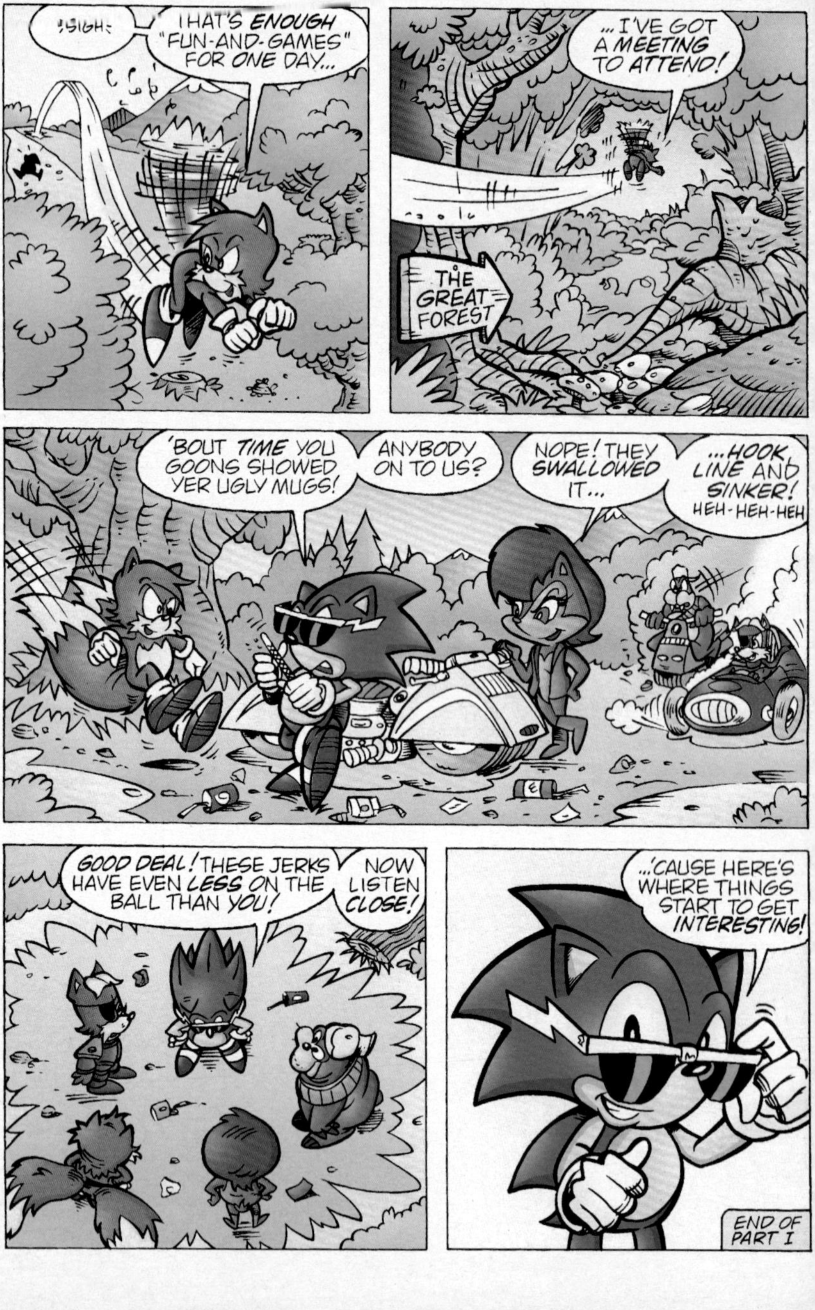
SIGH
THAT'S ENOUGH "FUN-AND-GAMES" FOR ONE DAY...
...I'VE GOT A MEETING TO ATTEND!
THE GREAT FOREST
'BOUT TIME YOU GOONS SHOWED YER UGLY MUGS!
ANYBODY ON TO US?
NOPE! THEY SWALLOWED IT...
...HOOK LINE AND SINKER! HEH-HEH-HEH
GOOD DEAL! THESE JERKS HAVE EVEN LESS ON THE BALL THAN YOU!
NOW LISTEN CLOSE!
...'CAUSE HERE'S WHERE THINGS START TO GET INTERESTING!
END OF PART I

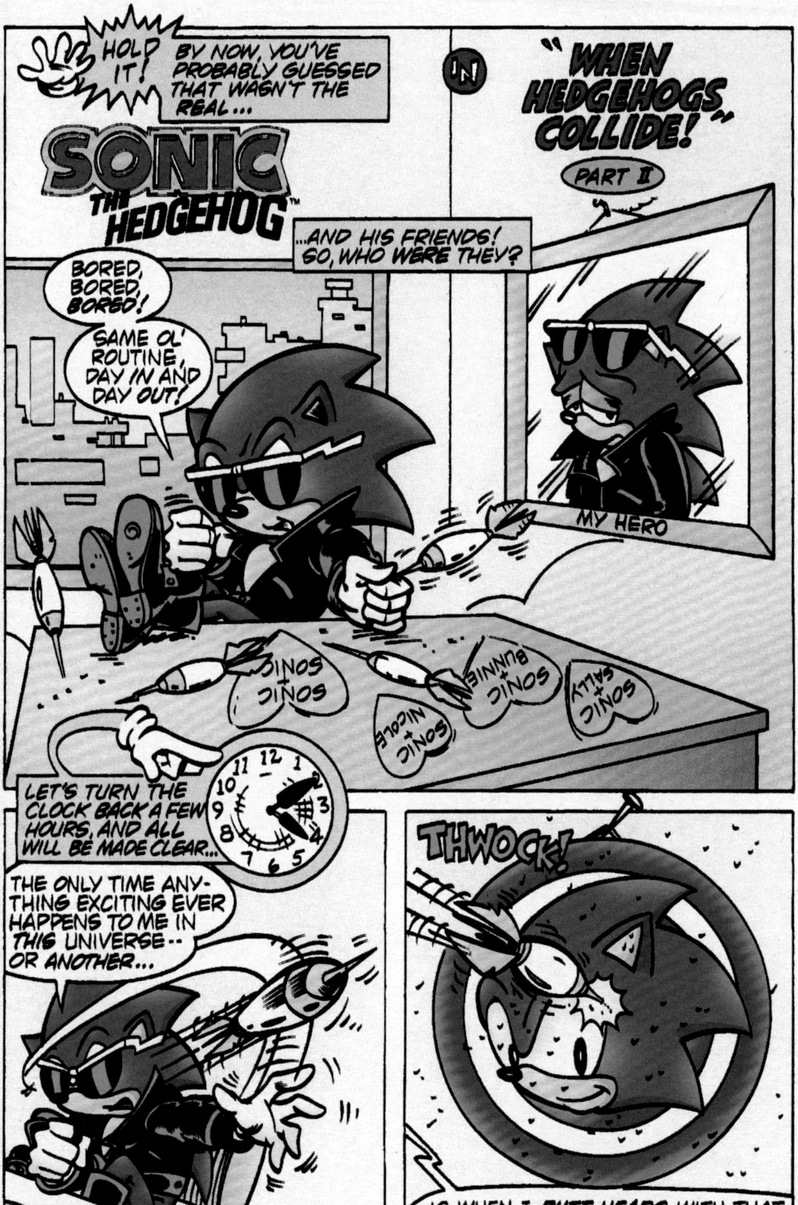
HOLD IT!
BY NOW, YOU'VE PROBABLY GUESSED THAT WASN'T THE REAL...
SONIC THE HEDGEHOG
...AND HIS FRIENDS! SO, WHO WERE THEY?
IN
"WHEN HEDGEHOGS COLLIDE!"
PART II
BORED, BORED, BORED!
SAME OL' ROUTINE, DAY IN AND DAY OUT!
MY HERO
SONIC + SONIC
SONIC + NICOLE
SONIC + BUNNIE
SONIC + SALLY
LET'S TURN THE CLOCK BACK A FEW HOURS, AND ALL WILL BE MADE CLEAR...
THE ONLY TIME ANYTHING EXCITING EVER HAPPENS TO ME IN THIS UNIVERSE-- OR ANOTHER...
THWOCK!
...IS WHEN I BUTT HEADS WITH THAT BUTT-HEAD SONIC THE HEDGEHOG!

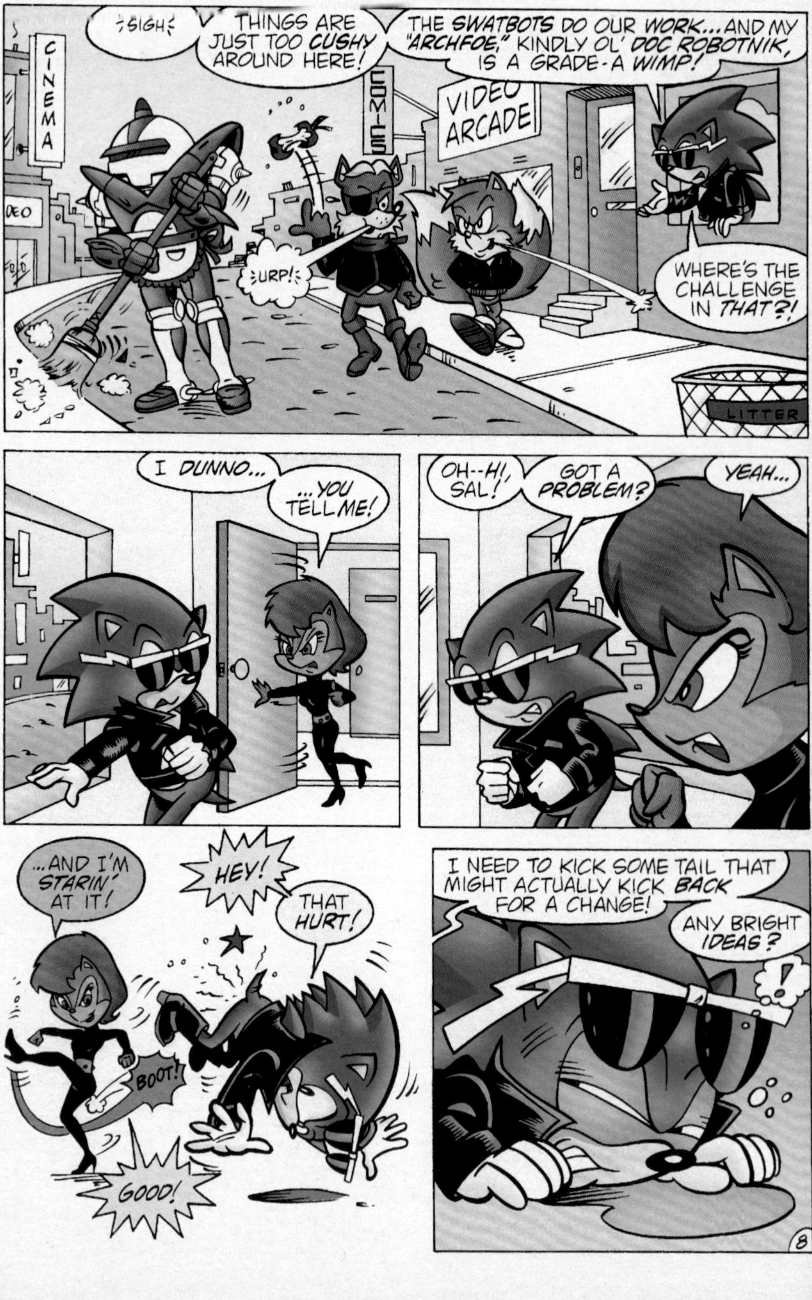

SIGH
THINGS ARE JUST TOO CUSHY AROUND HERE!
THE SWATBOTS DO OUR WORK...AND MY "ARCHFOE," KINDLY OL' DOC ROBOTNIK, IS A GRADE-A WIMP!
CINEMA
COMICS
VIDEO ARCADE
URP!
WHERE'S THE CHALLENGE IN THAT?!
LITTER
I DUNNO...
...YOU TELL ME!
OH--HI, SAL!
GOT A PROBLEM?
YEAH...
...AND I'M STARIN' AT IT!
HEY!
THAT HURT!
BOOT!
GOOD!
I NEED TO KICK SOME TAIL THAT MIGHT ACTUALLY KICK BACK FOR A CHANGE!
ANY BRIGHT IDEAS?
!

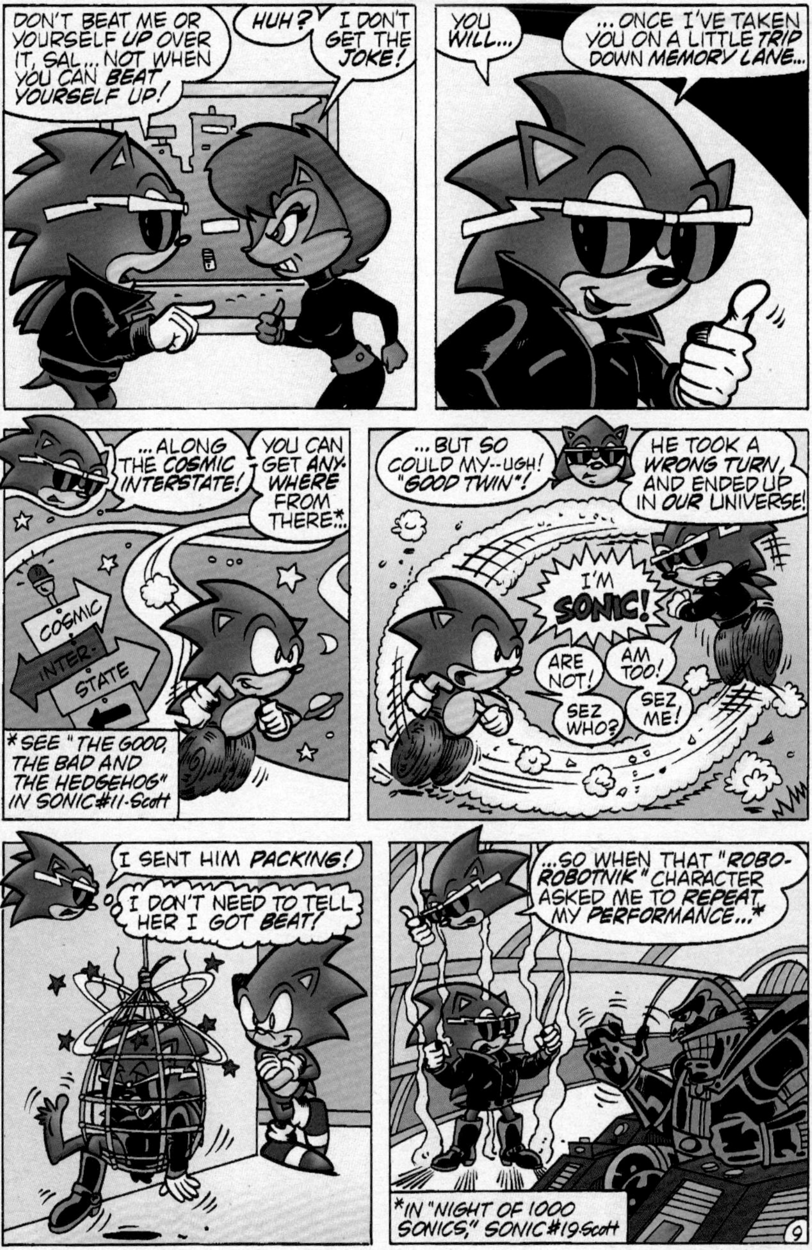
DON'T BEAT ME OR YOURSELF UP OVER IT, SAL... NOT WHEN YOU CAN BEAT YOURSELF UP!
HUH?
I DON'T GET THE JOKE!
YOU WILL...
...ONCE I'VE TAKEN YOU ON A LITTLE TRIP DOWN MEMORY LANE...
...ALONG THE COSMIC INTERSTATE!
YOU CAN GET ANY-WHERE FROM THERE!*...
COSMIC
INTER-
STATE
*SEE "THE GOOD, THE BAD AND THE HEDGEHOG" IN SONIC #11-Scott
...BUT SO COULD MY--UGH! "GOOD TWIN"!
HE TOOK A WRONG TURN, AND ENDED UP IN OUR UNIVERSE!
I'M SONIC!
ARE NOT!
AM TOO!
SEZ WHO?
SEZ ME!
I SENT HIM PACKING!
I DON'T NEED TO TELL HER I GOT BEAT!
...SO WHEN THAT "ROBO-ROBOTNIK" CHARACTER ASKED ME TO REPEAT MY PERFORMANCE...*
*IN "NIGHT OF 1000 SONICS," SONIC #19-Scott
9

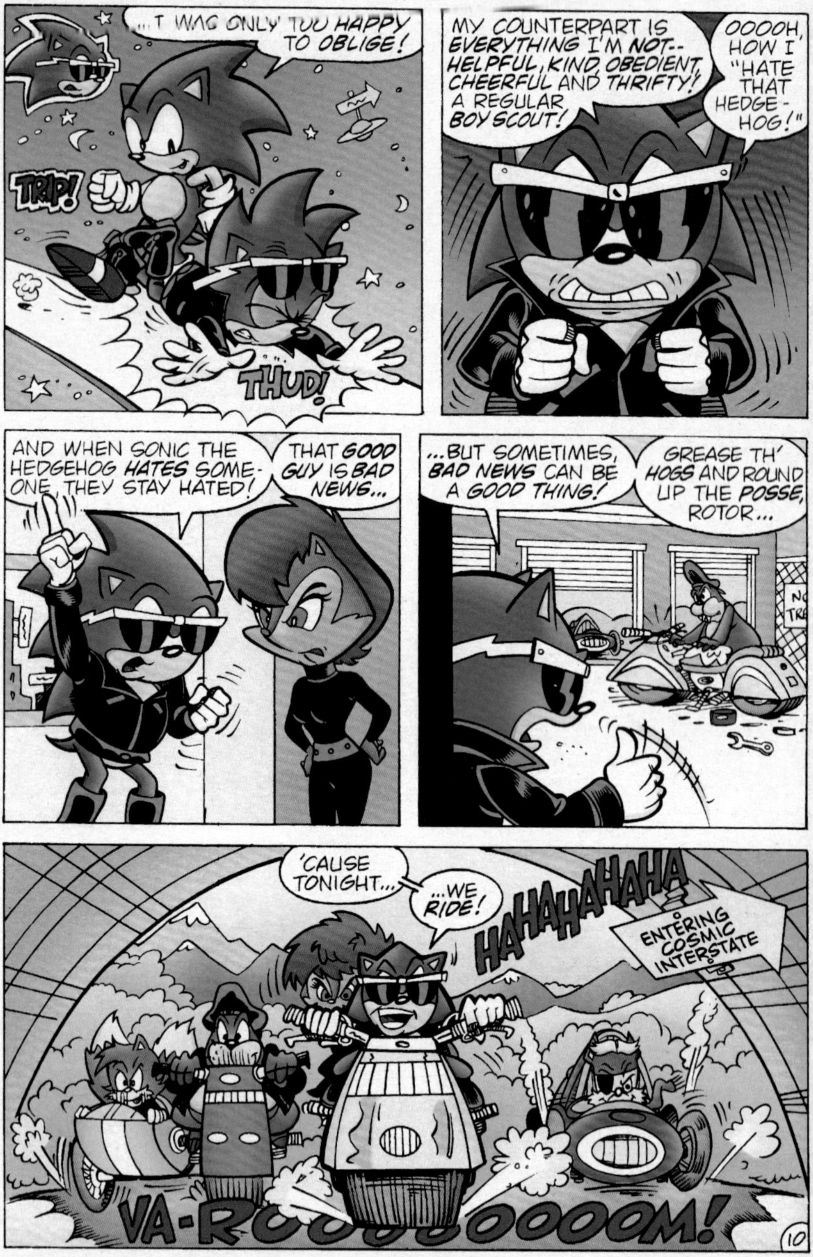

...I WAS ONLY TOO HAPPY TO OBLIGE!
TRIP!
THUD!
MY COUNTERPART IS EVERYTHING I'M NOT-- HELPFUL, KIND, OBEDIENT, CHEERFUL AND THRIFTY! A REGULAR BOY SCOUT!
OOOOH, HOW I "HATE THAT HEDGE-HOG!"
AND WHEN SONIC THE HEDGEHOG HATES SOME-ONE, THEY STAY HATED!
THAT GOOD GUY IS BAD NEWS...
...BUT SOMETIMES, BAD NEWS CAN BE A GOOD THING!
GREASE TH' HOGS AND ROUND UP THE POSSE, ROTOR...
'CAUSE TONIGHT...
...WE RIDE!
HAHAHAHAHAHA
ENTERING COSMIC INTERSTATE
VA-ROOOOOOOOOOM!

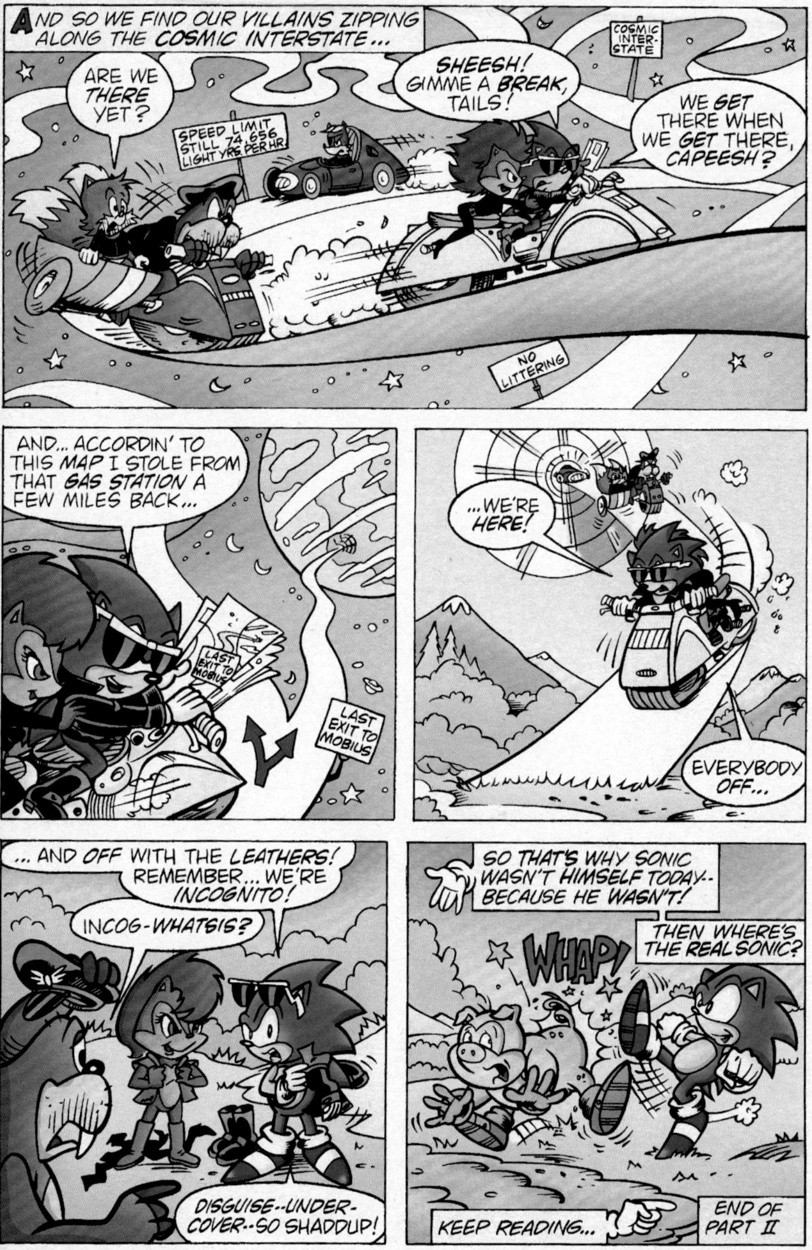
AND SO WE FIND OUR VILLAINS ZIPPING ALONG THE COSMIC INTERSTATE...
COSMIC INTER-STATE
ARE WE THERE YET?
SPEED LIMIT STILL 74,656 LIGHT YRS. PER HR.
SHEESH! GIMME A BREAK, TAILS!
WE GET THERE WHEN WE GET THERE, CAPEESH?
NO LITTERING
AND... ACCORDIN' TO THIS MAP I STOLE FROM THAT GAS STATION A FEW MILES BACK...
LAST EXIT TO MOBIUS
LAST EXIT TO MOBIUS
...WE'RE HERE!
EVERYBODY OFF...
... AND OFF WITH THE LEATHERS! REMEMBER... WE'RE INCOGNITO!
INCOG-WHATSIS?
DISGUISE--UNDER-COVER--SO SHADDUP!
SO THAT'S WHY SONIC WASN'T HIMSELF TODAY-- BECAUSE HE WASN'T!
THEN WHERE'S THE REAL SONIC?
WHAP!
KEEP READING...
END OF PART II

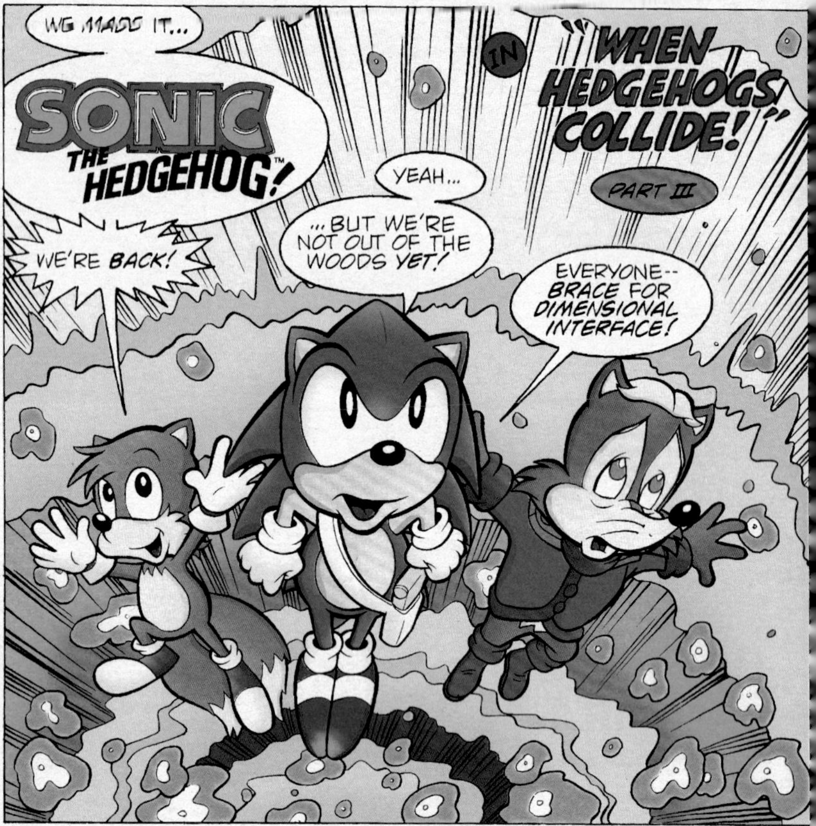
WE MADE IT...
SONIC THE HEDGEHOG!™
IN "WHEN HEDGEHOGS COLLIDE!"
PART III
WE'RE BACK!
YEAH...
...BUT WE'RE NOT OUT OF THE WOODS YET!
EVERYONE-- BRACE FOR DIMENSIONAL INTERFACE!

PENCILLING & INKING CHAPTERS 3 & 4: ART MAWHINNEY & RICH KOSLOWSKI

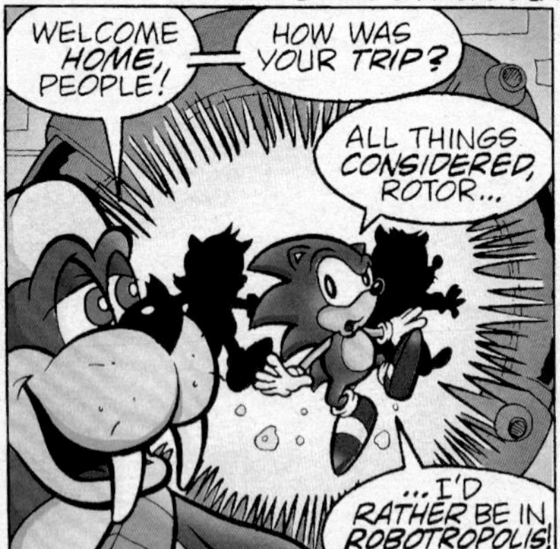
WELCOME HOME, PEOPLE!
HOW WAS YOUR TRIP?
ALL THINGS CONSIDERED, ROTOR...
...I'D RATHER BE IN ROBOTROPOLIS!

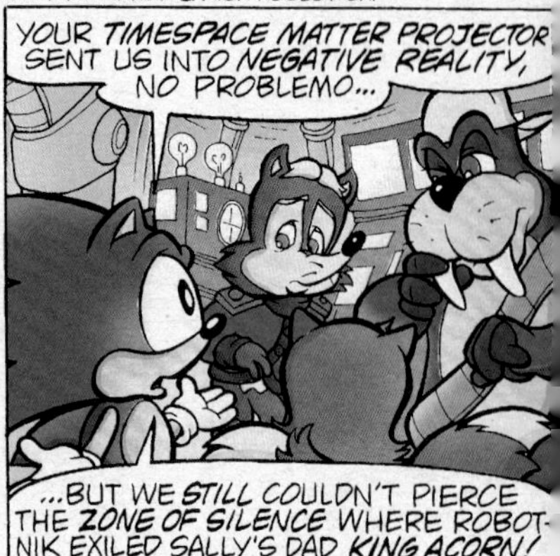
YOUR TIMESPACE MATTER PROJECTOR SENT US INTO NEGATIVE REALITY, NO PROBLEMO...
...BUT WE STILL COULDN'T PIERCE THE ZONE OF SILENCE WHERE ROBOTNIK EXILED SALLY'S DAD KING ACORN!

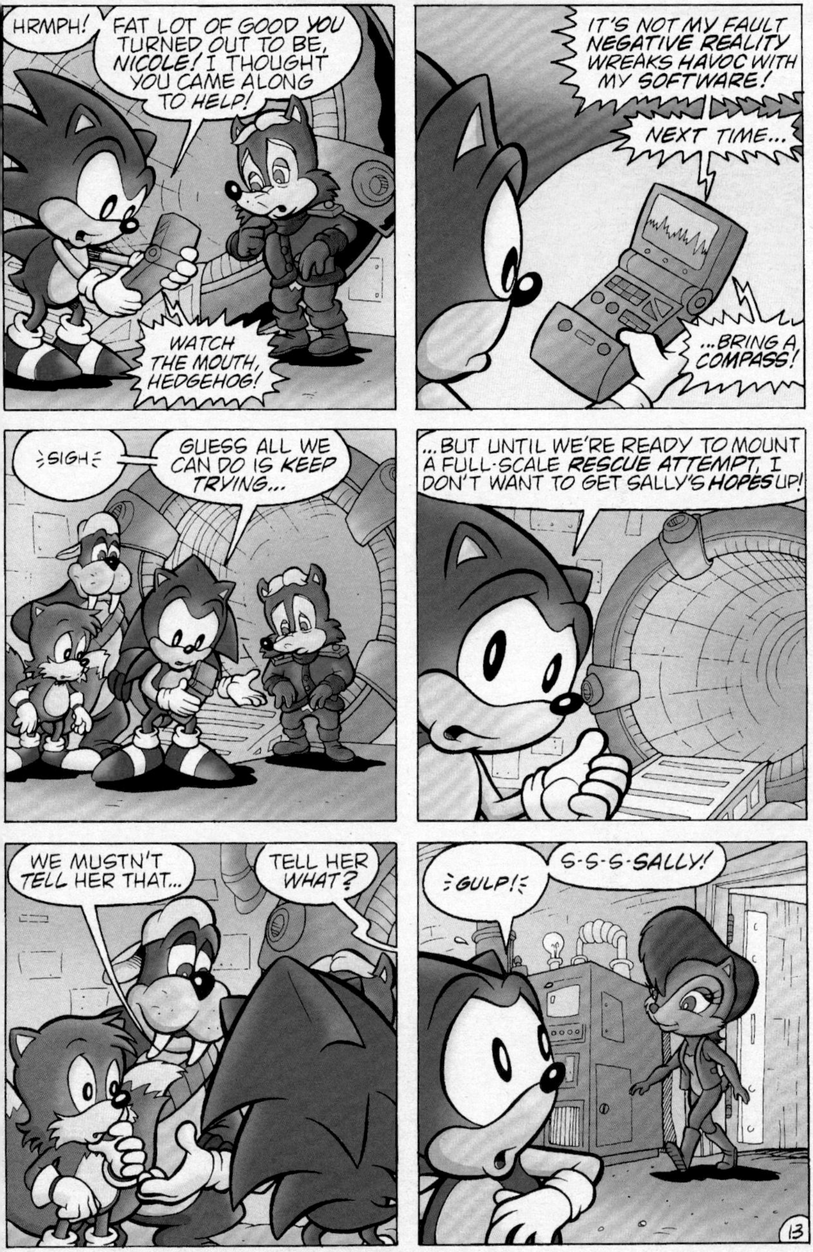
HRMPH!
FAT LOT OF GOOD YOU TURNED OUT TO BE, NICOLE! I THOUGHT YOU CAME ALONG TO HELP!
WATCH THE MOUTH, HEDGEHOG!
IT'S NOT MY FAULT NEGATIVE REALITY WREAKS HAVOC WITH MY SOFTWARE!
NEXT TIME...
...BRING A COMPASS!
SIGH
GUESS ALL WE CAN DO IS KEEP TRYING...
...BUT UNTIL WE'RE READY TO MOUNT A FULL-SCALE RESCUE ATTEMPT, I DON'T WANT TO GET SALLY'S HOPES UP!
WE MUSTN'T TELL HER THAT...
TELL HER WHAT?
GULP!
S-S-S-SALLY!
13

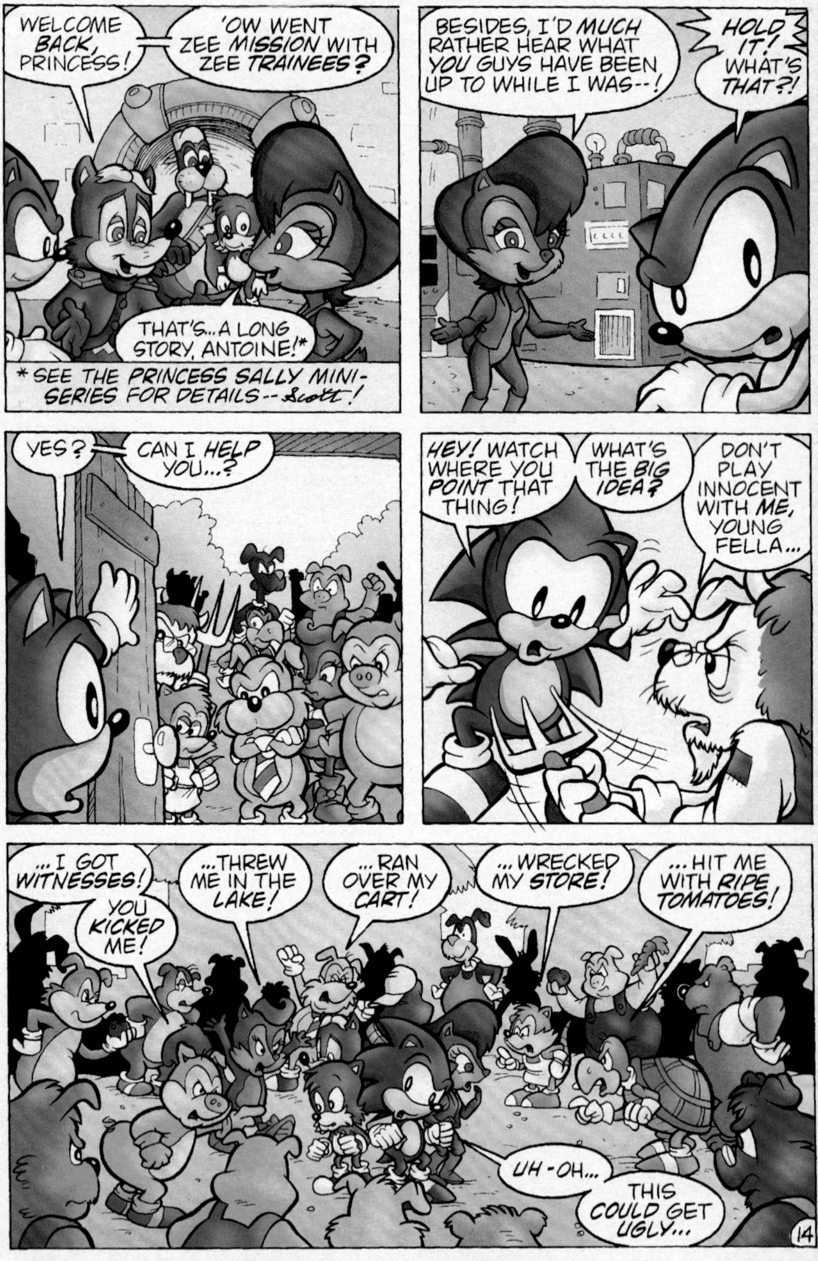
WELCOME BACK, PRINCESS!
'OW WENT ZEE MISSION WITH ZEE TRAINEES?
THAT'S...A LONG STORY, ANTOINE!*
* SEE THE PRINCESS SALLY MINI-SERIES FOR DETAILS -- Scott!
BESIDES, I'D MUCH RATHER HEAR WHAT YOU GUYS HAVE BEEN UP TO WHILE I WAS--!
HOLD IT! WHAT'S THAT?!
YES?
CAN I HELP YOU...?
HEY! WATCH WHERE YOU POINT THAT THING!
WHAT'S THE BIG IDEA?
DON'T PLAY INNOCENT WITH ME, YOUNG FELLA...
...I GOT WITNESSES!
YOU KICKED ME!
...THREW ME IN THE LAKE!
...RAN OVER MY CART!
...WRECKED MY STORE!
...HIT ME WITH RIPE TOMATOES!
UH-OH...
THIS COULD GET UGLY...
14

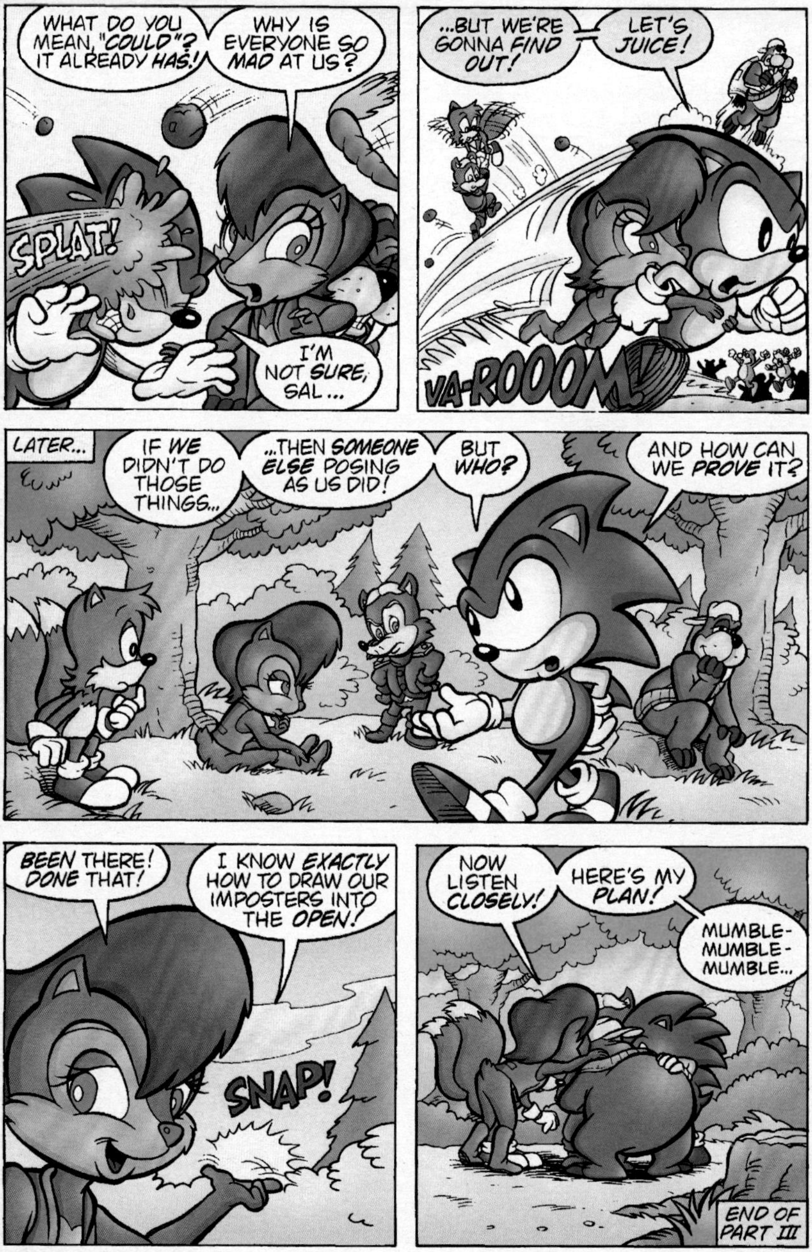
WHAT DO YOU MEAN, "COULD"? IT ALREADY HAS!
WHY IS EVERYONE SO MAD AT US?
SPLAT!
I'M NOT SURE, SAL...
...BUT WE'RE GONNA FIND OUT!
LET'S JUICE!
VA-ROOOM!
LATER...
IF WE DIDN'T DO THOSE THINGS...
...THEN SOMEONE ELSE POSING AS US DID!
BUT WHO?
AND HOW CAN WE PROVE IT?
BEEN THERE! DONE THAT!
I KNOW EXACTLY HOW TO DRAW OUR IMPOSTERS INTO THE OPEN!
SNAP!
NOW LISTEN CLOSELY!
HERE'S MY PLAN!
MUMBLE-MUMBLE-MUMBLE...
END OF PART III

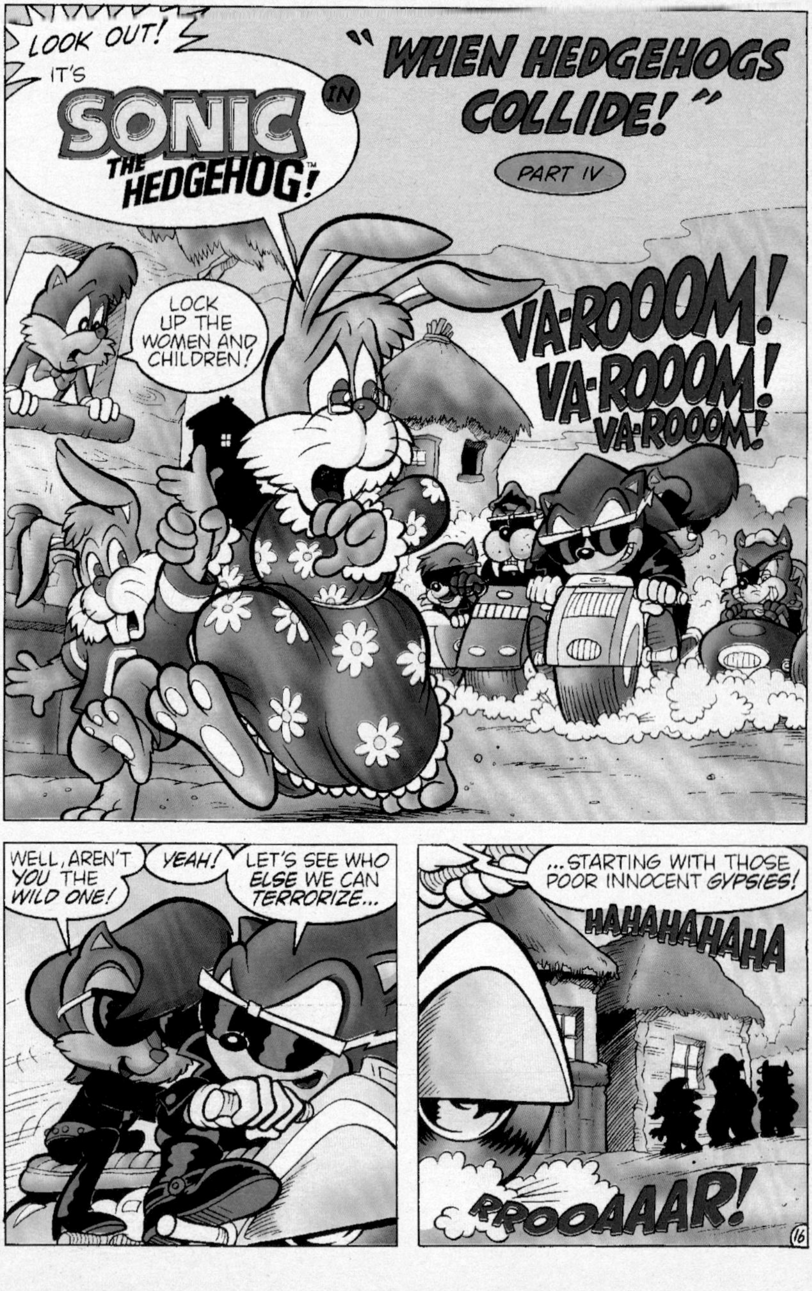

LOOK OUT! IT'S SONIC THE HEDGEHOG! IN
"WHEN HEDGEHOGS COLLIDE!"
PART IV
LOCK UP THE WOMEN AND CHILDREN!
VA-ROOOM! VA-ROOOM! VA-ROOOM!
WELL, AREN'T YOU THE WILD ONE!
YEAH!
LET'S SEE WHO ELSE WE CAN TERRORIZE...
...STARTING WITH THOSE POOR INNOCENT GYPSIES!
HAHAHAHAHA
RROOAAAR!

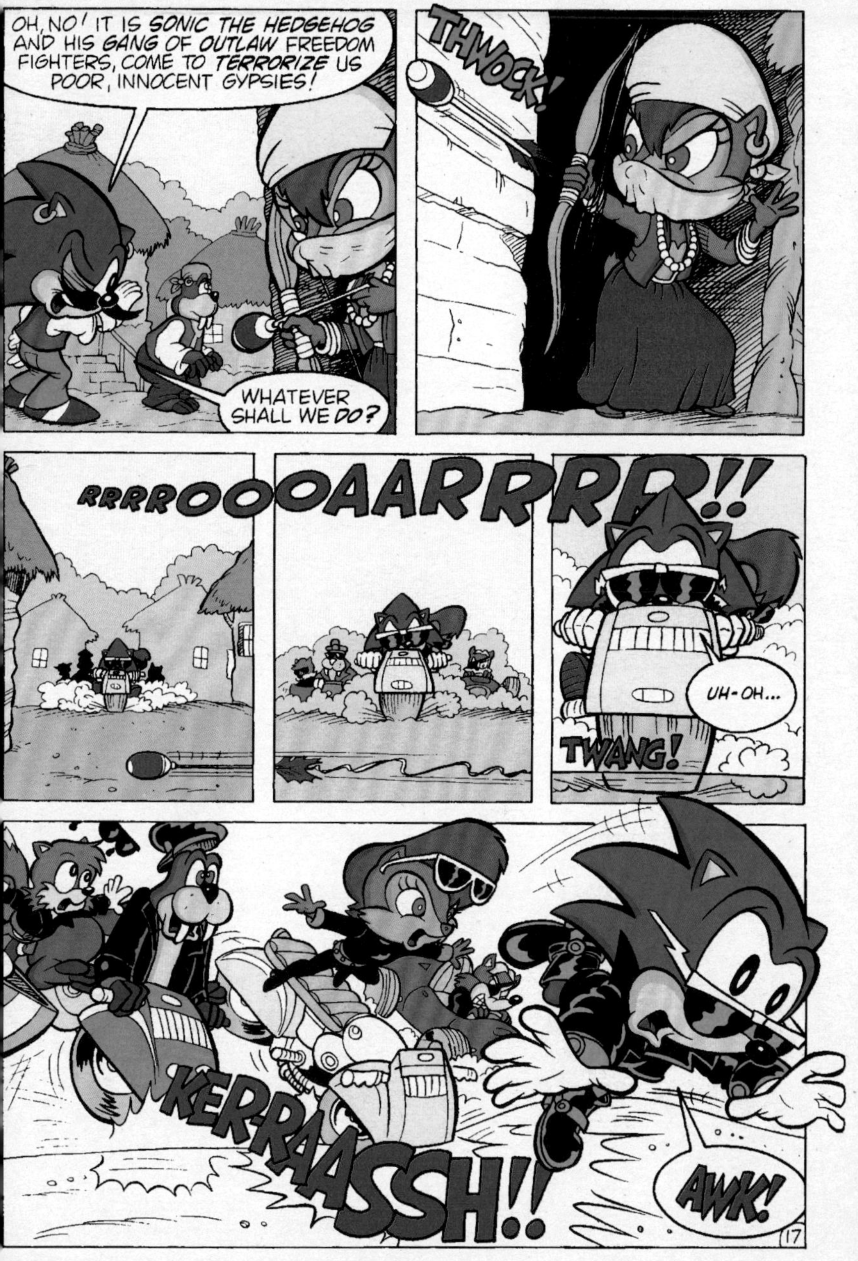
OH, NO! IT IS SONIC THE HEDGEHOG AND HIS GANG OF OUTLAW FREEDOM FIGHTERS, COME TO TERRORIZE US POOR, INNOCENT GYPSIES!
WHATEVER SHALL WE DO?
THWOCK!
RRRROOOOAARRRRP!!
UH-OH...
TWANG!
KER-RAASSH!!
AWK!

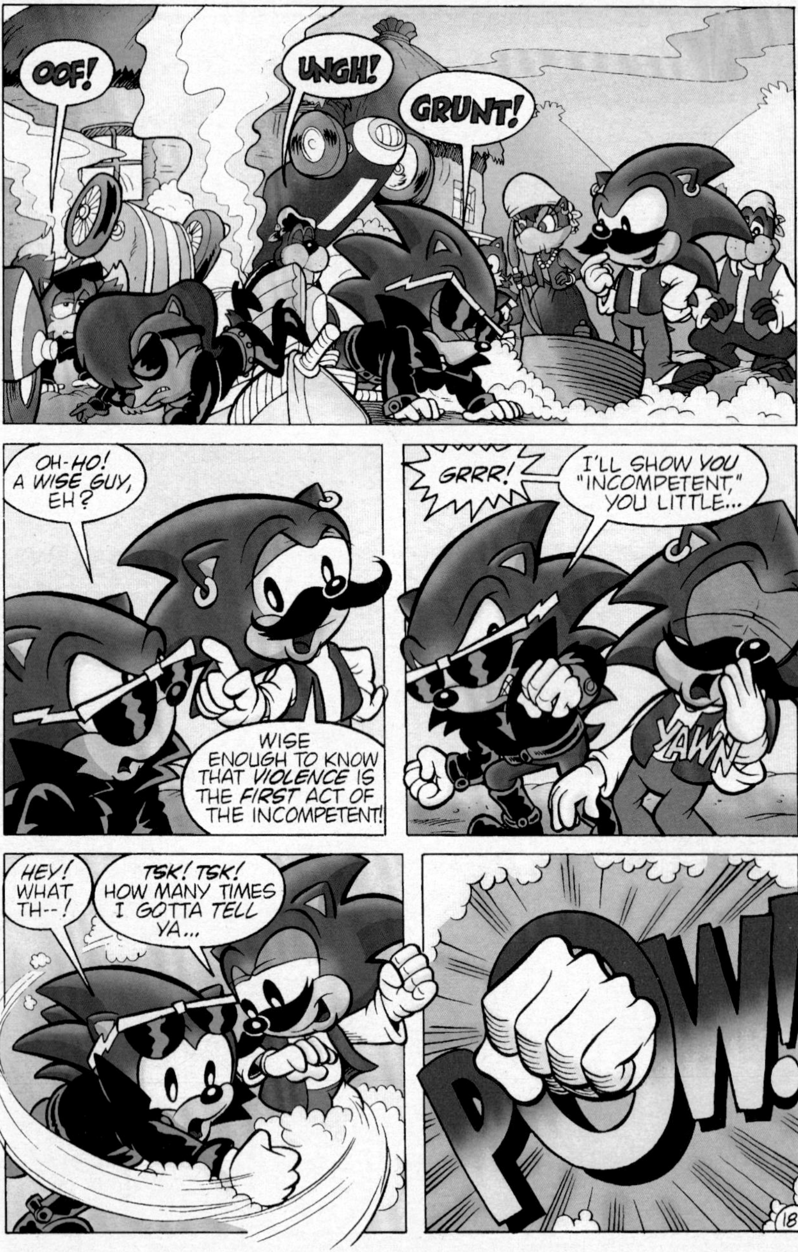
OOF!
UNGH!
GRUNT!
OH-HO! A WISE GUY, EH?
WISE ENOUGH TO KNOW THAT VIOLENCE IS THE FIRST ACT OF THE INCOMPETENT!
GRRR!
I'LL SHOW YOU "INCOMPETENT," YOU LITTLE...
YAWN
HEY! WHAT TH--!
TSK! TSK! HOW MANY TIMES I GOTTA TELL YA...
POW!!

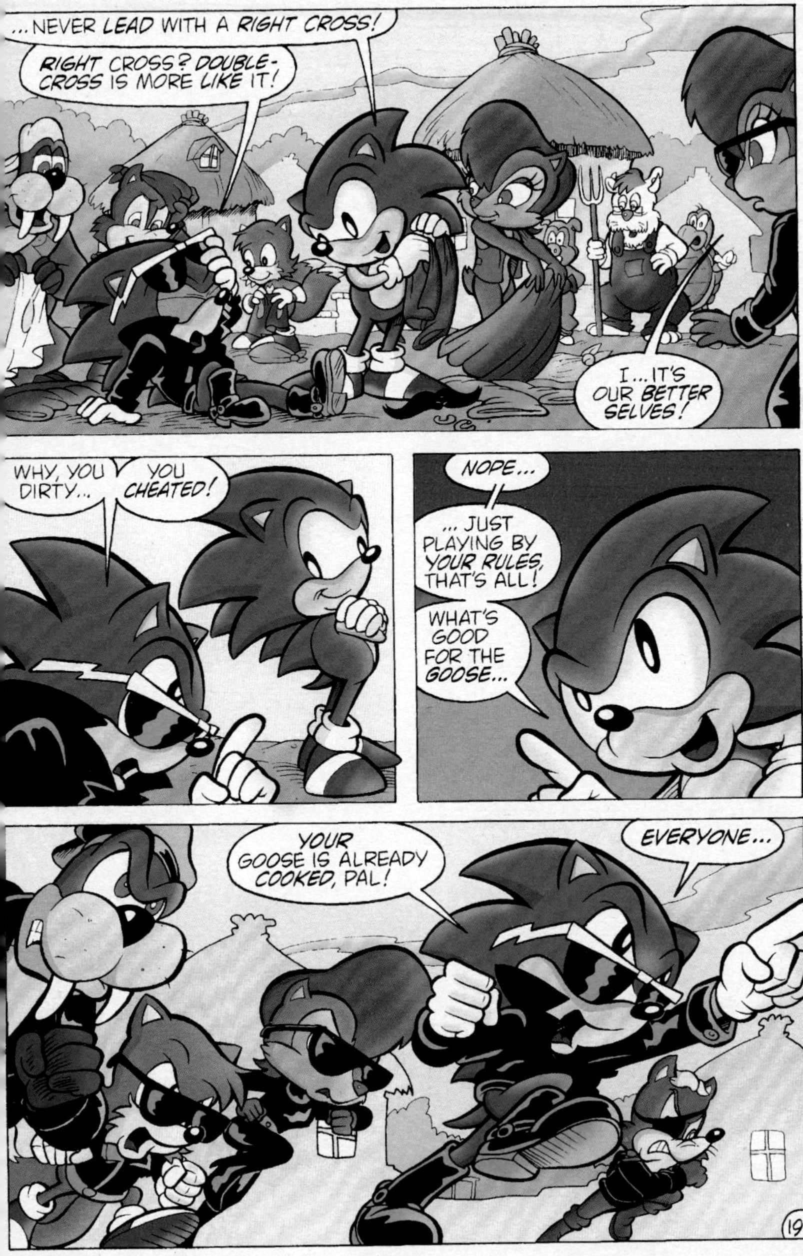
...NEVER LEAD WITH A RIGHT CROSS!
RIGHT CROSS? DOUBLE-CROSS IS MORE LIKE IT!
I...IT'S OUR BETTER SELVES!
WHY, YOU DIRTY...
YOU CHEATED!
NOPE...
...JUST PLAYING BY YOUR RULES, THAT'S ALL!
WHAT'S GOOD FOR THE GOOSE...
YOUR GOOSE IS ALREADY COOKED, PAL!
EVERYONE...

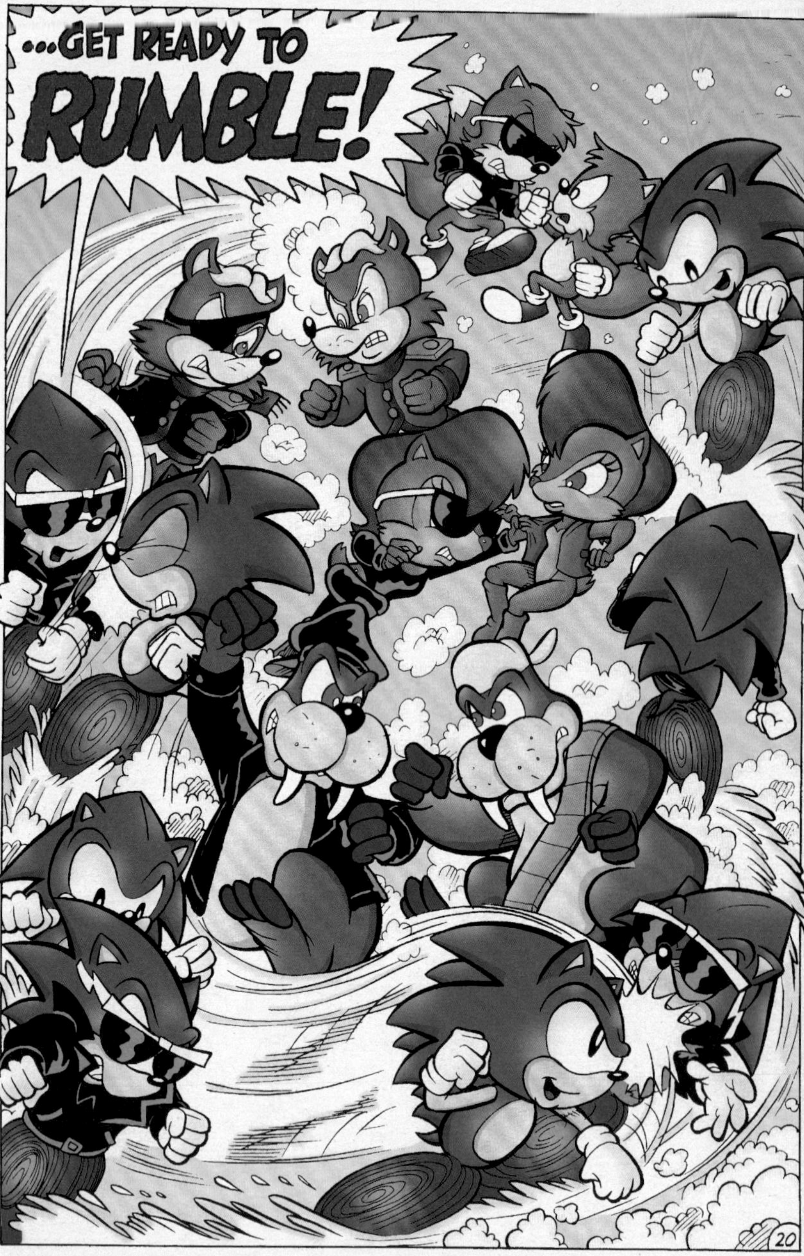
...GET READY TO RUMBLE!

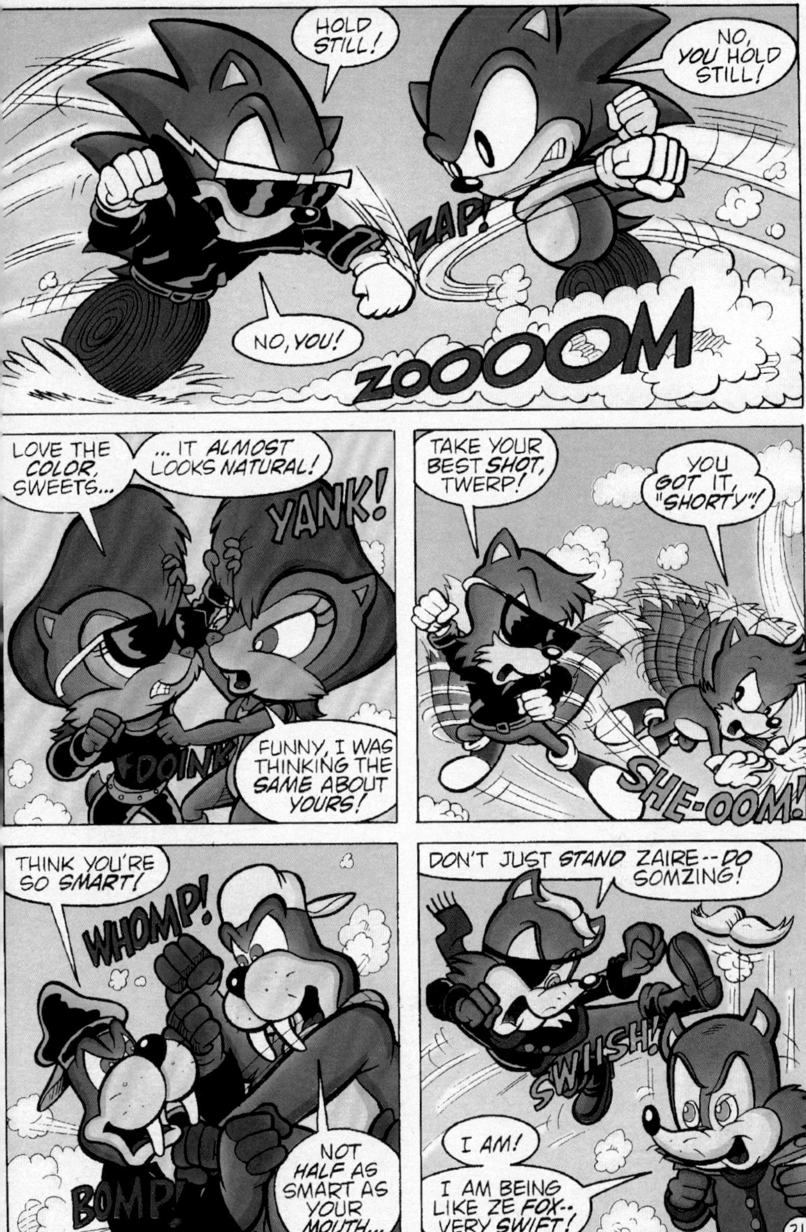
HOLD STILL!
NO, YOU HOLD STILL!
ZAP!
NO, YOU!
ZOOOOOM
LOVE THE COLOR, SWEETS...
... IT ALMOST LOOKS NATURAL!
YANK!
FDOINK!
FUNNY, I WAS THINKING THE SAME ABOUT YOURS!
TAKE YOUR BEST SHOT, TWERP!
YOU GOT IT, "SHORTY"!
SHE-OOM!
THINK YOU'RE SO SMART!
WHOMP!
BOMP!
NOT HALF AS SMART AS YOUR MOUTH...
DON'T JUST STAND ZAIRE--DO SOMZING!
SWIISH!
I AM!
I AM BEING LIKE ZE FOX-- VERY SWIFT!

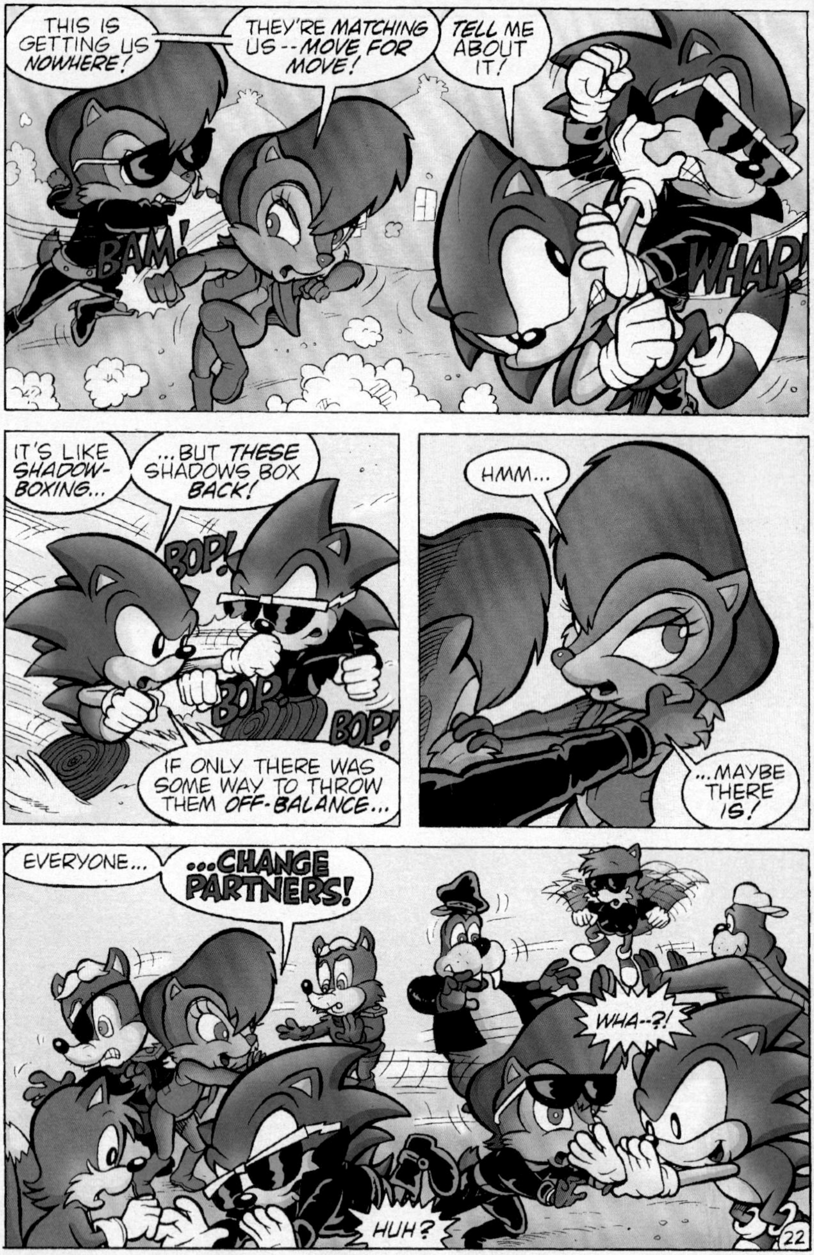
THIS IS GETTING US NOWHERE!
THEY'RE MATCHING US--MOVE FOR MOVE!
TELL ME ABOUT IT!
BAM!
WHAP!
IT'S LIKE SHADOW-BOXING...
...BUT THESE SHADOWS BOX BACK!
BOP!
BOP!
BOP!
IF ONLY THERE WAS SOME WAY TO THROW THEM OFF-BALANCE...
HMM...
...MAYBE THERE IS!
EVERYONE...
...CHANGE PARTNERS!
WHA--?!
HUH?

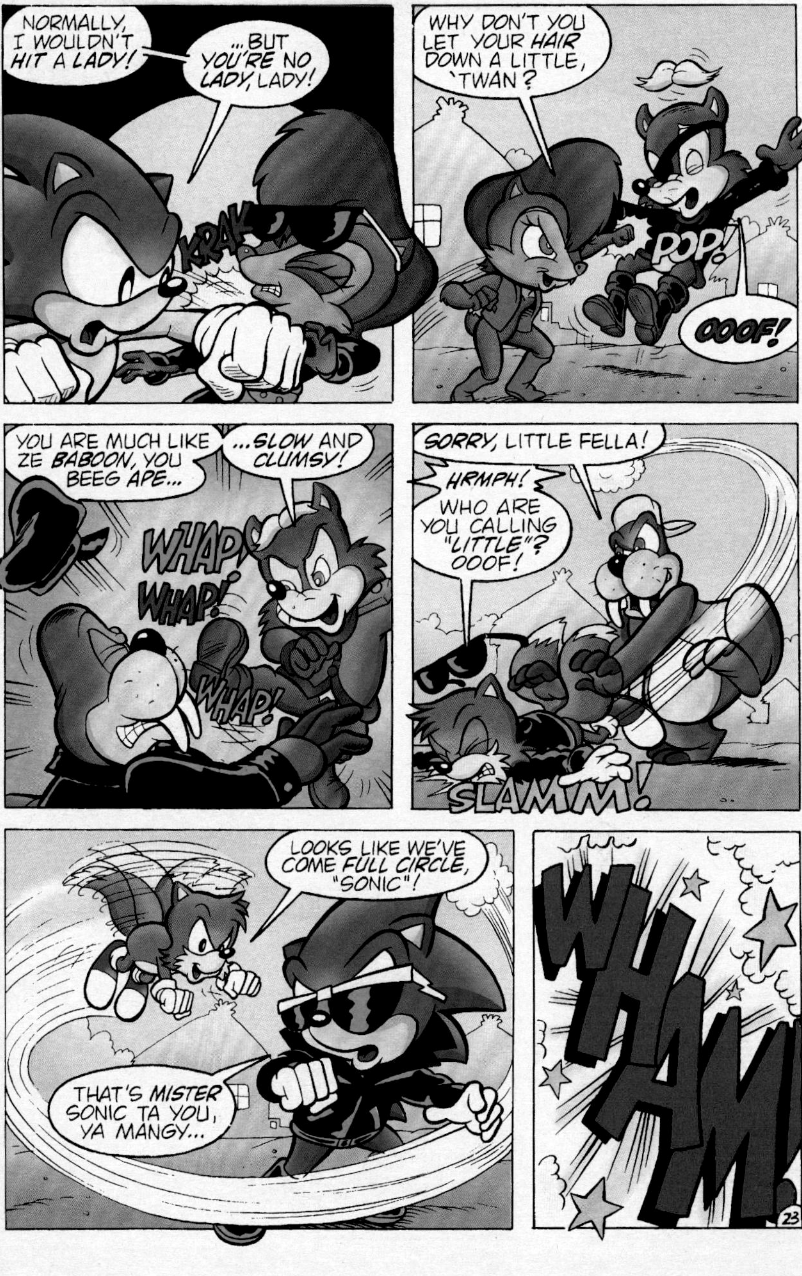
NORMALLY, I WOULDN'T HIT A LADY!
...BUT YOU'RE NO LADY, LADY!
KRAK
WHY DON'T YOU LET YOUR HAIR DOWN A LITTLE, `TWAN?
POP!
OOOF!
YOU ARE MUCH LIKE ZE BABOON, YOU BEEG APE...
...SLOW AND CLUMSY!
WHAP!
WHAP!
WHAP!
SORRY, LITTLE FELLA!
HRMPH!
WHO ARE YOU CALLING "LITTLE"? OOOF!
SLAMMM!
LOOKS LIKE WE'VE COME FULL CIRCLE, "SONIC"!
THAT'S MISTER SONIC TA YOU, YA MANGY...
WHAM!

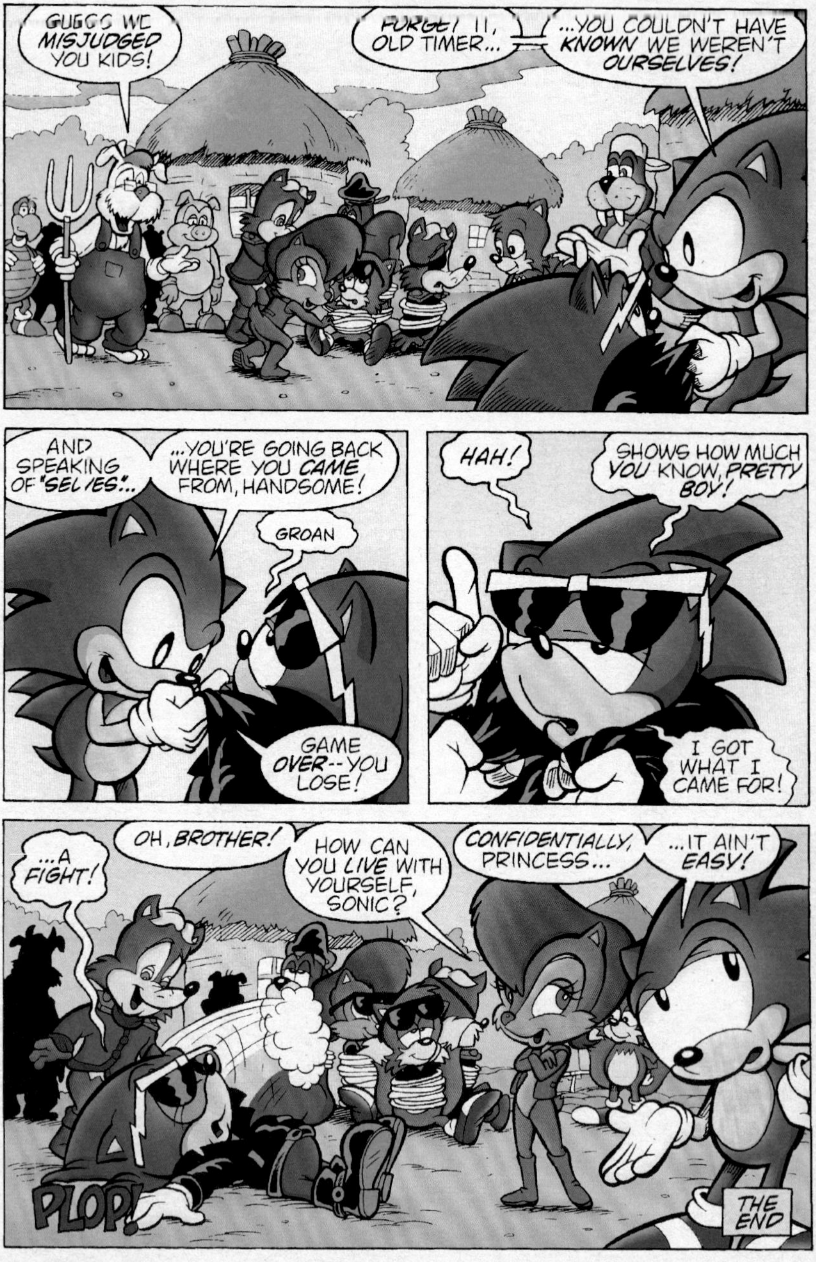
GUESS WE MISJUDGED YOU KIDS!
FORGET IT, OLD TIMER...
...YOU COULDN'T HAVE KNOWN WE WEREN'T OURSELVES!
AND SPEAKING OF "SELVES"...
...YOU'RE GOING BACK WHERE YOU CAME FROM, HANDSOME!
GROAN
GAME OVER--YOU LOSE!
HAH!
SHOWS HOW MUCH YOU KNOW, PRETTY BOY!
I GOT WHAT I CAME FOR!
...A FIGHT!
OH, BROTHER!
HOW CAN YOU LIVE WITH YOURSELF, SONIC?
CONFIDENTIALLY, PRINCESS...
...IT AIN'T EASY!
PLOP!
THE END

SONIC THE HEDGEHOG ™

Welcome to a brief who's who
of the Sonic universe.
You have just read some
of the earliest
and most loved stories from the
Sonic comic. We thought
you'd like to learn a little extra
about a few of your
favorite Sonic characters.

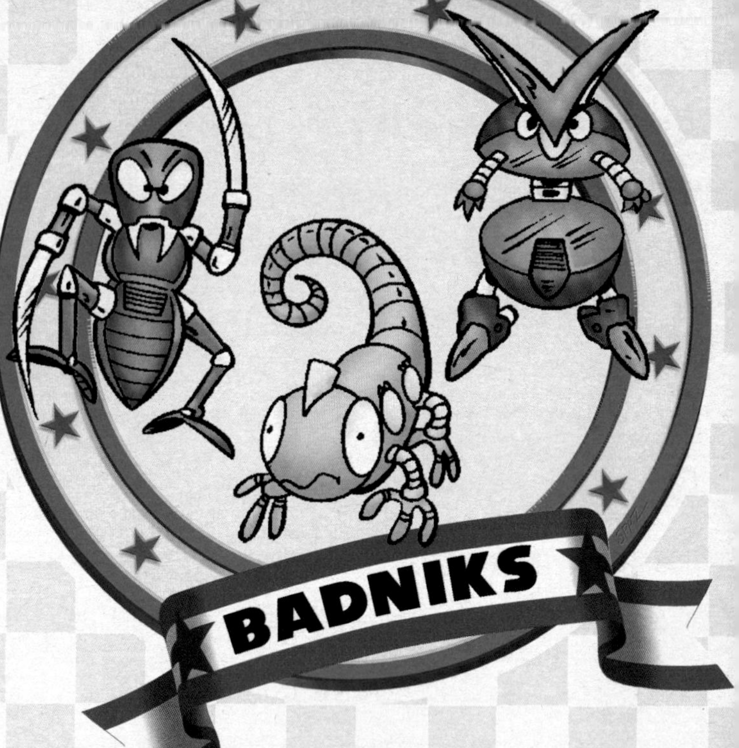
BADNIKS

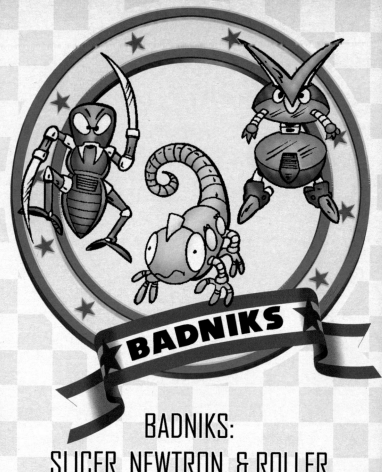

BADNIKS:
SLICER, NEWTRON, & ROLLER

More badniks of Robotnik's creation, these evil 'bots are going for the jugular! Armed with various abilities to battle Sonic and his friends, these mechanical misfits are still no match for our true blue hero!

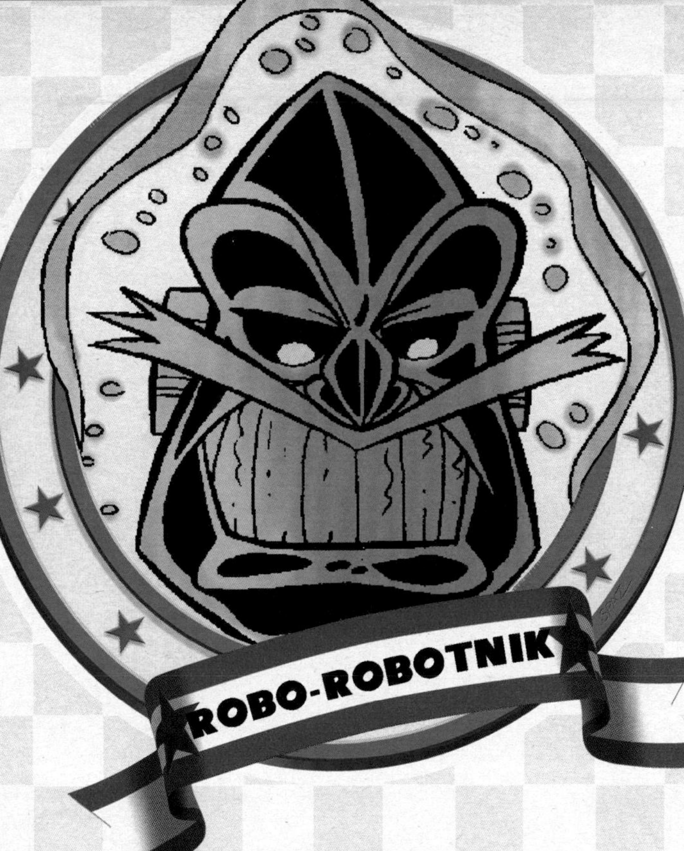
ROBO-ROBOTNIK

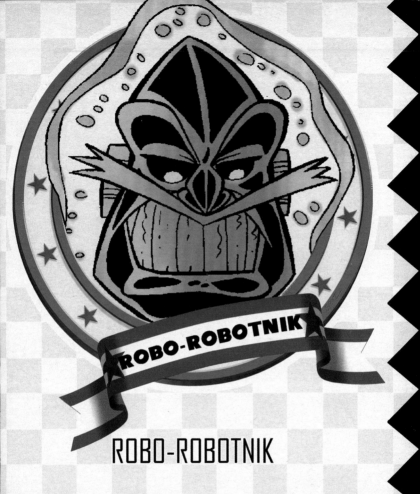

ROBO-ROBOTNIK

Can it be? Another Robotnik from a parallel dimension! Yikes! This Robotnik is just as evil as the one we know, and in his dimension, he successfully defeated Sonic and has now turned his sights on the Sonic of the Mobius we know and love! Can our heroes find a way to defeat him, or will they need some help... or maybe lots of help?!

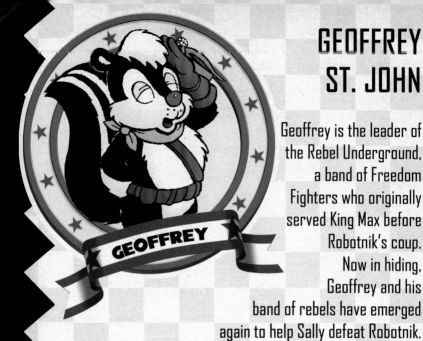

GEOFFREY ST. JOHN

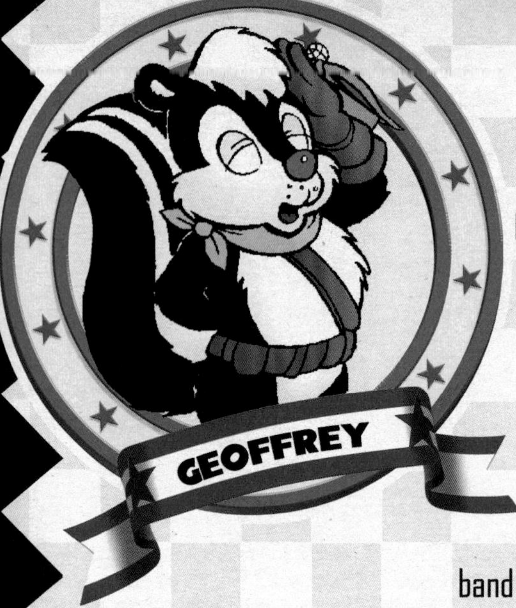
GEOFFREY

Geoffrey is the leader of the Rebel Underground, a band of Freedom Fighters who originally served King Max before Robotnik's coup. Now in hiding, Geoffrey and his band of rebels have emerged again to help Sally defeat Robotnik.

NICOLE

One night, Sally saw a strange-looking shooting star, and upon investigating, found Nicole. A thinking computer of mysterious origins, Nicole is both an analytical machine and a supportive friend to Sally, who has been struggling with keeping the Freedom Fighters together and searching for her lost father.

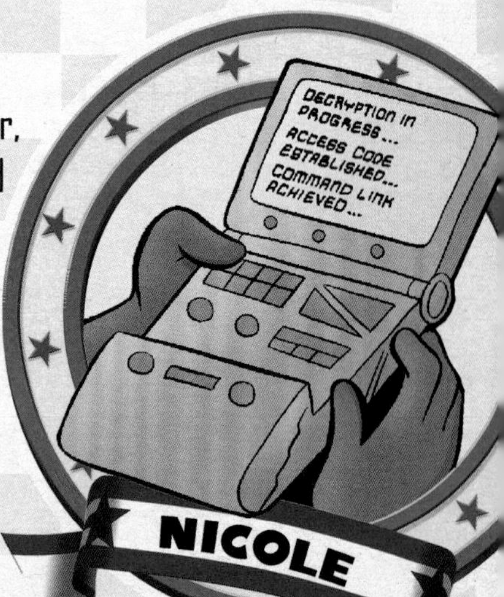
DECRYPTION IN PROGRESS...
ACCESS CODE ESTABLISHED...
COMMAND LINK ACHIEVED...
NICOLE

EVIL FF

EVIL
FREEDOM FIGHTERS

In the alternate Zone where Sonic found his evil
doppelganger, "Evil Sonic," there exists a group of
Freedom Fighters who fight against freedom,
not for it! Now, they have somehow made their
way to our version of Mobius, and they've decided
to make a reputation for their lovable
alternates: a BAD one!

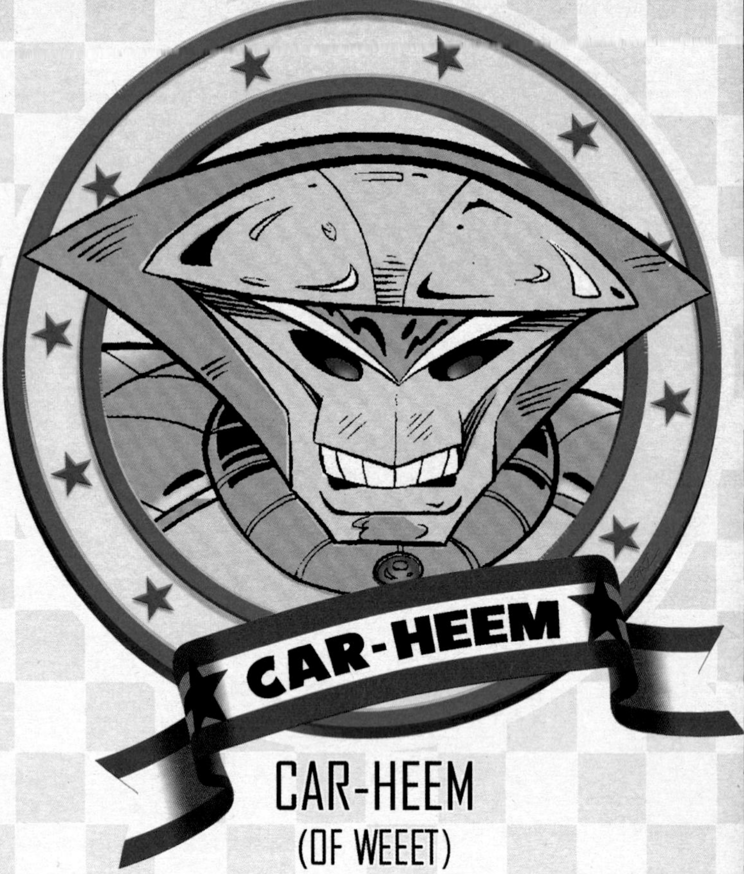
CAR-HEEM

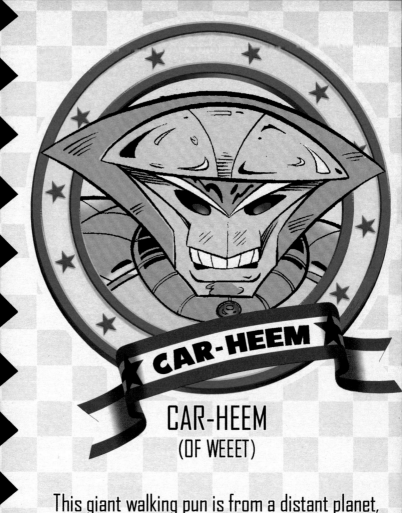

CAR-HEEM
(OF WEEET)

This giant walking pun is from a distant planet, where all creatures live alone out in space. As a pastime, Car-heem takes on a hobby many people share: collecting. The only difference is that Car-heem doesn't collect rocks or stamps, but rather living beings! When he sets his sights on Mobius, the Freedom Fighters have to join with an uneasy ally to outsmart the extraterrestrial.

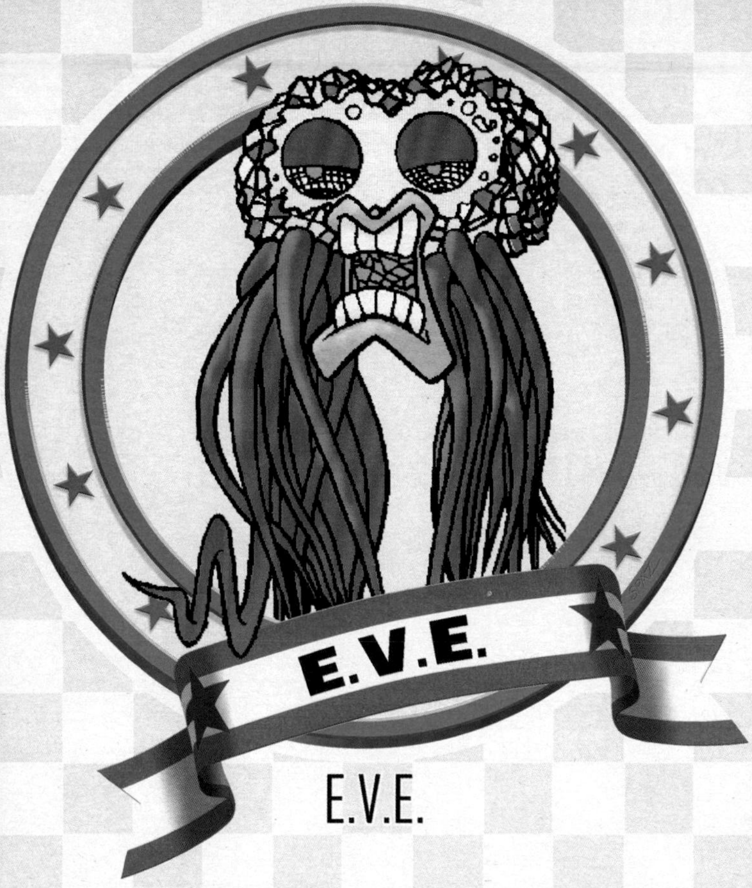
E.V.E.

E.V.E.

Standing for Exceptionally Versatile Evolvanoid, E.V.E. is by far Robotnik's most sinister creation. A machine made of miniature robotic "molecules," E.V.E. can never be destroyed! Rather, "she" takes the knowledge gained from battle defeats and evolves into an even stronger being!

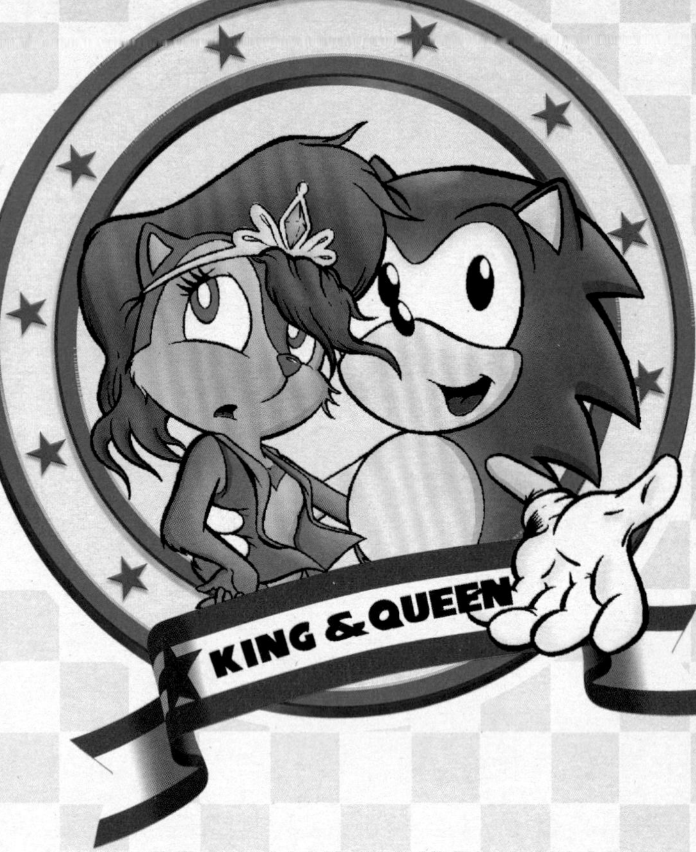
KING & QUEEN

KING SONIC AND QUEEN SALLY

In what may be a possible timeline,
Sonic and Sally have finally tied the knot!
Now, 25 years later, Sonic serves as
King of Knothole along with his wife, Queen Sally.
Is this the true future? No one knows for sure what
the future may hold...

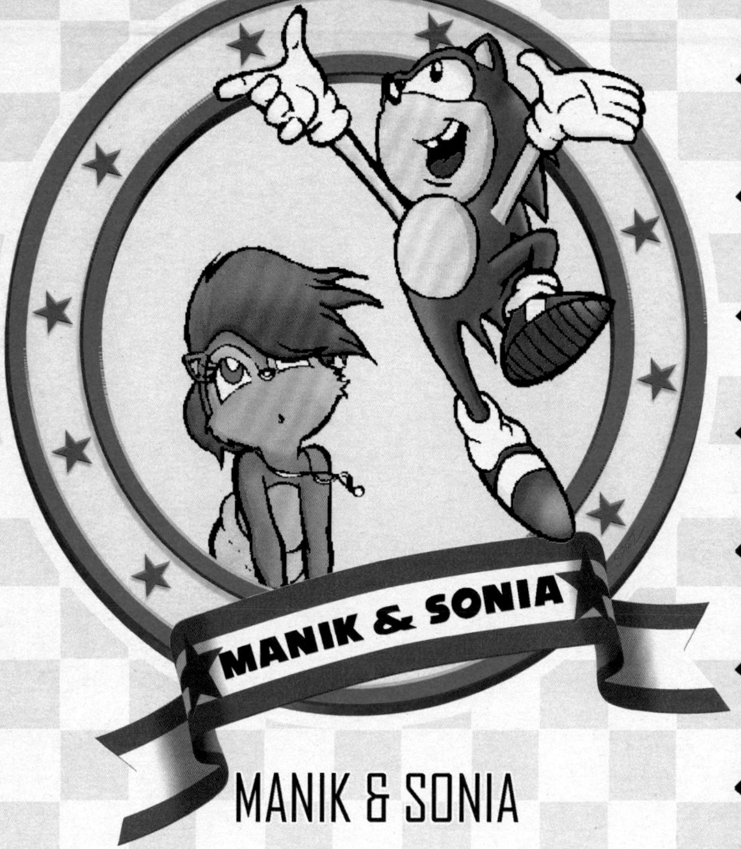
MANIK & SONIA

MANIK & SONIA

Sonic and Sally...with kids?
That's right, folks! In this timeline,
King Sonic and Queen Sally have had two children,
Manik, who takes after his father, and Sonia, who
takes after her mother. But what other traits of
their parents do these two possess? Stay tuned to find
out, as this "royal family" is sure to make an
appearance again!

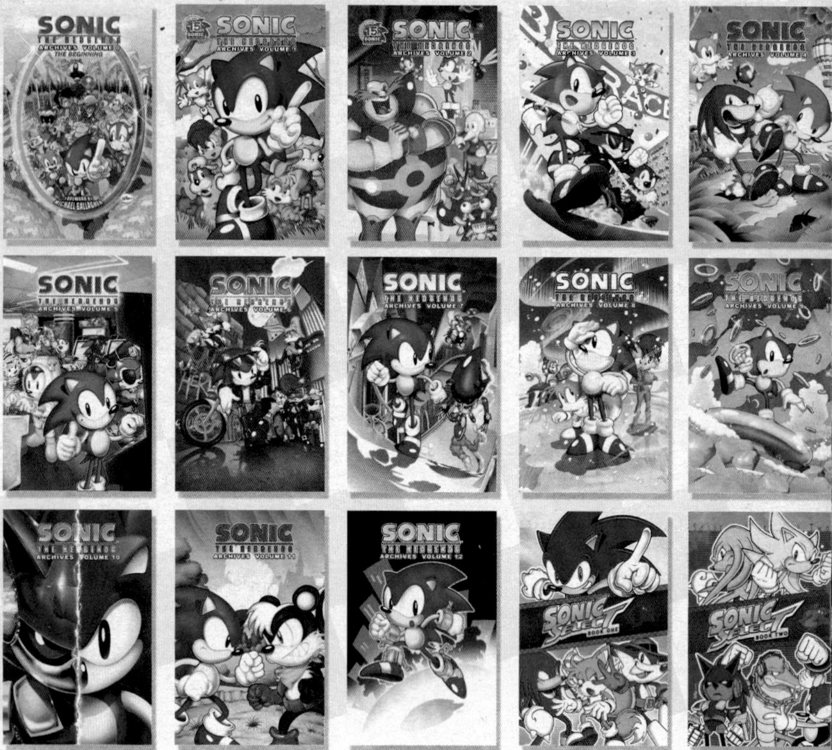

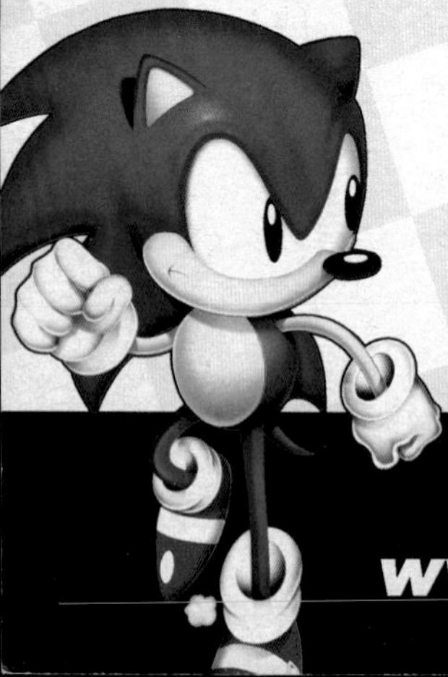